Livermore Write  *Country Literary Harvest*

2006

An Anthology of stories and poems

from

People Who Write and Tell Stories

edited by
Karen L. Hogan and Selene Steese

All materials in this publication remain copyrighted by the respective authors. No part of this book may be reproduced in any manner whatsoever without written permission except in the case of brief quotations embodied in critical articles or reviews.
For information, address WingSpan Press, P.O. Box 2085 Livermore, CA 94551.

Cover and Interior Design: Karen L. Hogan

ISBN: 1-59594-120-7
EAN: 978-1-59594-120-6

Dedicated to

*Cask and Mask
Auxiliary Players
May School Theater*

The weight of this sad time we must obey;
Speak what we feel, not what we ought to say.

from King Lear
Act V, Scene III
by William Shakespeare

Table of Contents

Foreword x
   by Lisa Tromovitch

Rubbing Shoulders With an Angel 1
   by Hector Timourian

What Am I Saying? What I Am Saying. 6
   by Tom Darter

The Cure 8
   by Mark Cabasino

John and Louise 10
   by Karen L. Hogan

Stream of Consciousness 32
   by Selene Steese

Charlene Writes a Poem 34
   by Charan Sue Wollard

Peacocks In Mourning 36
   by J.D. Blair

The Terrible Haiku 43
   by Jason Hambrecht

On a sleepless night in spring 44
   by sandra kay

Life's Just a John Prine Song 46
   by Peter Bray

Damp Eucalyptus 48
   by J.D. Blair

The Mailman 49
   by Steve Workman

Uncle 64
   by J.D. Blair

JoHanna James 65
   by Thomas Lofgren

The Pages 69
    by K E Froeschner

Death Valley And the "Unknown Prospector" 70
    by Harold Gower

A Fish in the Desert 75
    by Cynthia Patton

Rhythm of the Rain 94
    by Sue Tasker

Mirror 96
    by Albert Rothman

Good Weather Sunday 97
    by Diana Quartermaine

Effie's Eulogy 98
    by DianaQuartermaine

Sister's Earthquake Story 100
    by Diana Quartermaine

Tiger and the Fish! 101
    adapted and told by Bobbie Kinkead

Nearly Bacterial Haiku 107
    by George Staehle

touches stone 108
    by Ethel Mays

My Kidney Stone Rocks! 110
    By David Hardiman

Death Has Pale Eyes and Greets Me with a Knowing Smile 116
    by Cara Mecozzi

A Villanelle 119
    by Harold Gower

Kathy 120
    by Pat Coyle

Bill 125
    by Pat Coyle

He Lives Alone, Much Like Unloading a Uhaul 131
    by Mark Cabasino

Coyote Laughing 132
    by Ethel Mays

Hollow, Man. 137
    by *Tom Darter*
On Building a Universal Spam Filter 138
    By *Peter Bray*
Amazing Grace Arrives From Cyberspace 140
    by *Karen L. Hogan*
The Blue Vase 142
    by *Diana Carey*
A New Thing Called Television 146
    by *Frank Thornburgh*
Her Last Smile 148
    by *Frank Thornburgh*
Eating My Way Through India 152
    by *Annette Langer*
Sol 162
    by *JD Blair*
Sometimes I Just 163
    by *Selene Steese*
The Monologue of Rainsworth, the One-Eared Cat 164
    by *Mark L. Cabasino*
Again 166
    by *K E Froeschner*
Doctor Visit 168
    by *Thomas Darter*
The Loch 170
    by *Diana Carey*
Mono Tome 178
    by *Jason Hambrecht*
Math Attack 179
    by *Phil K. Mitchell*
Calculus 183
    by *Charan Sue Wollard*
3 of 9: Can't Wait! 184
    by *sandra kay*
Shooting Moon Rocks 192
    by *Charan Sue Wollard*

NanoFiction: One Billionth of an Oeuvre 206
   by Jason Hambrecht

The Sunrise Ritual 207
   By: Cara Mecozzi

Atlas of the World 212
   by Calvin Roberts

The Electric Lady 217
   by Vanitha Sankaran

destiny's token 221
   by Ethel Mays

The Trilogy of DEATH!* 222
   by Tom Darter

Good Daughter 230
   by Camille Thompson

The Island 234
   by Ben Jones

Poor Claude du Bois 240
   by Leslie Flannery

My First Enterprise 248
   by Frank Thornburgh

Buckarooing 250
   by Harold Gower

Kiss Dancing 251
   by Selene Steese

Hoppe's #9 252
   by Frank Thornburgh

Red Wing Shoes 255
   By Frank Thornburgh

Flight Path 257
   by Mary Druce

Discarded Things 258
   By Judy Clement Wall

The Ladder 269
   by Mary Druce

Moon Ride 270
    by Ethel Mays
Jihad American Style 278
    by Joy Montgomery
America's Rising Heart 281
    by Karen L. Hogan
Give War a Rest 282
    by George Staehle
I Pledge Allegiance to Freedom 284
    by Charan Sue Wollard
Anthology Contributors 286
Index of Authors 291

Foreword
by Lisa Tromovitch

With great respect and pleasure I write this foreword for the second annual Livermore Wine Country Literary Harvest. I'm not a writer, but as a theatre artist I am a literary artist. When I began attending Karen Hogan's grassroots group, People Who Write and Tell Stories, about two years ago, I experienced what I sensed was the genesis of theatre: people in the community had stories to tell; they wrote them down. Then, one-by-one, they stood up and shared their stories aloud. This component—the live sharing, the literal giving voice to their stories—is what captured my attention. It's said, "It isn't theatre if there's no audience." Theater is about community and so are stories. I was invigorated.

There were short stories, parts of longer pieces, poetry, fiction, nonfiction, works "inspired by" and "embellished." Editor Karen Hogan has created an opportunity for the community to share its stories and its literary work. This book represents a true literary harvest—a harvest of what writers in the Livermore Wine Country have grown this year: comedy, tragedy, irony, reflections on the past seasoned with new perspectives; "new vine" and work from "seasoned oak." Young and old perspectives are included: prose, poetry, documentary and nanofiction—our cab, chardonnay, merlot and petit sirah, perhaps.

As Shakespeare said through the voice of Albany in *King Lear*, " . . . speak what we feel, not what we ought to say."

Many of these pieces of work were ripened at People Who Write and Tell Stories. This book represents the local bottling of the fruits of the harvest, now made available to the rest of the community.

Salut! Enjoy!

Lisa Tromovitch
Theatrical Artistic Director, Shakespeare's Associate
Livermore Shakespeare Festival
Livermore, California

Rubbing Shoulders with an Angel

From Gifts From America

by Hector Timourian

Masses of people poured out from several ships, moving slowly and forming endless lines. They were being told to move, then to wait, then to get in another line. And then, their documents had to be checked one more time.

"I can't believe it, Sarkis, at last we're here!"

"Yes, isn't it wonderful. We're finally in America!" Uncle Sarkis was standing behind Aunt Hilda hugging her as they both stood in yet another endless line. They had never seen so many people. There were several thousand immigrants—from many different countries—being processed together with them at Ellis Island.

"We've waited many years for this moment," Uncle Sarkis said as he stood behind her, pressing his chest on her back. He could feel his strong heartbeat and whispered in her ear, "Are you as excited as I am?" Gently reaching under her breast, he felt her wild heart beating almost twice as fast as his. As he held her tight against his breast, he overlooked her hair's musty odor—a contrast to the lovely fresh jasmine that usually identified her presence.

The United States had established a quota limiting by national origin the number of people—especially from eastern

European and Asian countries—who would be accepted. Uncle Sarkis and Aunt Hilda had waited many years for their chance to immigrate. But once their turn came up, they were notified, and were given a short time to accept the invitation and to arrange for the long trip from Istanbul to America. Although they had waited a long time for the trip, they felt rushed as they closed all their affairs and got ready to leave their country, family, and friends.

First they took a small ship from Istanbul to the port of Marseilles in France. There they had to wait until they could board a big liner that took them to New York. The ship was full of people who were also starting a new life in the United States. All of them were carrying their few possessions in one or two suitcases or bags.

Having lived in Istanbul—an international city—they were able to identify the nationalities of many of the people on board ship, mainly by the languages they spoke. But language was not the only way to identify their differences; Uncle Sarkis became aware of how differently people smelled. Each person had a lingering scent, a peculiar mixed odor of sweat and spices characteristic of and peculiar to their mother country. Once on land, after the long trip without a chance to bathe, everyone's odor was mixed into a stench that became overwhelming as the masses of people pressed against each other, pushing—trying to gain a few minutes—to make up for the many years of waiting. Then, all of a sudden, the crowd began to move as guards guided them into forming several lines. They started to move quickly and were directed to enter a large warehouse type of building, The Great Hall. Uncle Sarkis and Aunt Hilda found themselves indoors where the people were being grouped and made to stand in different lines leading to a row of physicians—wearing white coats—who were conducting physical examinations. After having all their documents checked, a health exam was the last obstacle before being accepted into the country.

As Uncle Sarkis and Aunt Hilda patiently waited for their turn to be examined, they noticed that once the brief exam was over, the doctors made a chalk mark on the back of the person's left shoulder. Almost everyone was being marked on his or her shoulder. Only a few, those who were not marked, were told to stand aside. Somebody said, "Those poor people are going to be sent back because they are sick. The chalk mark means that you are healthy enough to be admitted into the United States of America."

The physical exam was rather hurried and brief, and the doctors spent only a few minutes with each person. First, Uncle Sarkis was examined. He stood quietly as the doctor, sitting on a stool, quickly examined and poked him, then without saying anything, grabbed his hips and turned him around so he could check him with the healthy chalk mark. Uncle Sarkis stepped aside, and waited as another doctor was examining Aunt Hilda. The doctor appeared to take more time as he listened to her heart. He then shook his head, and said, "You have a heart murmur." Without marking her shoulder, he pushed her aside, then turned around and started the next examination.

"What is going to happen to us?"

Uncle Sarkis and Aunt Hilda looked at each other, an unknown fear engulfed them, and their faces turned white with terror. They had never heard of a heart murmur.

A guard asked them to move and join others, who had been examined, in another area of the building. Soon they were in a big crowd again. Everyone started to move and push—they were being guided to a small doorway on the other side. There, guards were checking the mark on each person's shoulder as people were going out.

Uncle Sarkis held Aunt Hilda's hand as tight as he could; he didn't want to let her go. "I can't go on without you. We'll both return to Turkey."

"You should keep going, I can go back home and live with my parents."

Uncle Sarkis felt as if his whole gut was tied in a knot. Painful spasms grabbed his chest and made it difficult for him to breathe. He felt as if he were drowning. The crowd, like an ocean wave, kept pushing them on. "I'll never be separated from you!"

But she insisted, "It isn't fair for me to hold you back; you've dreamed of a new life in America. I'll be fine back home with my family."

Both of them started to get nauseous as they became aware of the crowd's stench. Aunt Hilda felt like she was going to faint. Her heart was beating like a wild animal wanting to escape her chest. She felt the pounding of each heartbeat throbbing through her whole body. There was a rush to get out. The multitude of people was pushing, trying to reach the door that meant passage to America. But Sarkis and Hilda wanted to slow down. It became even more difficult to move slowly when an old man walking backwards started pushing against Hilda with his back. Sarkis, remembering how men would get more strength by pushing backwards, resented the old man, "He must really want us out of the way." And like a wagon stuck in the mud, Sarkis held on to her hand. He didn't want to lose her.

What was going to happen when they reached the guards? What were they going to do when the guards noticed she didn't have a chalk mark? Uncle Sarkis was preparing—in the best English he could—to say, "I will stay with her and we will return together."

He was sure he didn't want to be separated; he would do anything to stay together. But he didn't know what was going to happen; they had no money to travel back to Turkey. Where were they going to go?

All their dreams of starting a new life together were tumbling down as they came to the door where guards were checking the shoulder chalk marks. A couple of older women had been asked to move aside; they had been refused passage. The black shawls over their heads prevented one from seeing their crying faces, but Aunt Hilda noticed uncontrolled sobs shaking their small bodies. "I am going to be like them, I can't hold my tears any longer."

As they reached the doorway, they noticed that one guard was a very tall man; he was like a giant compared with most of the people going through. He was looking for the chalk marks on everyone's shoulders and, without missing a beat, the giant guard directed both Sarkis and Hilda through the door.

Once outside—in the light of the sun—Uncle Sarkis noticed that Aunt Hilda had a faint chalk mark on her shoulder. The old man, walking backwards, had rubbed enough chalk on her shoulder to enable her to pass.

The brightness of the sunlight could not match their joy. They hugged and cried. They felt as if a dam had broken. Their pent-up fears and doubts were instantly dissipated.

Then the crowd overtook them and forced them to keep moving on their way to a new life. Suddenly, a gust of sea breeze blew away the crowd's stench. As they took a deep breath, they became aware of the fresh scent of liberty.

What Am I Saying? What I Am Saying.

by Tom Darter

> *I have nothing to say and I am saying it and that is poetry.*
> — *John Cage*

Do I have anything to say?
Or am I just saying it?
    (And is that poetry?)

Are words a tool,
    or something to hide behind?
And who am I fooling,
    myself, or you?
        (And is *that* poetry?)

Is meaning too slender?
Do rhymes help or hinder?

If measured by meter,
    are words better, neater?
Or is it just singsong to
    to move things along so?

Will I know when each line's done?
Or will I go on too long and create a line that doesn't match any of the others?

Should I
        splay   the words
            out   on
              the page
  with   Kirk-like
          diction
                  to   suggest the
      rhythm   of   thoughts?
or should I just let all the words run together
in a huge Bloomin' pound-cake mass to
suggest thoughts that spill all over each other?

Should everything be on topic,
        or should I throw in something random?
Was Eve a victim
        of serpent's stance?

Can I use anything but
        rhetorical questions?
Oh, I think I can manage that. . . .

Maybe poetry is as poetry does.
        (But—what is *that*?)

Maybe it's a poem if you call it a poem.
        (that is What I Am Saying.)

The Cure
by Mark Cabasino

> *I must fight this sickness, find a cure.*
> — *"Pornography,"* Robert Smith

Once again the forest is a series
of messy hands and empty wings,
not beating, I'm ebbing
like a taxed and tactless heart.

She's a sign for a missing persons
once pinned to a tree trunk, adamant—
only staples remain, and flecks
of a frayed color flier, like gashes.

Eventually I will arrive in the clearing
of an evening with an absence of stars
and nothing will scintillate for miles, days, save
the sweat of my soul leaking through pores.

And then it hits me:
things serrate.
Notched like leaves, they
stagger away
like jagged, stubborn, independent drunks
ruing the day
they first kissed me.

The baby will grow teeth and leave.
The girl will become cold and also leave.
Furthermore the adolescent will up and leave for college.
No sooner will the grandfather succumb to tumors and leave
then the father will inherit the same disease and leave.
And that doesn't begin to cover the loss of the mother.

Broken leaves under my boots,
ribcage like a sunken vessel,
I've forgotten that the verb to cleave
can also mean to cling.

O woman,
remove the slogan,
peel away the cotton tee,
reveal your sheen to the moon,
look behind the barren trees
and there you will find a man
eating bark for sustenance.

John and Louise
by Karen L. Hogan

The slap-slap sound of the wipers filled the Ford Coupe. Louise had been silent since they left the picture show. After eight years of marriage, John had learned to read the tone of her silences. He went over the evening in his mind, trying to think of what he had done to upset her so.

Finally, as they turned into the driveway, she spoke. "You embarrassed me in front of my friends."

He turned the key in the ignition and the engine stopped. He gripped the steering wheel with one hand and held the key in the ignition with the other. He thought back to the night before, when the O'Kelleys came over for pie and ice cream after Wednesday night Bible Study. His mind had barely begun to picture the evening when her next words ripped through his heart.

"That," she declared, "is why I want a divorce."

He knew that once she made up her mind, there was no stopping her. So two days later he drove her to Reno, then drove back alone to Livermore, the quiet ranching town in Northern California they had moved to two years ago, shortly after VJ Day freed him from the Navy. While she stayed in Reno the six weeks necessary to establish residence, John packed her things and sent them back to Missouri.

The divorce papers arrived on his birthday. "Extreme mental

cruelty" appeared in bold letters next to "Reason for granting divorce" on the first page.

He went over that night with the O'Kelleys. It must have been when he brought her the wrong pie server. She didn't say anything. She just had that look—frightened humiliation covered by anger. Her iron will belied the fragility that lay beneath.

Extreme mental cruelty. The words wandered aimlessly in his mind.

Anger rose up on one side of his heart.

What does she know about cruelty? I was the one at the end of my father's belt.

Shame rose up on the other side of his heart.

How could I have been so cruel to her, humiliating her in front of her friends. Please forgive me. Forgive me for . . . but the words wouldn't come to him. How could he be forgiven when he didn't even know his sin?

The words on the page screamed at him: Extreme mental cruelty. Extreme mental cruelty. Extreme mental cruelty.

Anger and shame battled in his heart, until, like any muscle when it can no longer endure the stress, it tore—a small jagged tear down the middle of his heart.

And, yet, his heart continued to beat.

He put the divorce papers on the table near the door, went to bed, and then, the next morning, drove to Ranahan's funeral parlor where he began his daily routine of preparing bodies for their final viewing. He did it carefully, knowing, sometimes hoping, that someone had once loved this shell of flesh.

At night, he would return to the house where they had lived together, and lay his hat as he always did on the table near the door—where it rested on top of the divorce papers. Without the scent of one of her mincemeat, lemon meringue, or gooseberry pies filling the rooms, the smells of the embalming fluid, death, and grief lingered in the air, carrying with them the possibility he had tended to a life that had been lived unloved.

Louise pulled the new cotton nightgown from the Schroeder's Emporium bag, and placed it in the suitcase. She was a good packer. She had been able to get all the clothes she needed for the trip across country into one suitcase. She could carry her toiletries in her train case. Opal would send the trunk after they left for California.

It had been over a year since that night she told John she wanted a divorce. She'd said that even though she loved John. She had proved she loved him when she endured his going to those places on her body, stoically receiving his stiff member and the sticky fluids he ejaculated into her, the smell opening the door in her mind where those words were hidden long ago: Look what you have done to me, you dirty girl. Now, God will send us both to hell.

But when he told her that he, as the other men in his company, had been treated for pubic lice before returning home, it created a barrier between her body and his that not even her love for him could overcome. Imagining his body crawling with filth she could not see, she could not bear to have him touch her. She shut him out of those places he wanted to go on her body, and then tried to shut him out of her heart.

But, she loved John. She knew he was a good man. And when he called to say he was in town visiting kinfolk and could he stop by just to make sure that Louise was all right, she knew that God had answered her prayers. He'd sent John back to her.

She placed her bath powder in her train case, clicked it shut, then carried both bags down to the entryway.

She went back upstairs, sat at the dressing table, removed the bobby pins and brushed out the tight curls until they framed her face—just the way John liked it. She opened her compact, made a light circle with the powder puff, shook it to get rid of the excess, and lightly powdered her pale skin. Finally, she applied the lipstick she'd bought the day before at Weinstein's Five and Dime. Ruby Delight.

She closed the compact, placed it with her new lipstick in her good blue purse and snapped it shut. She removed a pair of white cotton gloves from the dressing table drawer, draped them over her purse and moved to the flower print chenille armchair next to the window.

Pushing the sheer lace curtains aside, she watched as a car turned the corner, then stopped in front of her parents' house. John had written that he bought a new car, one of the first they made after the War was over. He stepped out, unfolded his suit jacket, put it on, and pulled at the lapels. His thick wavy hair was as red as it had been ten years ago when he first came to court her.

Opal, her baby sister, was already married by then—had already borne two children. Opal always got things first. "She's my little gem," their mother would say.

Well, now it's my turn, Louise had thought back then. And John was a good man. She liked cooking for him, pleasing him with the pies she'd bake for him on his birthday—he didn't like cake. If only she'd known how physical married life would be.

John's come to take me back with him so I can have a family. God will help me endure our sins.

She watched him place the boater on his head, pause at the

bottom of the porch stairs, then grab the rail and climb the steps one by one. Ten years ago he had taken them two at a time.

The doorbell rang.

"Well, now, John, you just git yourself in here." she heard Opal say. "You look real nice. Is that a new suit you got on?"

The spicy scent of Louise's mincemeat pie greeted John. He placed his hat on the table near the door—the divorce papers had disappeared the day after Louise and he returned from Missouri—and entered the kitchen, where Louise was scrubbing at the remnants of flour on the pastry board.

"I've talked to the minister," Louise announced. "He can marry us tomorrow afternoon at four. The O'Kelleys are gonna stand up for us. I've pressed your blue suit, so be sure to be home by three so you can take a bath and get that funeral home smell off you before we go to the church."

She wiped her fingers on her flour-dusted apron. "Now, dinner will be ready in about ten minutes. You go wash up. We're having mincemeat pie for dessert."

He loved her mincemeat pie. She used left-over roast beef, then sweetened it up with spices.

The two sides of his divided heart began to battle. He was grateful that she had forgiven him for his acts of extreme mental cruelty. He had wondered how he could ever be forgiven for what he did, and was ashamed that he still didn't even know what it was.

Anger rose on the other. What does she know about cruelty? I was the one at the end of my father's belt.

He washed his hands, splashed Old Spice on his face to help cover the smells of grief and mortality he carried home with him. Then they sat down to the dinner of fried chicken, mashed potatoes, green beans, okra, and corn. He ate his mincemeat pie with a dollop of whipped cream.

The phone rang in the middle of the night. He rose from the couch—she would not sleep in the same bed with him until they were married again—and answered it after just one ring. Young Jim Sampson had finally used up his nine lives. John scraped him off the pavement, then set to work making him look whole again for his family.

He returned home by three, just as she had instructed, bathed away the smell of death and formaldehyde, then drove with her to the church where, for the second time, a minister pronounced them man and wife.

They had dinner with the O'Kelleys. She made her famous strawberry rhubarb pie, and this time, he was careful to bring her the right pie server.

That night he climbed into bed next to her. "What are we gonna tell people about this?"

"About what?" She folded the top of the sheet over the blankets and stroked it to make it smooth. "The folks back home don't know we got divorced. "She turned out the light and rolled over on her side.

"Now, you let me know when you want to start a family," he said to her back.

John switched on the light. He worried that the ringing phone would wake Louise, but as his sleep-fogged mind cleared, he remembered she was in the hospital, their twin sons in incubators.

He moved quickly to the telephone. He wondered who it would be this time. Old man Sweeny wasn't expected to live out the week. It was probably him. But you never knew whose life

15

had ended when he got one of these calls in the middle of the night.

"John?" It was Dr. Matthews. "John, I have some bad news. One of them didn't make it."

The grandfather clock whirred, then began to chime. John steadied himself, placing his hand on the pile of diapers he had bought that day. It had been late when he came back from Miller's Emporium, and he was tired from the long night of waiting with the other fathers. He'd placed the diapers on the chair next to the telephone table.

The grandfather clock finished its third chime.

"John? Did you hear me?"

"Now, which one was it?" he finally found his voice.

"The second one."

"Well, how's Louise taking it?"

"She's sleeping. We haven't told her yet. You're gonna have to go get it and take it to Ranahan's, then we'll go in the mornin' together to tell her. And John, it was a pretty rough birth. She's not likely to have more children. But I don't think we should tell her that now."

The tick tock of the swinging pendulum filled the room. John noticed the dent his fist left in the pile of diapers.

"John, are you there?"

John removed his hand from the diapers and rubbed his temples.

"Yeah, I'll go get Billy. What time do you want to meet me to tell Louise?"

"Let's let her have breakfast first. How about nine?"

John put the receiver back in its cradle, and looked at the dent his fist had left in the pile of diapers. Using both hands, he smoothed the diapers until the dent disappeared.

Then he dressed and, as the grandfather clock chimed the quarter hour, he climbed into his car to go tend to death, just as he had done countless times in the middle of the night. Rain started falling as he left the driveway. He turned on the wipers. The slap-slap sound filled the car.

"And how are we feeling today?" Ethel chirped as she rolled the folded, white-pleated, metal-framed screen to the foot of Louise's bed. Louise hadn't seen her in her nurses uniform before. She was big boned and fleshy, like Louise. They'd just played bridge two weeks before.

It had begun to rain again, the wind rattling the window over Louise's bed.

Kathleen, the tiny blond daughter of Moira O'Kelley, fluffed Louise's pillow, poured her a glass of water from the ice-sweating pitcher and handed it to her. "Did we sleep well last night?" she smiled. Just two months ago, the bridge club had all told Moira how good it was that Kathleen was a nurse's aide. It would tell her if nursing was her calling.

Louise examined the ward, received the chatter of the three other new mothers and their husbands. *Why am I the only one getting this kind of attention? And where is John?*

She sipped from the glass. *I don't like ice water; Ethel should know that.*

Kathleen began brushing Louise's hair. "We want you to look pretty for the doctor," she smiled. Louise's hair hung straight and limp around her face.

Ethel pulled on the sheet at the foot of the bed and deftly tucked it in, then motioned to Kathleen that it was time for her to disappear.

Louise had felt uneasy ever since yesterday, when Ethel told her her sons were in the incubators. At least that's where Ethel told her she took them.

Ethel busied herself smoothing the sheet, raising Louise's arm so she could create a nice, neat fold.

The sound of squeaking wheels entered the ward. Kathleen pushed the wooden cart to the first bed, lifted out a bundle of flannel, and placed it in the outstretched arm of the young woman in the first bed. Her husband gazed wistfully into the bundle and they began cooing. Kathleen pushed the cart to the next bed and lifted a bundle of flannel.

"The doctor will be here in just a few minutes." Ethel began unfolding the screen around Louise's bed.

The squeaky wheels moved across the room. Ethel's back was to Louise now as she began carefully arranging the pleats.

The cooing sound of the couple across the room reached Louise. Ethel continued arranging the pleats as the squeaky wheels moved out of the ward.

Now mine are in the incubators. That's where they take the ones that come as early as mine did. They weren't supposed to come for two more months. That's why they aren't bringing me mine.

A shallow breath of dread filled Louise's chest, unleashing the memory of the conversation she'd had with John just last Saturday at Miller's Emporium, right after Dr. Matthews told her she was bearing twins. "Now," she stated, "a lot of times with two, only one lives. So let's just get enough diapers for one. Then if both live you can go get enough diapers for both."

Louise opened the door to the room in her mind, shoved the memory of the conversation into it, then slammed shut the door.

Ethel, satisfied with her arrangement of the pleats, turned around. A baby cried. Yellow liquid dripped from Louise's breasts and stained the front of her gown.

"Let me just get that," Ethel pulled off Louise's gown, swabbed the nipples with an alcohol-soaked piece of cotton, then helped her put on a new, clean gown. "We want you to look nice and fresh for the doctor, Dear." Ethel gathered up the alcohol and cotton swabs. "He'll be right along." She disappeared behind the screen, leaving Louise encased in the white-pleated womb.

Louise didn't like Ethel seeing her naked breasts. Didn't like her touching them, even with a cotton swab.

The sounds of the new mothers and fathers filtered through the pleated screen. She was older than the others —she was 37—and this was her first pregnancy. There were so many babies being born, now that the War was over and the men were back.

"We call this 'the twilight'," Dr. Matthews had said, as Ethel placed the mask over Louise's face. "You won't feel a thing."

Louise inhaled and a tule fog consumed her mind, erasing the door she so carefully guarded. From far away she heard Dr. Matthews' demanding voice:

"Forceps!"

"Oh, he's so small!" It was Ethel. Louise heard hurried steps disappear, and then return.

"I've got the next one." Dr. Matthews' disembodied voice wandered through the fog. "They sure are little. They came pretty early so their lungs are still young." Dr. Matthews' words wandered through the fog, looking for a home.

"Oh! Another boy!" The sound of Ethel's voice, followed by hurried steps leaving the room, tried to find an anchor in Louise's mind.

"Ethel!" Dr. Matthews' voice demanded in the fog. "We've

got a problem. Give her more."

Ethel's quick efficient footsteps returned to the room.

Louise felt something cover her face and the tule fog grew denser. Reverend Cole's hand reached out through the fog and took her hand. He sat next to her on the pew, the rain lashing at the stained glass windows.

"That's a lovely dress you're wearing," he smiled at her. "Isn't today your birthday? How old are you now?"

"I'm 13 today." Louise lowered her eyes and with her free hand smoothed the pink pleats of her taffeta skirt. She'd woken early so she had time to iron it, avoiding the suspicious look her mother shot her with the admonition, "Vain girls are selfish creatures."

She wanted to look pretty for Reverend Cole. He made her feel special, assigning her passages from the Bible, inviting her into his study where he read her lessons and assured her she was on the path to becoming a good Christian woman.

Louise's heart quickened when he took her hand in his, anticipating a mystery that rose from deep in her body.

Reverend Cole covered her hand, placed it on his lap. "We must be right with the Lord," he said softly, moving her hand up and down the rough wool, a look of rapture filling his face as he looked heavenward. Louise felt a growing presence under her hand and a knot forming in her stomach.

He moved her hand to his thigh and held it tight. With his other hand, he unbottoned his fly. "Louise, you have made me this way. Now you must touch it so you will know what your sin has brought on me."

Louise watched as he pulled out what looked like one of the huge sausages her mother had cooked for dinner the night before, wrapped her hand around it with his, then began yanking up and down, up and down, crying out to God, until the thing she held throbbed, his body shuddered, and he cried out. "Look what you have done to me, you dirty girl. Now God will send us both to hell!"

The white thick fluid spitting out of the thing she held smelled of the musty sheets she pulled off her parents' bed and carried to the laundry room—smelled of secrets and shadows and life out of control.

The thick viscous liquid dripped through his fingers and onto her hand.

"I will tell no one of your sin," he whispered. "Let us pray." He bowed his head, removed her hand from him and placed it on her lap. "God," he began, "please have mercy on Louise; forgive her her sins that she might one day enter into your Kingdom."

Louise grasped a handful of taffeta with her soiled hand, trying to get rid of the sticky mess. It crinkled the carefully ironed pleats of her dress.

The sound of Dr. Mathews' voice pulled her back into the room.

"That's it. Take her back now."

"Everything will be fine, dear. They're in the incubators." Ethel's voice and the squeaking sound of the gurney wheels followed Dr. Matthews' voice through the fog.

As the fog began to lift, the door in her mind reappeared, trapping behind it the memory of Reverend Cole and words that formed one sentence: "Their lungs are still young; just get enough diapers for one."

John's face came into focus. "Well, they're pretty small, but they look good to me."

"Name the youngest one William Brian, after your dad and

mine," she said, groggily. "And let's name the older one John Steven—after you. You go tell Ethel so she can make those little bracelets with the beads that spell their names—Johnny and Billy. And then you go on over to Miller's Emporium and buy some more diapers on the way home."

"Well, that sounds just fine to me," he said and kissed her lightly on the cheek.

She'd drifted off wondering who was taking care of her tiny new sons, alone in their incubators.

Now, surrounded by white pleats, Louise sipped her ice water. "He's so beautiful," she heard the woman in the next bed say.

The sound of swift footsteps moved closer to her, and then John and Dr. Matthews appeared. John kissed her lightly on the forehead, then took her hand in both of his as the doctor began to speak.

"Well, how are you doing today, Louise?" He drew deeply on his cigarette then picked a stray piece of tobacco from his tongue.

She looked at John, then back at the doctor. "What's wrong?"

"Well, Louise. I'm sorry, but one of them didn't make it." His exhaled smoke formed a cloud over his head.

The baby in the next bed cried. Yellow liquid dripped from Louise's breasts.

"Which one?" she asked.

"Billy," John said and squeezed her hand.

Louise looked to Dr. Matthews.

The doctor drew deeply on his cigarette. "Now, these things just happen, Louise. His lungs were just too young to handle it." The smoke slowly leaked out of his mouth as he spoke.

The baby in the next bed whimpered.

"Now, John Steven seems to be doing just fine."

Louise looked at John, then back at the doctor.

"When will they bring Johnny to me?"

"Well, now, we've got to be safe. Those lungs of his are pretty young. So we'll just keep him in the incubator for a while longer. We can take better care of him than you can right now."

"Where is Billy?" Louise implored.

"Well, I called John earlier and had him take it over to Ranahan's. Now you have a son left who's going to need you." He patted her on the hand. "And you'll have more children to take Billy's place. So don't you worry. It's all going to be just fine. We're lucky they both didn't die." He shook John's hand then disappeared around the screen.

Louise stared straight ahead. John held her hand.

"John, I want you to bring Billy here after you prepare him." She didn't notice the look of horror that flashed through his eyes. After all, it made perfect sense to her. John worked at Ranahan's. He prepared bodies all the time.

John bent down to kiss her lightly on the forehead, then disappeared around the screen, the sound of his footsteps receding down the ward.

Louise, alone in her white pleated world, listened to the rain beat against the window above her bed. *It was Ethel. If I'd been with him, Billy wouldn't have died.*

Footsteps entered the ward. Reverend Wilson appeared from around the white pleats, his hat in his hand, beads of moisture on his coat.

"Well, Louise, I thought you might like some comfort," he said, pulling the brim of his hat so it turned round and round in his hands.

A baby gave a soft cry as it pulled away from its mother's breast. Reverend Wilson looked down, as if he were ready to pray.

"Well, now, Louise, we know God works in mysterious ways," he said. "We were all so grateful that he answered your prayers. Given your age an' all, it was almost a miracle you conceived."

"I don't understand. If He meant me to have a singleton, why did He give me two?"

"Louise." Reverend Wilson played with the brim of his hat. "We have to submit to God's will. It's the path to His love. Pray with me now." The door to the room in Louise's mind opened to receive the prayer. The memory of the shudder of John's body and the smell of his sticky fluid escaped.

"Dear Heavenly Father, we know you loved Billy so much that you wanted him to be with You—*you dirty girl*—Give our sister Louise the strength to submit to Your will —*Look what you have done to me*—so that one day, she can be welcomed into your Kingdom—*Now God will send us both to hell*—and be reunited with her darling Billy. We ask this in Jesus' name. Amen."

Louise gazed vacantly at Reverend Wilson.

"We'll pray for you at church tomorrow," Reverend Wilson said, then disappeared around the white pleats. His footsteps receded down the ward.

God loved Billy so much, he wanted him for himself. The words lingered. Louise forced them into the room in her mind, then slammed shut the door.

A baby gave a quick gasping cry. Yellow liquid dripped from her breasts.

John removed Billy's beaded bracelet from his thigh—it was too big for his wrist—and placed it on the marble slab next to his son. Billy's wrinkled face made him look like an old man in the body of a tiny infant. His skin had the grey pallor of the dead. His arms and legs had stiffened in the pose of a puppy lying on its back.

John picked up Billy and lay him on the scale. Three and a half pounds.

He placed his son back on the flannel blanket to shield him from the cold hard marble of the slab, calculated how much embalming fluid he'd need to pump through his son, then searched for two small tubes.

First he worked on closing Billy's mouth. That was always the hardest part, getting the mouth to look natural. Then he sponged him off, warming the water first, adding just a drop of disinfectant so he wouldn't hurt Billy's fragile skin.

Carefully, he began flexing Billy's legs, gently pushing and pulling them, then massaging his arms to relieve the rigor mortis. Billy looked even smaller with his arms lying by his side and his legs extended.

John picked up a scalpel and made a small incision on the right side of Billy's tiny neck. He inserted the tube connected to the embalming fluid into his son's carotid artery and the drain tube into the jugular vein.

He wasn't seated properly. That's why he didn't make it. She pushed me away before I hardly finished. He never got the chance to take hold and grow.

A sob tried to ascend from deep in his body.

But his father's voice erupted instead, along with the memory of the belt snapping against his bare back, the lashing more fierce than any delivered before. "I got 25 cents for him from someone over in Miller's Creek. Times are too tough for you to have a dog!"

Buster hadn't come to greet John when he came home from school that day. Buster had been John's solace since they moved into town after the bank took the farm away; his only link to the open fields he roamed. John's tears flowed before he could stop them. That's when the beating began.

"I'm sorry, Father. I'm sorry, Father," he pleaded as the lashes tore through his skin, though he did not know his sin.

"I'll teach you to be a man!" His father raised his hand and delivered the final blow that drove John's head into the wall. John crumpled, urine running down his legs, blood trickling down his face. But the tears had stopped.

His father hovered over him, contempt and shame in his eyes. "Men make tough decisions. And they don't cry." He threw the belt at John and strode away.

The words from the divorce decree tumbled through John's mind: extreme mental cruelty.

Louise left me, and now, Billy, you died to escape my cruelty.

John turned on the pump and watched the embalming fluid slowly course through his son's body, turning his grey pallor into a newborn pink, pushing the pooled blood through the draining tube into the bottle he held in his hand. There was so little. Just over half a cup.

The tear ripped deeper into his heart. And, yet, it continued to beat.

The squeaky wheels entered the ward again. Louise received the sound of the cart as it moved from bed to bed, collecting its bundles of flannel, then receded into the hallway, carrying its cargo to the nursery.

The swift footsteps of the new fathers followed their murmered goodbyes. The cheery, light chatter of the new mothers stopped suddenly as the sound of John's familiar footsteps entered the ward.

John appeared, cradling a tiny white coffin in his arms.

Louise stared at the coffin.

"I want to see him," she commanded finally.

He opened the lid.

Billy's tiny head was swathed in a clean, white flannel blanket. John had done a good job preparing Billy to meet his mother. His lips looked as if he had just finished suckling at her breast. He appeared to be sleeping peacefully.

Louise reached out to touch his face.

It was cold and hard.

She pulled her hand away, turned from John and Billy and pulled the covers over her shoulder. John closed the lid. "I'll take him away now."

Louise listened to his footsteps recede down the ward, carrying the cold, hard body of her son away.

John had no trouble digging into the rain soaked ground. The grave was as deep as most, but much shorter. It didn't take him long.

He placed a rope around the tiny white coffin, tied it with a slip knot, and lowered it into the grave. He pulled the rope through the slip knot and wound it figure-eight style around his forearm.

He began shoveling the damp earth onto his son, tamping each layer, until Billy was safely buried. Meticulously, he worked around the edge of the grave, tucking in the dirt, so a clean neat seam formed between the bare earth of the grave and the lawn next to it.

John picked up the rope and began making his way back to

the car, covered with the mud of his infant son's grave, stepping around the headstones of those he had tended to so carefully, his heart aching with the sob that would not rise.

The heavy skies opened and God rained down his tears.

Louise stayed in the hospital a week, visiting John Steven's incubator every day, walking past the mothers cradling their babies, her arms feeling the phantom pain of the child she would never hold, her breasts aching with milk that had nowhere to go.

As Louise walked into the nursery on her last day in the hospital, she eyed Ethel putting John Steven back in his incubator. *It's her.* Ethel pulled the beaded bracelet from the pocket of her crisp, white uniform and placed it on John Steven's thigh. Louise remembered that she hadn't seen Billy's bracelet. *I bet she took it for herself.*

"Now doesn't he look just like his daddy?" Ethel said and patted Louise on the arm. "Don't worry about your little Johnny. We can take better care of him than you can right now. Let me get you some ice water."

Ethel crossed the room with a crisp, efficient squeaking and rustling.

Louise gazed down into the incubator at her sleeping son. John Steven's tiny body looked fragile, too little for his diaper, his umbilical cord black and shriveled.

God loved Billy so much, He wanted him to be with Him.

Louise stole a look at Ethel, her back to her, pouring ice water into a glass. She aimed her gaze back down on her sleeping son and whispered, "Not even God will love you more than I will."

Ethel crossed the room and handed the sweating glass to Louise, who tipped the glass to her lips. *She should know I don't like ice in my water.* The coldness of the water burned her.

"So we're going home today," Ethel chirped. Louise handed her the glass. Ethel took it, and turned to place it next to the pitcher.

Louise looked down into Johnny's sleeping face. "My love," she whispered.

"Don't you worry," Ethel slipped her arm through Louise's and walked her to the nursery door. "I'll take good care of your little Johnny, just like he was mine."

John had stopped at Smith's Flowers on the way to pick her up. The wreath sat on the back seat, next to the umbrella. They drove the six blocks to the cemetery in silence.

John helped her from the car, then opened the back door to pull out the wreath and umbrella. Their feet sank into the wet earth as they carefully made their way around the headstones to a small mound of fresh earth. John placed the wreath on top of it, then stepped back, opened the umbrella and put it over Louise's head.

They stood silently, not touching, listening to the sound of the rain spattering on the ribbon of the wreath.

"John, I want you to buy the burial plots next to Billy." They were the first words she had said to him all morning.

"I already bought one for you and me right next to him," John assured her.

"I want you to buy one for Johnny, too."

He took her arm, and they carefully made their way through the wet, soggy ground, picking their way around the headstones and back to the car.

They rode home in silence, the wipers slapping back and forth across the windshield.

The house was cold and dark. Louise removed the hat pin and placed her hat on the table near the door, next to the stack of telegrams.

"I'll go make a fire," John said.

She picked up the opened telegrams and began reading them.

Congratulations. Twins. Love to John and Louise. Opal and Fred.
Welcome Johnny and Billy. Love to you all. Joe and Betty.
So sorry. In our prayers. Love Opal and Fred.
Must accept God's wisdom. We pray for you. Joe and Betty.

Louise carefully folded the telegrams, gathered the unopened ones, placed all of them in her pocket, then walked into the nursery.

John had already taken down the extra crib. Two piles of diapers sat on the changing table next to the closet. John came to her side and put his arm around her shoulder.

"We shouldn't have bought so many diapers," she reported. "We expected too much. God doesn't want us to expect too much. That's why He did this to me."

She walked out of John's arm and crossed the room to the changing table.

God, give me the strength to understand Your will. Make me worthy of Your love so I can join Billy when my time comes.

Her back to John, she opened the door to the closet, picked a diaper from the extra pile, carefully folded it, and placed it in the back of the shelf. She picked up another diaper, folded it once, placed a telegram on top of it, finished folding the diaper, then placed it on top of the other diaper in the back of the shelf. She continued until all of the extra diapers were neatly stacked on top of each other, telegrams carefully tucked inside them, in the back of the shelf.

"This way I'll know where to find them. I'll go make us some dinner now," she said, closed the closet door, and left the room.

John stared at the closed closet door, then at the romping lambs that covered the walls. He had finished putting up the wallpaper just two weeks ago, working carefully to match the pattern so no seams were visible.

He placed his hand in his pocket and pulled out the beaded bracelet he'd removed from Billy's leg at Ranahan's. He ran his fingers over the lettered beads. B. I. L. L.Y.

"Did you know I loved you?" John said aloud, though he knew no one could hear him. The sob, so firmly lodged in his heart, grew until the weary muscle could bear it no longer—his heart broke.

And yet, it continued to beat.

The browning roast sizzled in the kitchen.

He knew she shouldn't be left alone for too long; her iron will belied the fragility that lay beneath.

John placed Billy's bracelet back in his pocket, closed the door to his son's room behind him, and left to join Louise in the kitchen.

Stream of Consciousness
by Selene Steese

In a moment, the path will bend,
and in a moment I will see
the stand of bamboo
by the road, across
from the needled, fragrant trees
awash in light from the burnished moon.

I come here, mostly,
in my dreams. Walk
this brambled path above this stream
of rushing, rushing, rushing, splashing,
leaping, swirling, blue-black blessings
touched and tipped with silver dripping
from the drifting, damask moon
and edges of the mica stars.

This is not where the words
lie waiting. Not where
my next poem lives.
This is where the silence dwells
that comes before the words creep in.

I make my way along this path
when I'm unquiet, or in wrath,
or feeling shamed, or grieving deep.

The bank beside the stream
is steep, and I descend into the sound
of rushing, splashing all around
and drink from the pure waters there.

Then comes the impulse
toward the words.

Then I ascend
to where the waking world
lies waiting
and once again
I place the pen
upon the page.

Charlene Writes a Poem

by Charan Sue Wollard

The wise woman
contemplates a pear
The color of it:
bright green softening into yellow
russet where the flesh
mellows inside
She holds its bowl bottom
succulent with promise
pinches the hard fist
that affixes a small brown stem
to the invisible pulpy spine
She presses it to her cheek
Its rough skin grates
keeps its fragrance
barely perceptible until

She bites into the pear
cuts it with her sharp teeth
dives into sugar meat
licks its tart, sweet juices
inhales full pungent scent
swallows pearness as she would
enlightenment
savors the juice of pear
as the essence of life itself runs down her chin
pours into her lap
She does not stop until
she has devoured it
Left no more
than the still-twitching core of pear
Its seeds spill at her feet

Peacocks In Mourning

by J.D. Blair

A peacock's call echoed off the creek at 6:30 and penetrated the meager windows of the doublewide on Lee's ten-acre ranch. Their squawk woke Ray and he felt Lee's warmth against his back as she stirred against him.

"Do you want to drive or toss?"

He smiled. Ray hated her aging pickup that served as the feeding truck. "I'll toss, thank you. You can wrestle with the beast this morning. It understands you."

She kissed the back of his neck and left the bed. "I'll make coffee."

Lee was a beautiful, tall brunette with large, dark eyes and full lips. She had the look of the young Ingrid Bergman. Lee harbored a passion for life Ray had never experienced before and in their ten years of stolen moments together there wasn't a time when he didn't want to make love to her. Lee had been on the ranch just three months. It was her life's dream and she boarded twelve horses including two of her own. Five were kept stalled and the rest pastured on six acres that fronted the house. Their weekends became a rhythmic tonic for them and as the weeks passed they worked on upgrading the doublewide, tending the stock and sharing the changes in the rural landscape as the seasons moved through.

With coffee cups filled they stepped into the morning as sunlight washed over the hills that formed the horizon east of the ranch. The air was heavy with the musty smell of damp hay and horses as they loaded bales into the truck.

As she steered the pickup along the dirt access road the peacocks squawked and fluffed, skittering out of the way as the truck made its way along the fence line. The horses loped along the fence waiting for chips of hay to fall their way. Ray clipped baling wire and tossed as Lee maintained a slow speed along the fence, the truck clutch chattered as she kept up the pace. When he had tossed the last chip, Ray pounded on the truck cab and Lee made the turn up the lane to the barn where the other horses were stalled. She backed the truck into the barn and Ray jumped out of the bed and lowered the tailgate. Before Lee could get out of the cab he got to her and laid her across the front seat of the truck and kissed her hard on the lips. He pulled back and looked into her dark eyes.

"Good morning."

Lee took hold of his jacket lapels, "Good morning yourself. You are a terrible feeder. You missed half of the spots you were aiming for and the chips were way too big."

"I like to spoil them."

"I'll go broke in a month if I let you toss."

He kissed her again. "Yes, but you will be rich in other ways. Where else can you get this kind of attention?"

She laughed, "Next door, dummy. Tom Neely at the next ranch has been after me for months and I ignore him because of you." She pulled him to her and kissed him softly. "Now get off me so we can finish feeding these critters and get some breakfast."

He did get off and they finished feeding and walked back to the house. She made breakfast while he showered and dressed.

They ate quietly and listened to the peacocks prattle at every movement of the livestock. Ray would be on the road into town in half-an-hour and Lee felt bad at the thought of being without him.

Their routine together was steady but incomplete. Ray lived and worked in town an hour and a half away and in a stagnating marriage shared a suburban home with his wife. He spent weekends on the ranch with Lee under the guise of work. Lee was divorced from an abusive husband and lived on the ranch, alone. Each week Ray arrived at the ranch on Friday evening and left on Monday morning. On this Monday morning a hawk circled and the peacocks sang and scattered as the weekend ended. Lee watched from the porch as Ray backed out of the driveway.

As he drove to town that morning Ray pondered the question he asked Lee over breakfast. It was something as simple as "How are you going to spend your day?" It was nothing that would cause Lee's response…a gaze of total confusion. Her blank stare across the table was so devoid of understanding that he questioned it. It's clear now that she didn't have an answer. Something had declared war on her consciousness and she didn't understand anything at that moment, let alone the meaning of how she would spend her day, or what a day was. Ray knew something was different that morning.

Aside from that moment over breakfast there wasn't anything in particular to signal a problem but he did notice Lee's growing reluctance to ride her favorite gelding, Bob. He was a gentle horse and she never had trouble with him. She often took him out on the rolling landscapes but lately had not saddled him.

"They've opened the gate to the park trail," prodded Ray, " you should take Bob out for a walk."

"He's skittish at the creek," said Lee, "he doesn't like it."

Her fear puzzled him. The gelding had crossed the small creek dozens of times.

"You bought this place so you and Bob would have a place to run and you haven't taken him out in weeks."

Lee had no answer for him and continued to pay the bills scattered over the dining room table.

On a late Saturday afternoon they were watching television and Lee confessed to having bad headaches.

"They're like tension headaches," she said. "They make me dizzy and my eyes get blurry."

"Have you seen anyone?" asked Ray.

"No, I don't know who to see. I'm sure it will go away."

In the weeks that followed Ray didn't badger Lee but made sure he paid closer attention. He thought he noticed lapses in her attention span and what he thought was an unsteadiness as she made her way through the house but she wasn't complaining so he let it slide.

It was a Sunday in late May when Lee's headaches and her worry finally collided. Ray was reading on the porch when she came to him.

"I think we need to go see somebody."

He put his book down. "See somebody? About what?"

"My headaches. They're getting worse and I'm dizzy all the time now. Can we go?"

Ray was already out of his chair. "Of course we can. We'll go to the emergency."

They didn't talk much on the ride to the hospital. There wasn't anything to say that would make Lee less scared and Ray less worried.

The hospital took her in immediately and began a series of scans and tests. Ray went outside to call her two sons alerting them to Lee's situation.

It took several hours to complete the tests and when they finished Lee was wheeled to a room adjoining the ER. Her beautiful raven curls where shaved back and fluids were flowing into her arm. When Ray came in her boys were already in the room. Lee smiled wanly and he went to her and held her close.

"I'm so scared," she whispered.

"I know," said Ray. "Try not to worry; we're here."

It wasn't long before a doctor came in. He scanned the room and acknowledged Ray and the boys.

"Well, we see a dark mass on the upper left part of your brain, about here." He pointed to the shaved patch on Lee's head. Lee held back tears and the others clenched their jaws. "We don't want to make any rush to judgment until we go in to see what we've got."

There it was in two brief sentences. Lee had something intruding on her brain and needed surgery.

Ray spoke up. "When do you need to do that?"

"Right away," said the doctor. He looked at Lee and applied light pats to her shoulder. "We should schedule it for tomorrow morning."

Lee's hands went to her face and Ray held her.

"Try not to worry," added the doctor, "there are several things it could be and we want to be sure about what we're dealing with before we decide what to do next. You get some rest."

The doctor left and the room was silent. There was nothing any of them could say and Ray knew then that his role in Lee's life would change. Her family would be forming around her and Ray would do what he could from the edges of her life.

Glioblastoma was the medical term for the web of deadly growth that was strangling Lee's brain. It is the most invasive of all brain tumors and there was little to be done outside of chemo, pain control, and medicine to treat her balance problems. In the preliminary surgery they removed as much of the tumor they could safely reach but it was too advanced to do more.

The day after the surgery Ray went to her. Lee's entire head was shaved and bandaged and the fear in her dark eyes was replaced by fatigue. Her recuperation from the surgery would be short and she would be released soon.

After she left the hospital their life rhythm returned to normal with the exception of medical matters that became part of the regimen. Ray put together a schedule for her to keep track of the cascade of medications she was now forced to take. Whenever he could, Ray became her taxi service to and from doctor visits . . . trips to specialists in San Francisco and Berkeley. None of them offered much encouragement other than to make the most of what time she had left. Her boys took over work on the ranch but Lee was still able to work with "Bob" in the corral. She and Ray took long walks around the ranch and had picnics along the creek.

As the weeks crawled by Lee became more and more dependent. Her sons and their wives spent time with her when Ray couldn't be there. Eventually Lee's mother made the decision to move into the doublewide. When Lee's condition reached the point where her mother couldn't cope the family called on Hospice for help. By that time Ray was a spectator and all of Lee's medical demands were in the hands of others. She became less lucid and was losing mobility. She would often struggle to remember who people were though she did know Ray when he came to see her. She spent longer periods of time in a hospital bed in the living room of the doublewide. Lee's ten acres had been reduced to the size of the bed.

Several times a week Ray talked with her family but only occasionally was he able to talk with Lee. He visited on weekends once or twice a month but Lee was barely lucid and even with Hospice care the family struggled to keep her at home. Inevitably the day came when her family put Lee in a critical care facility.

The idea of Lee in the facility saddened Ray and he visited her often. Every time he went by to see her, she was alone. Her dark hair had turned into a mass of mousy gray clumps. She wore a diaper and a bout with seizures now called for the use of restraints. Lee was tied to a bed and unable to control any of her bodily functions.

On what turned out to be Ray's last visit he stepped into her room and Lee became agitated. She was hallucinating and was having trouble seeing him. She couldn't talk and was thrashing, tugging at her restraints. The tumor had done its work. Her faculties were snatched from her and what had been the love of Ray's life was now a crazed and feral animal. He left her for the final time and cried in his car in the parking lot.

A week after Ray's last visit, Lee died. There was a small gathering of friends and family at the ranch. Lee's boys rode on horseback to the ridgeline of the hills behind the doublewide. They carried a small box containing Lee's ashes. They tossed her into the wind and she swirled lightly over the road and along the fence line where the hawk circled and the peacocks shrieked their goodbyes.

The Terrible Haiku
by Jason Hambrecht

Dear Christine
You are beautiful
In all categories

On a sleepless night in spring
by sandra kay

        my mind insisted on telling me a love story. "it will help you fall asleep," she whispered.   and so i agreed to listen   —but with my eyes closed.

"at a small oak table," she said softly, "there sat a very handsome man who could solve gigantic mathematical problems in an instant. No paper. No pencil. No machines. —he was a genius," she said smiling, "and although everyone within earshot knew his answers were correct, still they insisted   —delighted in— proving with a calculator.

And I started to recall scenes from the movie Good Will Hunting . . . then saw Robin Williams, then scenes from The Fisher King, Dead Poets Society; Mrs Doubtfire. And I tossed and I turned, but she waited patiently for me to settle back down and then continued:

"The fanfare attracted a beautiful woman who was quick to fill in the empty seat directly across from him," she said, "and in an instant, she knew they would fall in love. No words. No time. No question.   —she was a genius too," she said smiling, "and although no one else within earshot could hear the wedding bells or baby cries, still she insisted   —delighted in—   looking in his eyes.

That's a sweet n' short, g-rated story, I said to my mind. Thank you. I think I can fall asleep now.

"Not so fast," she said, "type it first, or it's gone forever after."

The End.

Life's Just a John Prine Song
by Peter Bray

He was blowing blue notes through the end of his horn,
wondering why in the world that he had been born
when I found him all alone with his music in the bowels of BART.

He said, "Life's just a John Prine song, it's sad and it's funny,
when you're living on love, 'cause ya ain't got no money,
and your teeth are all aching and saying Goodbye to their neighbors."

I said, "Kleenex your heart and help Phoenix your friends,
you'll never know whether your fortunes may end
and your heroes are homeless when they're making amends,
and love's on the backroads being made by your friends."

He said, "Life's just a John Prine song, it's sad and it's funny,
when you're riding on bald tires, 'cause ya ain't got no money,
and your life's just a scream 'cause you're wondering which one will go first."

I said, "Kleenex your heart and help Phoenix your friends,
you'll never know whether your fortunes will end,
and your heroes are homeless when they're making amends,
and love's on the backroads being made by your friends."

He said, "Life's just a John Prine song no matter how it ends."

Damp Eucalyptus
by J.D. Blair

The first time you smacked my senses into awareness
was in the park near the lake in the dampness of
an early Sunday morning in the grasp of summer in San Francisco.
Another time, in bed, as the Richmond District woke to
June I stirred with nostrils full of you pulling at me
through those drafty Victorian windows that were
burdened with layers of design.
Yet again, in the still wetness of four A.M.,
in a Sunset District bungalow low in the avenues
loving my dangerous lack of judgment with
a brown eyed lady whose hair smelled of you and who
loved me well, and often.
You came again in the denseness sliding across Morro Bay
in blankets pulled inland as I walked beach ward
with your pungent, camphor scented drops
               in cadence.

The Mailman
by Steve Workman

My uncle was not particularly outstanding in terms of appearance or occupation. He had a chubby face that reminded me of Santa Claus without the beard. His potbelly was well honed from years of drinking his favorite beer, although almost any beer would do. The calves of his legs were muscular and hairless from the constant rubbing of his pants as he walked thousands of miles over the course of his lifetime delivering mail to the unassuming town of Frankfort, Indiana.

He had a gentle manner about him. His favorite pastime consisted of doing laundry. An ancient washer and dryer were located in one corner of the garage. Once the clothes were loaded, he would grab a folding aluminum chair and place it carefully in the same position near the garage entrance where he kept his pipe and tobacco on a small metal ashtray stand. Once lit, he would throw his head back in quiet celebration and gaze into the distance as both machines hummed and whirred.

There was a cornfield across the road from his house that seemed to hold some fascination for him. I could never understand why. There was nothing particularly different about this cornfield that made it stand out from any other. In the state of Indiana, there is never much question about what type of crop should be planted. There was only the question of when to plant the corn, when to harvest the corn and when to ask God for a little help along the way. Nevertheless, by summer's end, when the corn stood tall, you could usually find Uncle Joe sitting at the entrance to his garage, staring at the cornfield and smoking his pipe in slow motion, inhaling and exhaling to the beat of a drummer that only he could hear as a sweet cherry aroma slowly filled the house with an ambiance that felt like . . . home.

It was on a Fourth of July such as this that I found my Uncle Joe sitting at the entrance to the garage. Being an only child from a broken family, I found the sameness of seeing him sitting there was comforting in a way. In that sense, he was more like a father than an uncle. And although I heard that they had tried, they never had any children. I always thought it was a waste that a person like Joe would never leave the footprints of his kindness in the heart of a child.

I pulled onto the gravel driveway and parked on the lawn next to Joe's pickup truck so I would not block the view of the cornfield. "OK if I do some donuts in your yard?" I said, gunning the engine.

"I was just sitting here thinking about doing the same thing," said Joe with a chuckle. It was always like that with Joe. You always started a conversation with a laugh and a smile.

Joe and Dottie had lived in the same three-bedroom home for as long as I could remember. Surrounded by farmland on an oversized lot, it had been added-to and patched-up over the years so that it took on a quirkiness that made you smile as you drove by. An expansive front porch looked out over a never-ending field of corn, while a meandering stream lined with sycamore trees defined the edge of their property in back. Dottie had crossed that stream hundreds of times over a makeshift bridge that Joe built for her so she could walk to the schoolhouse nearby, where she taught fourth grade. Despite these peaceful surroundings, Joe inevitably preferred to sequester himself in the garage.

On one wall of the garage Joe had hung a number of vintage automobile license plates. There were 32 in all. Twelve of them were from Indiana, eight from Illinois, and the rest scattered across various states east of the Mississippi River. Other than a small lake near the Indiana-Michigan border where Joe would occasionally go fishing, he had never traveled to any of those places. But knowing that he was trying to collect them, the customers on his route would religiously be on the lookout for a particular license plate he wanted whenever they ventured outside the friendly confines of Frankfort. I always assumed he would eventually collect all 50, but when I asked him about it one day, he simply shrugged and told me that he had collected all the plates he needed for the time being. I never pushed the subject further. Looking back now, I wish I had.

 I walked into the garage, grabbed another folding chair and sat down next to him. Joe was hard of hearing in his left ear so preferred to have you sit to the right of him. The left side of his face was pockmarked making it difficult to shave. Sure enough, it looked like he had cut himself shaving again, as he wore a band-aid on that side of his face. I smiled as I sat down and noticed he was wearing white socks with his black loafers.

 "I think there's a class at the local college called Shaving Do's and Don'ts," I told him.

 "I know. They use my face in their course material. I'm hoping to retire on the royalties." People tended to view Uncle Joe as a simpleton. He never went to college, never graduated from high school and never seemed to venture far from Frankfort. But for me, he seemed to draw from a hidden wellspring to find wit, wisdom, and irony in the mundane.

 "Joe, I need you," said a voice from inside the house. By all accounts, Aunt Dottie wore the pants in the family. She dominated the conversation with her daily exploits as a teacher at the local elementary school. The subject of Joe's latest near-death encounter with the pit bull down the street was usually drowned out by another one of Dottie's tirades on Washington politics and the inevitable moral winter that awaited us all once her fourth graders reached voting age.

He put his pipe in the ashtray, stood up, and, with a wink-of-a-smile, wondered what "Nurse Ratchett" wanted this time. Uncle Joe never showed a hint of anger. And, except for the occasional migraine, he was in a jovial mood most of the time.

So I sat there and did the only thing there was to do . . . listen to the laundry and stare at the cornfield. Rows of corn stretched as far as you could see in almost every direction, finally disappearing over a hill in the distance. The corn was getting tall at this point of the season. The stalks waved lazily back and forth in the late afternoon breeze as several hawks circled overhead. The sun had already dipped below a line of thunderheads building on the horizon, their edges glowing like embers left over from the heat of the late summer day. It would be a good evening to watch the fireworks, if they could get them in before the storm hit.

Whatever it was that Dottie wanted seemed to be the source of some disagreement, as snippets of an argument could be heard over the sound of clothes drying. The sound of a marriage in trouble was one I was already too familiar with. After several minutes, Joe finally emerged with Dottie in tow. "I didn't hear you pull in. Going to see the fireworks tonight?"

Dottie wore a bright yellow dress that screamed summer, along with a strand of white pearls and earrings. I gave her a hug and noticed her perfume was a little strong. She was an attractive woman for her age. People wondered how she and Joe got together. Dottie was forever the cosmopolitan with an opinion on almost everything, while Joe delivered the mail and did the laundry. Wherever she was going tonight, Joe was obviously not going with her. He sat down in his chair and relit his pipe.

"I was thinking you might want to watch the fireworks with me," I said. "I can drop you off at home on my way back to school."

Dottie looked at her watch. "Why don't you guys go. I have a school function to go to tonight." Joe shot her a penetrating glance.

"Either way, the two of you will probably have more fun without me. There's plenty of beer in the fridge. Just make sure you don't overdo it. You don't want Frankfort's finest pulling you over tonight on the way back home," said Dottie.

"That won't be a problem. He can stay here," said Joe more to himself than either Dottie or me. There was a moment of silence.

"Joe, don't you think . . ."

Joe cut her off in mid-sentence with an uncharacteristic irritation in his voice. "I said it's OK. He can spend the night."

Dottie stared at Joe, who now seemed indifferent to her presence as he slowly smoked his pipe. "I'll get my keys then." She turned and walked back inside the house.

Now, it had not gone unnoticed by the rest of the family that my aunt and uncle never had anyone stay overnight. Nor did they stay overnight at anyone else's house. And whenever there was an occasion for the family to be together, like Thanksgiving or Christmas, they would always leave a little early while everyone else continued on in half-drunken merriment. My mother always said they were private people and just preferred it that way. As I got older I sensed she knew something more.

Dottie came back outside, opened the door to the pickup truck and stopped for a moment. "Joe, make sure you take your sleeping pills. I put them on the kitchen counter. And stay out of trouble you guys!" I waved. Joe said nothing as she drove away.

"Hell, I've been looking to find trouble in this town for the last 20 years," said Joe. "I remember we had some trouble here once." He paused as if to remember the particulars of a robbery or a shooting that must have happened years earlier. "Someone stole a catfish from the Anderson's pond." Joe looked at me.

"That was probably the best damn catfish I've ever had." We both laughed.

We decided to stay home for the evening instead of driving to the fairgrounds to watch the fireworks. The county fairgrounds were less than a mile away on the other side of the hill, hidden from view, but you could easily see the fireworks that were shot into the air from where we sat. As darkness settled in, fireflies started to appear, their yellow beacons flashing in a haphazard "catch-me-if-you-can" fashion. "I heard that some people catch them by the thousands and sell the phosphorous in them," I said.

Joe looked at me and smiled. "Yeah, I tried using that story once when I stayed out too late with the guys. Trust me, it won't work." The smile on his face quickly faded with the flash of several bombs that signaled the start of the fireworks show. As the sharp rumble of the first bombs hit us, I thought I saw him flinch out of the corner of my eye.

We continued to talk over the fireworks, mostly about things that didn't matter. Joe never liked talking about politics or world affairs. Didn't need to. I suspect Mark Twain would have liked my uncle. He probably could have written a book or two about the daily exploits of delivering mail to the townsfolk of Frankfort. And while Dottie and others mostly talked over him, I found his stories filled with lessons in life that ultimately define the kind of person that we all should aspire to be.

We drank another beer following the fireworks finale, before turning in around midnight. You could see lightning in the distance and smell the sweet fragrance of wet farmland that blew ahead of the rainstorm. We closed the garage and went inside to get ready for bed. I noticed the sleeping pills on the kitchen counter. Joe walked past them.

"See you in the morning, Joe."

He hesitated at the entrance to his bedroom and looked at

me as though he wanted to say something. A moment of silence was finally punctuated with a "see you in the morning." As he closed the door to his bedroom, I noticed that he also locked it.

While they had no children of their own, their guest bedroom seemed to have been decorated with one in mind. A full size bed in one corner of the room was covered with a quilt blanket and several pillows imprinted with images of zoo animals. A toy rocker with a teddy bear sat in one corner of the room next to a small desk that must have once seen the inside of Dottie's classroom. Pictures of Dotties's fourth grade classes adorned one wall. I could hear the echo of children laughing as I moved from one year to the next. Thirty years of teaching had taken their toll on Dottie, as she seemed to smile less and less over time while her lips thinned and the lines in her face grew more prominent. I noticed that pictures of Joe were conspicuously absent. Apparently, the life of a mailman did not warrant an honorable mention in this shrine to a purpose-driven life. It suddenly dawned on me that as much time as I had spent with my uncle, even I did not have a picture of him.

I walked to the window and opened it so I could hear the storm and feel the cool damp air. I took my shoes off but was too tired to bother with the rest and collapsed onto the bed. I laid in the dark watching the curtains move lazily back and forth as the storm outside began to breathe. Sleep came easily . . . at first.

I cannot say exactly when, but at some point during the night I heard the creaking sound of a door being opened very slowly. Not knowing the sleeping habits of my aunt or uncle, I ascribed no particular importance to it. Perhaps Joe had decided he needed to take his sleeping pills after all. But there was an uneasiness that I could not ignore as I laid in the dark and listened for him to return to his bedroom. He never did.

The distant rumblings of thunder were getting louder, interspersed with an occasional crack of lightning that lit up the bedroom. They said the storm that was coming might be severe which, in this part of the country, usually meant tornado weather. Perhaps Joe was outside making sure things were not going to get blown away.

All of a sudden, for a brief moment, as the wind sighed and the night paused, I thought I could hear the distant sound of someone crying. Not as if they were hurt, but more like a cry of torment. It was an other-worldly sound that sucked the air from my lungs as I tried to listen for it a second time. I suddenly noticed that the curtains were being pushed against the screen window, which meant that a breeze was blowing from somewhere inside the house. The front door must have come open.

Too old to be scared of the dark but just young enough to remember how it felt, I pulled the covers up just a little higher and remembered the quiet whispers that surrounded my Aunt and Uncle as I was growing up. They say that everyone has a dark side, although it was hard to believe that someone who liked to do laundry could possibly have one. I was quickly embarrassed at myself for considering the possibility. Joe was probably injured and needed my help.

With this self reassurance, I quickly got up and put on my shoes. I walked to the window and pulled the curtains back to look outside. The fireflies and frogs had settled in for the evening. Large drops of rain were starting to tap the gutters of the house. But there was no sign of Joe. As I turned from the window, I heard it again...the melancholy moaning sound of someone in pain.

I could feel the pulse of my heart quicken as I walked by Joe's bedroom. The door was wide open but Joe was not in his bed. I noticed the sleeping pills were still on the kitchen counter where Dottie left them. Sure enough, the front door was wide open.

"Joe?" I yelled from the front porch. I strained to listen for a response. Nothing. I walked quickly to the side of the house and yelled again, but still there was no answer. The rain was beginning to come down harder now, as I sprinted back to the front porch and stood at the bottom of the steps waiting for the next bolt of lightning to spray the countryside with a moment of daylight. Where the hell is he?

I didn't have to wait long. A bolt raced down from the sky striking a tree at the top of a ridge nearby. It was quickly followed by an ear-piercing snap and a thunderclap that faded into the same muffled cry I heard before. And then suddenly, it swept over me. Joe was out there . . . in the cornfield.

I ran to the edge of the road and looked out across the top of the corn, their tassels now churning like foam on a stormy sea. Sheets of rain blew directly into my face as I filled my lungs with air and shouted Joe's name again and again. I stumbled along the edge of the road until I thought I saw an opening where he might have entered. And so, not knowing or understanding, I closed my eyes and pushed my way several yards into the cornfield, before finally stopping to listen through the wind and the rain for that the tell-tale sound of torment that would surely lead me to my uncle.

I stood still for several minutes with water pouring down the back of my neck, as my clothes became heavy and began to melt against my skin. I noticed the cornfield had grown strangely quiet and I began to feel foolish for putting myself in this position. Joe was probably going to be standing at the front door when I returned, wondering what in the world I was doing outside in the rain.

But as I stood there . . . in the cornfield . . . in the storm . . . in the darkness, I felt my skin begin to creep with the feeling that I was being watched. I slowly turned around and was suddenly confronted with the silhouette of Uncle Joe floating like an apparition just a few feet away from me. Neither one of us spoke. Neither one of us moved as the rain poured steadily down upon us. Adrenaline raced through my veins as I clenched my fists, ready to protect myself from the stranger that now stood before me.

And then, just as another flash of lightning shot between the clouds above us, I saw a face of my uncle that I had never seen before. It was a face of pain and anguish that must have been forged in some crucible of horrors that he kept locked away in a dark corner of his mind. He looked skyward, but his eyes were closed and his jaw was clenched. And though the raindrops pelted down upon his face, I could still see the tears that streamed from the corners of his eyes. He suddenly dropped to his knees in front of me. I ran over to him and cupped his face in my hands. "Joe! What's wrong? Wake up!"

"I didn't want to," he whispered over and over. But not to me.

"Joe, we need to get inside now. We're going to get drenched." I helped him get up, put his arm around my shoulder and half-dragged him back to the edge of the cornfield.

As we stood there for a moment, I thought I heard him say, "We're almost there."

"That's right, Joe. We're almost there." We made our way slowly back to the house. He said nothing as I helped him pull off his wet clothes and got him into bed. I couldn't tell if he was awake or asleep or somewhere in between.

I stumbled back into bed exhausted and listened to the storm while I tried to comprehend what had just happened. Whatever it was, I knew my relationship with my uncle would never be the same.

I woke up late the next morning. Jumping out of bed, I ran to the kitchen glancing into Joe's bedroom as I went by. He was already up. Opening the kitchen door to the garage, I looked out to see Joe sitting in his usual spot smoking his pipe. The washing machine was already running.

Neither one of us acknowledged the other as we both sat and

stared at a cornfield that now seemed to hold a secret of some kind. The look in his eyes told me that whatever he wanted to say to me was not going to come easy. He finally put his pipe down on the stand next to his chair and looked at me. "You once asked me about the license plates," he said, pausing to scan the wall where they were hung. "I never really gave you an answer. But after last night . . . I guess maybe it's time I did."

Uncle Joe was in the third wave that landed at Normandy in June 1944. He was a spotter for an artillery unit. It was his job to crawl forward into the face of the enemy and radio back the small adjustments needed to hit their target. The thunderous noise from the explosions near him would eventually cause him to be partially deaf in his left ear.

During the first two weeks after landing, his unit made their way inland several miles to a position near the town of Rouen. Crawling through the underbrush, he found himself in front of a German machine gun position. He lobbed a grenade that hit a branch, dropping just short of its intended target, but close enough to kill the two German soldiers inside as they looked up to investigate. Shrapnel from his own grenade struck the left side of his face. Years later, pieces of metal would periodically ooze from his skin. The headaches were particularly severe when they did. To most people, it looked as though he had cut himself shaving.

He continued to crawl forward several hundred yards through a cornfield and soon found himself in a bomb crater in the middle of that field. Hearing gunfire behind him, he realized that he was probably surrounded. And so, without any hope of escape, he called in adjustments as round after round of artillery came in on top of a German tank division nearby. The bombing would continue for the next three days.

Sometime during the third night, it began to rain and the

bomb crater he was in began to fill with water. Night can be a treacherous ally in the middle of a battlefield. Mix in a little rain and a soldier will find the rough edges of his own sanity as he listens sleeplessly for the tell tale snap of a twig amid the constant patter of raindrops.

At some point, he thought he heard the crunch of a footstep. Not wanting to give away his position, he reached into his pocket for a knife that a friend had sent him from home, flipped it open and waited. He had hoped it was just ghosts moving through the cornfield as the stalks rustled in the evening breeze.

Suddenly, a German soldier emerged at the edge of the crater. Before he could do anything, Joe leaped up and thrust the knife into his mid-section. He could feel the knife hitting bone as he pushed it in as far as it would go. They both fell backwards into the bomb crater.

In the darkness, both men only knew of the other from their labored breathing. And from the groans, he could tell the other soldier was probably not in a position to do him harm. He thought for a moment that he should finish what he started, but then there was always something more personal in killing another human being with your own hands.

Now and then the crack of lightning would light up the night and, for a brief moment, each could see the other's face, like snapshots that could never be thrown away. From the sparse stubble on his square jaw, Joe could tell that he was young, like him. Clutching his right side now stained a bright red, the soldier stared wide-eyed at Joe as he lay sprawled on the bank of the crater across from him.

Periodically, the soldier winced in pain. Afraid that the noise would draw the attention of more Germans, Joe finally decided he had to do something and crawled through the water over to him. The soldier shut his eyes and whispered a prayer hoping that the end would come quickly. Joe positioned himself behind his head, lifted it onto his lap, and reached around his mid-section to pull out the knife . . . and held him. Joe was like that. The young soldier began to cry. They both cried.

At daybreak, he placed two fingers on the young German's neck to feel for a pulse but couldn't tell for certain. It was hard to feel anything anymore. He looked skyward for an answer. The morning mist that hugged the ground providing a blanket of cover the last two mornings was no longer there, but he had no choice. He reached for his mud-covered rifle, shoved the barrel into the ground and carefully placed his helmet on the butt of his gun. He pulled off the soldier's boots, gun belt and pack to lighten the load and, resting on his knees, lifted him over his shoulder. He slowly stood upright and walked out of the crater to the edge of the cornfield. He took one step into the open startling a flock of birds, and waited briefly for a hail of gunfire to take them both down.

He would walk over a mile along a winding country road back to his artillery unit carrying a dead enemy soldier on his back. The men in his unit were speechless as he walked up to a medic and asked him to look after his "friend" and then, almost without pausing, asked for a rifle so he could go back. In the grotesque confusion of war, Uncle Joe could no longer tell the difference between life and death. They sent him home not long afterwards.

Sometime after the war ended, he discovered that 32 members of his unit never would come home. Twelve of them were from Indiana, eight from Illinois, and the rest scattered across various states east of the Mississippi River.

Twenty years later . . .

I stood overlooking the cornfield remembering the events of that evening so many years ago. My uncle died that same year in the fall. Dottie sold the house not long afterward and moved to another city nearby. But I still come here every year on the Fourth of July, more out of fear that I will forget than to remember. This year there was a sign in the distance advertising the future site of a new housing development. By this time next year, the cornfield would be just a memory. Like my Uncle Joe.

"Daddy, why are we here?"

I looked down into the expectant face of my six-year-old son and smiled. "To remember," I told him. "To remember something important that happened a long time ago."

"What happened, Daddy?"

I stroked the top of his head and said a silent prayer hoping that he would never come to know the hell of war. "Well, it's a little complicated Joseph." I paused to reflect on how to answer without really answering. "Before I tell you, I want you do something. I want you to take a picture of this cornfield with your eyes so you'll always remember when I tell you the story. Will you do that?"

He looked back at the cornfield and blinked slowly.

"Good. Now let's go watch the fireworks."

Ordinary people are asked to do horrible things in war. Sometimes they do noble things instead. My uncle never mentioned the medals that gathered dust in a box in the attic. He never put a sticker on his car that he was a wounded veteran. He never talked about what happened in that cornfield in France . . . except at night . . . in his sleep. The nightmares became less frequent over the years, but the ghosts would never leave. Periodically, he would wander outside in his sleep in the middle of the night looking for a young German soldier to emerge from a cornfield across the road from his house hoping that their meeting would somehow end differently this time.

Included in my uncle's affects was an article about the German Tank Commander Erwin Rommel, who was killed for his involvement in the attempted assassination of Adolph Hitler toward the end of World War II. Rommel's wife would tell friends afterwards that the turning point for him came when he watched through his binoculars as an American GI carried a dead German soldier on his back through no-man's land.

I know my uncle was not particularly outstanding in terms of appearance or occupation. But he was a hero just the same.

Uncle
by J.D. Blair

He shared his space with the darkness,
his right thumb severed at mid-
knuckle with the nail-less, rounded stump
twitching as he sat in that shadow
in the rocking chair near the shaded window
rocking to the tock of the mantle clock.

Tumbler of whiskey on the lamp stand,
thumb stump wrapped around the glass
with condensation tracing rivulets
around the nub leaving little pools at the base.
Seventy-nine in his thin, angular frame,
looking sickly.

Bald with steel gray eyes intently watching
through horn rims, a Cowboy who
carried the brand and wore it well.
Lasso, limber gait, horseback etiquette,
silent and straight, a man of few words
with his back to the wind and his heart
in the high country.

He watched the world through eyes of an ancient
Cowboy true and blue and died alert to the ways of the range
as his saddle, soaped and smelly, poised but unused, sat on
the sun porch of a mobile home in San Luis Obispo
County.

JoHanna James
by Thomas Lofgren

The eyes of JoHanna James are quite remarkable—so deeply brown you had to call them black. It was as if they were in a state of constant dilation. When I sat across from her and began speaking, those ebony orbs would focus on my every word. It led me to believe she used them as her primary organs of hearing. Yet this slim girl of twelve, with a train of black hair to match her eyes, could not, even with this intense concentration, understand anything I was saying.

JoHanna James is autistic. She is also a savant. Her place among other autistic savants is quite unique. She can do little of anything well, but there is one thing she does very, very well. She is capable of remembering and reciting everything that was ever said to her—not only the words, but who was speaking, what they were wearing, the nuances of the speaker, the accent, the facial expressions, body language, and the placement and gesturing of the hands. Johanna's eyes are, astronomically speaking, great black holes sucking in every detail of a one-on-one conversation. She then files them in a most elegant manner, and is able to efficiently retrieve them when called upon to do so. Even more amazing, each detail seems to be methodically time stamped. Given a date, JoHanna is able to fully describe all conversational elements on that day, in their order of occurrence. During one of my sessions with her, I tried to see how far back JoHanna could remember. I talked with her parents to determine when a simple repeating of what mommy said changed into a serious diagnosis. That revelation occurred around age two. When I maneuvered

JoHanna back to this age, response from her memory bank prompted a touching scene as mom and dad could hear how they each had once talked to their infant girl.

JoHanna's recall was phenomenal. She remembered and could restate every word of mine from every session we had together. She never got mixed up on which session was which and that internal clock kept everything in order and paged. She could pull out any part of a session and continue up to whatever end time you asked of her. I made intricate notes of what I said and tried to keep them in tight sequence. I would test her, slurring a few words, mangling others, inserting some in French, but she passed all these exams with flying colors.

We had a peculiar type of fun, JoHanna and I, bringing back some statements of mine from past sessions. She could mimic my accent, my pronunciations, mispronunciations, mannerisms, habits, smiles, and even a grimace followed by a slap to my head after a dumb grammatical error. She would laugh her girlish laugh, perhaps not because she understood the irony of her unusual talent, but more likely from the startled, amazed look on my face when she launched into her reiterations. I reflect fondly on all those wonderful moments we had together.

I no longer visit JoHanna. I cannot allow myself that pleasure due to an allegation that popped up soon after my final session. Some insidious peepster, a shameful gossip with a depraved imagination, someone perhaps with a window facing that of the room in JoHanna's parents' house where our sessions were held, accused me of improprieties. Someone who did not know me and did not know JoHanna, but claimed to have seen or heard something that should not occur between a man my age and a girl JoHanna's. Although I bristled at the suggestion, my being a professional and licensed left no recourse but to be charged.

JoHanna's parents had attended some of the sessions. I felt I had gained their trust and the fact that they would testify in my defense confirmed it. Other times, I was left alone with JoHanna and I had done or said nothing to make her distrust me. I at first insisted that JoHanna not be involved in the trial. It would be a doleful and strange intrusion into her simple life. After much inner grappling, and at the urging of my lawyer, it was decided to have her take the stand. JoHanna's parents approved, along with their daughter's life-long doctor. My lawyer convinced the DA that JoHanna knew of me and could answer, in her own way, questions regarding my behavior. The prosecution smugly accepted, as they had arranged to have a noted psychologist examine JoHanna and testify on the credibility of someone who would not understand the proceedings, the questions asked, or the consequences of anything to which she testified.

JoHanna had been very protected and secluded in her life. She knew well only her family. She was cognizant of me, and through me, my lawyer. My lawyer's methodology was very simple. He began with questions about the initial visit. From JoHanna came, in her best mimic job, my words, my inflections, my mannerisms, right down to the pulling of my mustache while pondering. She described in amazing photographic detail the pattern on my tie, the chair, the rug, the wall behind. A forty-minute conversation was broken down to its simplest components, like a computer program, in precise order of event. It was, in effect, an impersonation of me. My lawyer then asked about other sessions, to emphasize JoHanna's exacting skill. He then introduced an aspect I had not brought out in any of my sessions—JoHanna's database of words and conversational attributes. He devised queries that involved suggestive or provocative words or movements. I assume this was used to take the steam out of similar tactics the prosecution may have contemplated using. JoHanna's search was diligent and silent. Through it all, not one improper word was repeated, not one inappropriate move, not even a leer.

When my lawyer felt his point proven, he challenged the

prosecution to ask of JoHanna what they wished. The district attorney's staff began with the times the witness claimed, then concentrated on the latter sessions, assuming if I were to make a move it would be after I had gained a friendly familiarity with JoHanna. The results of the cross examination were a mirror image of ours. The state's attorneys tried all they could to get JoHanna to remember any suggestive word I had used, any casual or direct movement towards her, any touching, looking, cajoling. JoHanna in profound silence delivered me clean and innocent. I was somewhat bemused by the thought that the Prosecutor's frustrations were being recorded by JoHanna in vivid neural video. I was also saddened by the placement of certain words and gestures into JoHanna's once pristine and elegant database. Just before the trial, the prosecution's self-proclaimed expert on autistic savants declined to participate. He stated that after interviewing JoHanna his testimony would be of no advantage to them. I was acquitted.

    I shall always miss JoHanna and the sessions I had with her. I am sorry I never had the chance to thank her for helping in my exoneration. Although I may be only a cataloged collection of sounds and images to her, I regret that I will not be able to tell her of the fractional immortality she has afforded me. For long after I am gone, my words and speaking personality that she placed in her virtual depositary, can now, by anyone so inclined, be withdrawn from the magic mind that resides behind the big black eyes of JoHanna James.

The Pages
by K E Froeschner

Only after many years
    of living life as a headlong dash
        into the future's mesh of days,

Only after many tears
    one learns that time is not quite so . . .
        single-minded . . . inexorable.

Then one puts aside one's fears
    and sees that the frantic rush of years
        can now be stilled by silent reverie.

Those days that thrilled
    are just as real in memory.

One's life is not a mechanically moving picture show.

It is a book.

The pages turn both ways.

Death Valley And the "Unknown Prospector"

by Harold Gower

I

Ha, Ha, yes indeed
That's my grin all right
The only photo ever taken of me.
My daddy was born in a covered wagon
Crossing the Kansas prairie
And I was born in the mining camp
Known as Rough and Ready.

After eighteen years I left my home
And on to wealth I rode
I panned and sluiced and worked in the mines
Of the fabulous mother lode
Each time there was news of another strike
I ran there to claim my share
And each time I got there a little too late
No one said this game was fair.

To Angels Camp and to Jamestown,
With hopes of striking it rich
Then on to Dogtown, and Bodie
And over to Pizen Switch.
The camps of Aurora and Tonapah
Were waiting just for me
And Rhyolite, and Beatty
Were tougher than all three.

II
Then I followed the Amargosa
Around that southern bend
With nothing but hope I entered a land
That surely God condemned
The air so dry and stifling hot
It bakes the mind and soul
A person has to be insane
To enter this fumarole.

We climbed to the sky my burro and I
Seeking a cooler clime
Sampling the earth determined to find
The wealth of the Breyfogle Mine.
Or perhaps I'd find the lost Gunsight Mine
That others had foretold
Then high in the Funeral Mountains
I found my ledge of gold.

III
I hadn't even noticed that
My water had run out
Till that doggone pesky burro
Chose to take a different route
I yelled and cursed and called her names
I set up such a squall
I swore I hissed I shook my fist
She would not heed my call

Always keeping just one step ahead
She led me down the slope
Better than I, she knew our need
I had not yet lost hope.

As we descended from the heights
The deadly heat increased
Calming down my anger for
The stupid lowly beast.

When we finally reached the flatland
She brayed and brayed and brayed
Returning all the epithets
That, descending, I had made.

I knew I couldn't beat her for
Only she could save my life
That stinky little burro now
More precious than a wife.
As I untied the diamond hitch
The pack fell on the ground
Dumping all my mining gear
And nuggets I had found.

I followed her and she her nose
We raced against the sun
Forgetting, now that ledge of gold
And riches I had won.
I shed my hat, I shed my shirt
In my delirium
I shed my boots, I shed my pants
Until at last I finally shed
My equilibrium.

IV

I was fifty yards from water
When my torso hit the ground
By then I'd shed my body
Without a sigh or sound.
I never ever felt again
That desiccating heat.
Nor felt again the scorching sand
Beneath my blistered feet

I'd never know that throat dry thirst
Nor inhale another breath
I found there's nothing fearsome 'bout
This awful thing called death.

It was early in the morning
While the coolest air maintains
When a pair of hungry coyotes
Discovered my remains

Watching very cautiously for
Any sign of life
One skulked up close his head held low
The other standing back.
The first one took a tiny nip
And then a solid bite.
The other moved in quickly then
To feast on this delight.
As the many stars were fading
Left the morning star alone
They'd stripped the dehydrated flesh
Like jerky off the bone.

V

Weeks later when a man rode up
And took a photograph
Audaciously he titled it
"Prospector, name unknown."
Thus wrote my epitaph.

Well I am here to tell you all
And set the record straight
I'm Leland Edgar Masterson
I found my wealth too late.

VI

If this tale sounds too ghoulish
To suit your refined taste
Don't follow the Amargosa
Into that lethal waste.

A Fish in the Desert

by Cynthia Patton

An open suitcase sprawled on the floor. I stared at my clothes, unable to decide how a good mother should dress. I modeled a pink suede jacket and tossed it on the pile. Easily stained. Oversized blue sweater? Sloppy. Grey velvet top? Trying too hard. If this were a job interview I'd select an outfit without a second thought. But I didn't know what to wear to meet a pregnant 22-year-old.

I discarded several skirts (way too uptight) and regretted my offer to drive to Sedona. It was early December, and Michael had suggested I plan for snow. An excellent idea, but it ruled out virtually all my shoes. I reluctantly pulled off my black stretch pants because they looked best with kitten-heel mules. Inappropriate footwear screamed bad parent. The pile of clothes grew to a mound.

I tried on jeans, swiveling for a backside view, and froze before the mirror. Allison didn't care about my ass. She wanted to know if I'd love her baby more than the other wanna-be moms. Jeans conveyed disrespect, as if I didn't appreciate the magnitude of her sacrifice, as if I didn't know the value of a child. I yanked them off and slid down the wall, huddling in my underwear on the bathroom tile.

Today I shake my head, unsure whether to laugh or cry. I want to tell myself it's not going to matter if I wear the raspberry blouse that makes me look fat or the brown pants that are half an inch short. The birthmother's reasons won't hinge on our wealth, clothes, or age. They are things I couldn't have predicted, things as unalterable as the features on my face. But when I remember the adoption process this is the scene I always come back to: me in my underwear surrounded by piles of rejected clothes.

At midnight Michael came upstairs and shoved khaki slacks, three plaid shirts, a pair of jeans, and his favorite belt into a duffle bag. He glanced at my empty suitcase and frowned. "You've been up here for hours. What's taking so long?"

"I don't have anything to wear."

He laughed. "You've got plenty to wear. Look at this mess."

I kicked the pile. "I need to make a good impression."

"You won't with bags under your eyes." He made a point of studying the clock. "We'll hit the road early. I didn't want to make the drive in one day, but now we've got no choice."

He turned to leave, and I grabbed his arm. "What should I wear?"

He pulled away with a scowl. "Just throw something in and zip it up."

I grabbed his arm again, whining about under-eye circles and frothing with panic. He shook his head, but didn't laugh. I loved him for that. I knew I was being ridiculous.

After surveying the wreckage, he pointed to a nubby, multi-colored jacket with thick silver buttons. "How about that? It looks nice on you and has Southwest flair."

I studied the jacket and my shoulders inched lower. "What color pants?"

"Ones that match," he said, and climbed into bed.

In the morning I checked and rechecked that we had everything: family photos, scrapbooks, digital prints from our trip to Provence. I added an article on open adoption agreements and joined Michael and Chinook in the Toyota RAV4. Michael backed out of the driveway and said, "Hmmm. Only two hours late. Not too bad."

For twelve hours I munched and munched and munched: cold pizza, dry cereal, peanuts, baby carrots, potato chips, string cheese, soy nuts, crackers. I inhaled a 64-ounce Big Gulp and remembered the agency's call five days earlier, the Monday after Thanksgiving. "We're one of five couples? She's having a boy? When's she due? Are you sure it's a boy?" I was hyperventilating. I'd expected a quiet paddle to the isle of childfree when life hit me with a sleeper wave.

Carol, the adoption counselor, laughed. "Relax. She's more nervous than you."

I phoned Michael with the news. I planned to contact Allison when he got home. "Are you crazy?" he shouted. "Make the call. I'll get there as fast as I can."

My head pounded as I dialed. Fear sat in my stomach like a lump of lard. A no-nonsense voice answered, and I said, "Hi, this is Cynthia Patton." Silence stretched taut on the line. I swallowed hard. "We're the couple in Livermore. My husband's name is Michael…."

"Oh, the Murdochs," Allison said. "The Patton threw me. Aren't you married?"

My chuckle sounded like a hiccup. Shit. Maybe she wouldn't pick us because I insisted on a stupid feminist statement.

When I muttered yes she seemed intrigued. "I never met anyone who kept her name."

I veered to neutral topics. "You're due February 10th. How

do you feel?"

We talked about family, the virtues of travel, her step-sister-in-law's adopted child. I learned Allison was the youngest of nine kids and grew up in Hawaii and Orange County. She had a hearty laugh. I imagined her as an all-American girl, a volleyball champ. She told me she worked as a waitress and asked what I did for a living. I told her about the job I'd left at Save The Bay. "I wanted something with less travel, but since I didn't find it, I guess I'll stay home with the baby."

"I hoped you'd say that."

I bit my nail. I planned to stay home six months. Any longer and my brain would melt. Was I obligated to clarify? I coughed. "So how'd your family end up in Hawaii?"

She told me her father was a missionary, but she no longer followed the Book of Mormon. Her opposition had a vaguely feminist slant, so I voiced support. She asked about my religious views, and I said I'd never found faith in church. "I'm closest to God in the wilderness. When I'm there, every breath feels like a prayer. I think that's why I loved my job. Restoring wetlands felt like God's work."

"That's how I feel when I write poetry."

I sucked in my breath. How cool was that? The kid would have a poet birthmom.

She asked about Michael and I described his job. When I told her we'd just celebrated our ninth anniversary, she said she was no longer with the baby's father. She described him with a surprising level of hostility, given he'd wanted to marry her. She'd left Las Vegas and dumped the guy. "An artist, going nowhere. Not what I wanted for me or the baby."

It struck me as funny coming from a pregnant waitress poet living in Sedona.

We talked about infertility and Allison's love of the ocean. She said, "The baby's going to be blonde like me." I asked how she could be sure and she said everyone in her family was blonde and in the father's family too.

Everyone in my family was brunette, but Michael's sister Debbie had been blonde. I revised my mental picture of Allison to a sun-bronzed surfer chick and glanced at my watch. To my surprise, two hours had passed. She said, "I've really got to pee, but I'd love to meet you guys."

I told her we'd come to Sedona, and later we'd have her up to meet the family. She said she'd like to see the baby's room, and for an instant I glimpsed sorrow beneath her shiny veneer.

"I'll check with Michael, but we can probably come down this weekend. Do we need to work around other candidates?"

"I've talked to everyone and right now, you're the only ones I'm seeing."

My eyes widened. "Wow. It's like I was picked first for dodge ball."

We both laughed as we said goodbye.

Michael was beside himself. "You talked about dodge ball? Did you mention my salary or the remodeled kitchen? Did you tell her your parents live close by?"

I shook my head.

"Honey, you have to tell her this stuff or she'll pick someone else."

What did he know? My heart said I'd just won the lottery.

Three days later Carol phoned to talk about our upcoming trip. "Be sure to avoid questions involving the other couple."

"What other couple?" I stared at the wall, my face numb.

"Oh, didn't Allison tell you?" Carol's voice had that saccharin tone that reminded me of so-called friends in junior high.

My mind spun with questions I didn't dare ask: Were they younger than us? Better looking? Where did they live? I wished I'd met Carol so I could picture her as she trampled my heart.

"Birthparents often interview backup couples to confirm their choice."

The blood flowed back to my face, and sorrow flashed through me for the nameless couple. Then Carol said Allison felt pressured, and I didn't know what to think. Allison had suggested our visit—or was it the other way around? Either way, it didn't make sense. We had such a good chat. Maybe the other couple got nervous, did a hard sell. I could see it happening. But I knew better. I'd been careful. Hadn't I?

I asked for specifics and Carol said, "I'm not at liberty to discuss a birthmother's conversations. I just want you to know she's under pressure."

The barren Mojave lumbered by my second time behind the wheel. Would Allison notice my gray roots or the gap forming between my bottom teeth? I down-shifted to pass a truck and obsessed about my outfit. Were the cowboy boots a mistake? Why did I choose red pants? I thought the color would make it easy for Allison to identify us, but now I remembered she knew what we looked like from our birthparent letter. Why did Michael pick that damn jacket? Red pants were the sign of a crazy woman.

Michael fidgeted in the cramped seat, grumbling about making the drive in a single day. When I didn't rise to his bait, he said, "What'll we do if she's hideous? You know, really ugly with bad skin and an overbite."

I kept my eyes on the road. "She won't be."

He kicked at the trash that littered the floor. "How do you know she won't be a dog?"

"I just know." I clenched my teeth so I wouldn't scream. We had bigger problems than unattractive birthmoms. What if she thought I was frumpy?

I drove east into the night, winding through squat mountains that hugged the road. Michael took over when we crossed into Arizona, the lights of Las Vegas staining the sky. Chinook whimpered in her sleep, and I tasted bile. I never imagined we'd compete for a child after we got the call. Screw that "when you meet the right one you'll know" crap. Allison would pick one couple and the other would be crushed, beating themselves up over what went wrong. I didn't want it to be us. I wanted the baby.

Trees loomed in the frosty haze as we sped east along Interstate 40. I tossed trail mix into my mouth and relaxed my grip on the arm rest. Allison had said we shared a strong vibe. I needed to trust my instincts.

Michael pulled into a truck stop near Flagstaff, and I sipped scalding coffee while he filled the tank. My breath mingled with steam from the cup.

I drove the last leg of our trip while Michael snored. The sky glittered like black ice. I studied the empty road and a shiver of regret traveled through me because Allison's baby wasn't my red-haired girl. For eight years Katie had sat on my shoulder, whispering in my ear, and I'd grown to believe she'd materialize. The yellow line split me in two. Then I shook myself, reminded my ungrateful heart that Allison's child was real.

Sunday morning dawned clear and crisp, no snow in sight. We slept in, then walked Chinook and criticized Bush for the war in Iraq. I was still in denial over the election results. "How could we elect him twice?"

Michael studied the scenery as if he were painting it. "I think it was the women."

I stopped walking. "The women?"

He nodded. "Lots of women voted for him. The whole safety and security thing."

Chinook yanked her leash and I followed in a daze. Had Allison voted for Bush? She'd spent her formative years in Orange County, followed by stints in Nevada and Arizona. I'd have to ask; I didn't want to parent the next Rush Limbaugh. Good grief. This could be a deal breaker.

Michael grabbed my arm. "Honey, are you okay? I criticized Dick Cheney and you didn't respond."

Back in our generic motel room, Michael pored over visitor guides. I sorted photos and wondered if we'd have anything to say when we sat face-to-face. At office parties Michael chattered about his Christmas village collection in excruciating detail. Would Allison roll her eyes as I'd been known to do?

At 1:00 Michael handed me the phone. I tossed it on the bed. We repeated the exchange until Michael snatched up the receiver with a grimace. I watched him as he dialed. He wore khaki slacks and a shirt the color of iron-rich Sedona soil. Its tiny checks played off his silver hair. Sure we were older, but we looked vibrant and confident. I could wear a size 10 again. The red pants were an excellent choice.

Allison proposed the Highway Café at 2:00. I paced the room. How in God's name were we supposed to wait? After three circuits I suggested an art gallery, and Michael stared. "You want to buy a painting now?"

"No, just kill some time. Get out of this damn room."

He grabbed his keys and we ran for the car.

We tied Chinook in the shade of a monstrous bronze eagle

with outstretched talons and descended a flight of stairs. The gallery door opened with a sucking sound. Before us stood a series of six-foot-tall metal shamans, all horned and pitted like something hammered from the earth, their feet weighted in stone. I fought the urge to fall on my knees and pray.

A young salesgirl glided to my side. "Beautiful, aren't they?"

"Uh huh," we said in unison without turning. I willed her to leave.

"You have exquisite taste," she said. "Which one is your favorite?"

"That one," Michael pointed.

I yanked his arm and he muttered, "Well it is."

The woman launched into a spirited dissertation on the artist, and I spun and faced her head-on. "Look, we're not in a position to buy. We're meeting a birthmother in an hour, and supposedly she's pressured but that doesn't make sense because we talked like girlfriends. It was a normal conversation—well, except for that religious riff. That came out of nowhere, I have to admit. But now we have to pull off another conversation and I feel like we have to defend ourselves, state our case in the clearest possible language or face a lifetime without parole. So I'm not interested in art right now. I'm focused on the kid. Do you understand? There's a baby at stake."

For a second I felt her withering scorn. Then she blinked and it was gone. She was once more smooth and polished as Barbie. "Would you like me to check shipping costs?"

We made for the door when she turned around. I stopped at the exit and watched her, the ash of regret bitter in my mouth. She was just like I was at her age: still convinced she held destiny in the palm of her hand. She'd never been backed in a corner by fate, didn't know some things are more precious than pride. Looking back I realize I was jealous. She didn't need to know what birthmother meant.

Michael shook his head. "No caffeine during lunch, okay?"

Three passes through town and no Highway Café. Michael stopped two men carrying 12-packs, and they pointed in opposite directions. He groaned and ran inside the Circle K. He returned breathless. "It's on the other side, four lights down."

We hit all four stoplights. I gritted my teeth as Michael ground the gears. The restaurant sat across from our motel. "Damn," Michael said. "I knew it seemed familiar."

We skidded into the parking lot. I didn't tell him to slow down because we were ten minutes late—so much for first impressions. We plunged into the silent restaurant, the door slamming behind us like a cannon shot. Well, I thought, that's one way to make an entrance.

Across the room a pregnant girl stood. She wore denim overalls and a white t-shirt, her blonde hair pulled into a loose ponytail. She had pale skin rather than the deep tan I'd imagined and a sturdy, wholesome appearance.

We slid into the booth facing her. "We had trouble finding the place," Michael muttered.

"No problem," Allison said. "I had some bread to calm my jitters."

I tried not to stare at her bulging stomach. "We're nervous too."

"Well, then." A smile warmed her brown eyes. "We're nervous together."

I guzzled water as Allison described her fractured family.

The waiter tried three times to take our order but I couldn't focus on the menu. The air felt bottled. On his fourth trip I ordered the turkey club because it was the first thing listed. Michael did the same. His leg jiggled so violently I thought the joints would crack. As Allison described life in Hawaii, I put my hand on his knee and pressed.

She asked about Europe and said one of the reasons she selected us was that we'd traveled so many places. "That's the life I dream for my child." She said the other factor was family size. With seven siblings between us, Michael and I had the largest. "I know you want to adopt more kids, but even if you can't, my baby will have lots of cousins. I want him to know the security of a big family."

I couldn't fault her logic.

Allison discussed the pros and cons of Hawaii and Las Vegas. She described her future plans (massage therapy) and where she wanted to live (Los Angeles). She had every detail mapped out, and I smiled at the memory of my younger self. In the midst of an unplanned pregnancy, Allison wanted everything under control.

When the food arrived, she dug in with a vengeance. The conversation skipped like the stones Dad taught me to throw on summer vacations, skimming across the shallows in effortless leaps. Michael asked if she had a photo of the birthfather and she shook her head. She caressed her belly and said, "When I was barely showing, a lawyer matched me with a Los Angeles couple who claimed to want an open adoption. I thought it was settled. But last month he sent me the contract and it turns out they wouldn't allow visits. I mean, isn't that the whole point?" Her words oozed bitterness.

I nodded like one of those dogs with bouncing heads you

see in back windows of Buicks and assured her two visits a year would not be a problem. Did she want more?

"I tore up the contract and told the lawyer off. I called your agency and said I needed to make a decision quick. They sent me a stack of letters by Federal Express. Really impressed me. I narrowed it down to five and made the calls that day."

I searched her voice for doubt or waiver and found none. Her eyes allowed no possibility of pity. "Wow," I said. "You fired the attorney?"

"Yeah—after he said I didn't have the luxury of being picky."

My sandwich lay untouched. It was all I could do to nibble the fries. Michael was pulling his apart, pushing it around the plate. How could anyone say that to her?

Her fork clattered on the tabletop. "Thanks to them, I'm behind schedule. I want this wrapped up next week."

I longed to put my arm around her, remind her it was a child, not a race.

Allison wiped her plate with a chunk of bread and popped it in her mouth. She leaned back and told us she left home at 16 to live with an older sibling in Michigan so she could "see the world." I asked about high school and she was disturbingly vague. Again the conversation veered to religion. Michael ripped his napkin and asked if she'd prefer a Mormon couple. Allison waved her hand. "Any religion is fine with me. I'm past all that."

I wasn't sure I believed her—am still not sure—but her poise and determination impressed me. I didn't even care if she voted for Bush. Besides, who ever heard of a Republican poet?

Too soon Allison announced she had to leave. Her shift started in an hour and she needed to change. We'd talked nonstop, our scrapbooks and photos untouched. She picked up the top photo and pointed to our nephew Jack. "He's adorable, and I love his name. I hope you'll name the baby that—or Kai, which means ocean in Hawaiian."

I reminded her Jack wasn't possible. Didn't say Kai wasn't an option. I stared at the stack of photos in my hand. Was it too much, not enough, wrong day, bad pants? "I'd like to show you more…."

"Let's do lunch tomorrow," she said.

"Really? We don't want to pressure you."

She gave me a hard look. "Did Carol tell you that?" When I nodded, she tossed her head. "I told her specifically it wasn't you guys. It was the other couple."

Michael grinned as we gathered our things. "Way to go," he whispered. "The ones with the most face time win."

Michael let Chinook stretch in the parking lot, and I crossed my fingers: please suck up to the birthmother. Chinook rolled to expose her tummy like a Disney dog, and Allison bent to pet her. "Did I mention husky was my favorite breed?"

We hiked near Coffee Pot Rock and the Sacred Pools and couldn't stop talking about her. The sky soared in an unending arc. Michael pulled out his camera, and I posed before copper cliffs burnished by the sun, their slopes dotted with juniper and pinion pine. "We should take photos of her," I said, "with us." The air smelled earthy sweet. "We can show them to the baby and say 'Here's the day we met your birthmother.'"

"Definitely." He snapped another shot. "My only concern is her nose."

"Her nose?"

"It's kind of big. Bulbous, really. If it was a girl I'd be

reluctant."

I stared, not sure if he was joking.

"Well, it is." He kicked the red dirt.

"It's a healthy baby, Michael. No drugs, no alcohol, not even caffeine. Didn't you hear her? She stopped wearing makeup and nail polish when she learned she was pregnant. It doesn't get better than this. We should be thrilled." Even if it's not a red-haired girl.

He adjusted the camera lens. "I know. It's just your baby would have been beautiful, Cyn."

Chinook bounded up, smelling of sage. I buried my face in her fur and blinked back tears.

The next day Michael phoned and got no answer. I paced the room, fiddling with our scrapbooks and snacking on cheese. "You're sure we're supposed to call at noon?"

Michael studied his hands in his lap. "You dial this time."

After two attempts I left a message saying we'd gone to the Red Planet Diner. We slid into a retro vinyl booth and debated if Allison had changed her mind. "You hardly opened your mouth," I said.

"You showed photos when she had to leave."

Outside a silver UFO decorated the low maintenance landscape. Standing in the corner booth, a toddler pressed his face to the glass. "What's that, Mama?" He pointed. "What's that?"

Michael tore at his turkey burger. "I can't believe she didn't call."

"She's juggling a lot of stuff right now." I watched the boy jump on the seat.

"She's inconsiderate, Cyn. Look at how she treated her boyfriend. And yesterday she cut our lunch short."

"She had to work."

He stuffed an onion ring in his mouth and practically spit pieces on me as he yelled, "Why are you making excuses for her?"

I stared out the window, hoping to avoid a full-blown fight. As a peace offering, I asked if he wanted dessert. We were polishing off an ice cream sundae when his cell phone rang. Allison's checkup had run late and she wondered if we could do dinner instead?

Another hike, another animated discussion. How could we make the guest room turned nursery more masculine? How would we manage two weeks in Arizona after the baby was born? If we rented a house, would my parents come? We circled behind Chimney Rock and I said, "I have a good feeling about this."

Michael studied the bleached horizon. "Don't get too excited. It's not over yet."

That night we shared Thai food, and my face finally relaxed. Allison asked us the secret of marriage, and Michael gave a long-winded answer that involved opposites attracting, timing, and my superior intelligence. Allison cocked her head. "Patience," I said, "and a sense of humor."

Allison said she'd just learned one of her brothers had moved to Livermore. I stopped chewing, and Michael smiled. "Maybe he could baby-sit."

Later Michael said Allison's face darkened like a cloud passing over the sun. Damn, he thought, why did I play the family card? I didn't notice because I was too busy considering his brilliant idea. I squeezed his leg and asked why her brother had moved.

"I don't know," she said. "We haven't spoken in years."

"Maybe you can re-establish contact when you visit us."

"I don't think so." She stabbed at her food, her voice tight. "He's strict Mormon. We don't see eye-to-eye."

I twirled Pad Thai onto my fork, unsure what to say. Was this about an illegitimate pregnancy—or something more?

Michael regaled her with travel stories and the mood lightened. Allison slid a photo across the table with the hint of a scowl. "Here's the father."

I studied the smiling face, lanky body, and tousled blonde hair. "How does he feel about the adoption?"

"We don't talk anymore. I don't want to have anything to do with him."

Michael smirked as I passed him the photo. I made a mental note to ask Carol how we could work around her attitude. I wanted our child to know both birthparents.

"Wow," Michael said. "This guy looks tall."

"Yeah, he's built like you." She handed me another photo. "My ultrasound."

She cupped her belly while I examined the blurred black and white image. "He has my profile," she said with surprising pride.

Michael stuffed his mouth with skewered chicken and studied the wall. I had to admit, her nose was on the large side. But when I looked at her, all I saw was courage.

"How can you tell?" I said. "He looks like a silver fish to me."

She smiled, and I laughed for the first time in days.

Outside, wearing a rough, fur-trimmed coat that made her look like a stout Mongolian warrior, Allison said, "I feel comfortable with you guys." She hugged me, then Michael. "I'd like to sleep on it. Let you know in a day or so."

I felt like dancing. "Take all the time you need. We'll be

home Wednesday."

Tuesday we hiked at the base of Cathedral Rock, shaded from the mid-day sun. Dirt puffed beneath our boots. We picnicked on a stone slab and scoured the real estate pages for month-to-month rentals. I didn't taste the food. My mind ricocheted from the nursery, to Allison, to clothes for the baby. Michael stared across the valley while Chinook begged for pita sandwich. She ate the hummus, but spit out all the sprouts.

On the hike back I breathed dusty juniper and tangy manzanita. When we visited in the past, I'd been annoyed with the people that flocked to Sedona. I'd scoffed at crystals and Chinese herbalist vets. But now it seemed the perfect place for an adoption. Why not take a crazy leap of faith in a place spinning with vortexes?

We crossed a dry streambed, and I stared up at burnt rock. Peace settled over me like the missing snow.

Back in town, we purchased Christmas gifts. I found a wooden egg painted with dancing lizards and held it up to Michael. "To remember this weekend—whatever happens."

He froze, then slowly nodded.

The next day Michael drove north through the Central Valley, dark clouds boiling overhead. It started to rain, and I said, "How do you like the name Devin? It means the poet."

Michel stared at the road. "Don't jinx it. No names 'til we know for sure."

As the sun sunk behind the Coast Range, I tried to picture Allison's blonde son. Compared to Katie, he was faceless, shapeless, and voiceless. I watched raindrops slide down the windshield and told myself Katie belonged in the comfort drawer with my letters and lost dreams. There was a baby in our future. He was Devin, the poet, a silver fish swimming through oceans to meet us. When he arrived, I needed to hold out my net to catch him.

By Friday I wished I hadn't told Allison to take her time. Four days had passed. I paced the house, unable to change the sheets or water the plants. Michael obsessed about the shower doors on the bathtub. How could we bathe a child with those damn doors in the way? Carol phoned and left a short message, her tone upbeat. "Just checking in," she said. I called back at 4:00, but she had already left.

At Save The Bay's annual holiday luncheon, I chatted with donors and former coworkers. I opened my mouth to talk about tidal marsh restoration and babbled instead about our trip to Arizona. I heard myself tell people I was okay however it turned out, surprised to find it true. Or mostly true. Secretly I was convinced it was finally going to happen—I'd be a mother in less than two months.

Michael glared at me. "We're one of five couples."

"No, she's down to two."

"It's five," he said, setting down his knife a bit too hard. "We're one of five."

Nothing could dampen my mood. A strange, gloating hope filled me.

On Monday Michael phoned the agency and learned Carol was out sick. He told me he was re-doing the bathroom, just in case. He yanked off the warped shower doors and rusted faucet and dragged me to the hardware store. He insisted on swapping the shower head with a hand-held version and purchased replacement parts for everything else.

As Michael worked in the bathroom, I left a message on

Allison's machine. She didn't call back. My heart settled into an old groove.

The phone rang Tuesday at 3 p.m. Michael was caulking the holes left by the shower doors, and we studied each other before he left to answer. I stood next to the tub and admired Michael's handiwork. Would we bathe a baby any time soon?

When he returned I knew what he would say before he said it. His eyes gave it away.

"The pushy ones?"

"I guess so. They live in Santa Cruz. Maybe they're willing to name him Kai."

Michael walked into his office and shut the door. I stared at the shower curtain I'd just hung. Black and yellow and purple fish swirled in a vibrant turquoise sea.

I went downstairs and stood by the window that overlooked the pool. I felt Devin slip away like the moon dropping below the horizon and couldn't muster the strength to cry. "Live long and prosper," I whispered to the unseen child who touched our lives for the briefest of moments, then swam away, carried off by the tide.

He was no longer Devin, my poet child. He was Jack or Kai or some other name. I leaned my head against the cool glass and couldn't decide if I was glad to have another chance to find my daughter. I was tired of waiting for the tide to change. I wished I had the comfort of anger or regret, but the truth was I was happy for Allison and her child, even if her happiness didn't include me. She'd proven the attorney wrong and picked her son's parents. I was grateful for that.

I turned from the window, and something bright caught my eye. A red leaf had fallen onto still water. I watched it make a slow circle, working its way toward me.

Rhythm of the Rain
by Sue Tasker

She dashes outdoors
To dance in the rain
Splashing through
Puddles.
Giggling and twirling
Under her
Polka dotted umbrella

Wet feet
Wet face
Wide smiles

She slips and slides
Her way inside to
Warm hugs,
Dry towels
Hot cocoa;

Listening
For the
Drumbeats of clouds.
She watches flashes
of fire in the sky.

Rivers of rain
Wind
down
windows,

Girl sits,
Gray cat curled
in the crook of her arm,
Turning the pages of her book
to the
Rhythm of the
Rain

Mirror
by Albert Rothman

hairy chin and moustache
define my gender
incomplete—
I miss the fullness
of a beard I had
in the sixties
a mature forest
that surrounded my face

Alas!
my upper cheek denies.
The forest now has clear cuts

Where are the environmental groups?

Good Weather Sunday

by Diana Quartermaine

Children squeeze on
    hand-me-down bathing suits
pull up
    faded Summer shorts
scuffle shuffle excitement
    —in outgrown flip-flops.
Mother, barelegged under
    madras skirt
packs familiar
    waxed-paper wrapped
        Baloney slices and American cheese squares
        mustard yellow on Kilpatrick's white
        —sure to get sand-dusted
    Church key opener for
family size pineapple juice tin can
        Del Monte promises Best Hawaiian
—will slake midday thirst
scratched purple green gold tumblers
      —with metallic after-taste
blue red plaid folded picnic blanket
      —that stakes spot
ragged rolled beach towels
    for pink-flush shivers
salty drips
      —sandy toe grit.
Father perches felt fedora on thinning hair
    dons old Flannel slacks
        with cuffs he will rollup
        —at water's edge
    buckles open-weave leather sandals
        —to jaunt forward.
Family restless for
    City bus trip
bumping to earth's end
their scramble down
    warm concrete seawall
      —through tangy air.

Effie's Eulogy
by Diana Quartermaine

Effie's *Oatmeal* habit was ritually
    witnessed by mourners
        —like children absorb an oft-heard tale.
Speakers, shy or bold
    recited that, upon Effie's household rising,
    children, grandchildren or guests
    bent to consume their servings
    at her 1940's Formica kitchen table.
    Effie joined them—ate remains
        large-spoon scraped
        heavy cooking pot
        lap-cradled.
Effie's middle-aged son declared—
    he loathed *Oatmeal*
        Then-and-Now.
Effie's grown daughter was commonly known to
    urge *Oatmeal* on her own family
    as their diet's staple.
    A pert young cousin
    admitted she tagged
    Effie's daughter's family
        —"*the Oatmeal People.*"

The Reverend's closing words
    reported his final visit with 96 years-old Effie.
    Effie divulged that daily *Oatmeal*
        was her secret to a long life.
Effie, perhaps would be satisfied
    that, by her example
    Oatmeal's goodness
    was so fostered in
    −her nearest and dearest's hearts.

Sister's Earthquake Story
by Diana Quartermaine

Barely old enough
    to remember–
my mind's eye– jolted

    Our living room creaked—trembled
    —jiggle—jiggle—jiggle
    —rumble—rumble—rumble
window panes' drum
    —rattle—rattle—rattle
Gathered into Mother's skirts
    encircled tight–
we huddled
    weathering wildness
and the chandelier's crazy swings
    –transfixed me.

Tiger and the Fish!

adapted and told by Bobbie Kinkead

A long, long time ago in ancient Korea, when the animals spoke to each other, Uncle Tiger wore a horsehair hat and smoked a long bamboo pipe. He was the King of the Beasts, the Guard of the West, greedy, cruel, and arrogant. All the animal cousins lived in fear of Uncle Tiger. He hunted them day and night for his pleasure.

Deep in the pine forest the animal cousins: rabbit, pig, deer, squirrel, skunk, rat, mice, duck, birds of all sorts, fox, bear, chipmunk, badger, lizard, snake, turtle, frog, and many others gathered to complain about Uncle Tiger, the beast.

"Uncle Tiger chases us as we walk in the bamboo grove," complained chipmunks.

"He pounces on us when we eat in the meadow," quacked the ducks.

"He stalks us when we drink in the river," yapped fox.

"He hunts us at night," growled bear.

"Wasteful," pig grunted.

"Uncle Tiger is mean," badger snapped.

"Selfish!" hissed snaked.

"He takes advantage of his power," peeped the birds.

"What are we to do?" squeaked the mice.

The animals debated for hours.

Finally, a decision was made.

Great Dragon, Guard of the East, would ask Uncle Tiger to stop his cruelty. "Who would ask the Great Dragon?" The animals quieted and looked at each other.

Cousin Rabbit considered. I could die of fright in Uncle Tiger's claws after a horrid chase; or, I could die for my cousins confronting the beast.

She stood up among the animal cousins.

"I will ask Great Dragon, if my Brother and Sister Rabbit come with me."

So it was settled. The Cousin Rabbits would ask the Great Dragon.

The three rabbits hopped down the mountain to the ocean. Far away the long, thin serpent appeared and disappeared in the waves. They crossed the beach and stood. The lapping of waves on the shore drowned their voices. The three yelled their loudest.

"Great Dragon, Guard of the East."

The long, thin serpent turned towards them. They watched Great Dragon swim to the beach. Larger and larger he grew as long and thick as the tallest pine tree. He stepped from the waves. He crawled onto the sand. His silver and gold scales flashed as crystals of water. On his paws rested claws sharper than spines.

His head held pointed antlers. Great Dragon bowed.

"Cousin Rabbits, you called?"

His breath hung as moist and cold as winter's fog and smelled of seaweed.

Cousin Rabbit bowed, "Great Dragon, Guard of the East, we need your help. Uncle Tiger is mean and selfish. He stalks us, he chases us, and he pounces on us. He hunts us day and night. We have no rest. You must tell him to stop."

Great Dragon's eyes shone as deep as the green pools in the river.

"Cousin Rabbits, you must ask Uncle Tiger to stop."

"We are afraid of him!"

"He is mean!"

"He will eat us!"

"Yes, Tiger is cruel, yes, actually greedy and vain. If you can talk to me, you can ask Uncle Tiger. Have a plan, in case he disagrees with your request."

Great Dragon bowed to the three, turned, and crawled to the ocean.

The three rabbits hopped back to the pine forest. All the animal cousins gathered to hear. "Great Dragon told us to ask Uncle Tiger to stop his cruelty; and we must have a plan if he disagrees."

The cousins argued about the best plan.

"Push him from a tree," owl screeched.

"Throw rocks on him," croaked the frogs.

"Tie him with long grasses," wolf snarls.

"Push him into the river," skunk gruffed.

"Block him in his cave," shrieked deer.

They argued a long time. Finally, they had their plan.

Now, who would talk to Uncle Tiger? The animal cousins looked at Cousin Rabbit.

"Sure, I am afraid of Uncle Tiger, still I will go, alone."

So it was decided Cousin Rabbit would ask Uncle Tiger to stop his wasteful hunting.

Cousin Rabbit hopped up the mountain to Uncle Tiger's cave. She noticed that Uncle Tiger watched every hop. Her dread weakened her. One swat of his paw and she was his lunch. She climbed carefully to show strength.

"Grrrooooowwwllll!" Uncle Tiger's roar shook the trees. His teeth shone sharper then ragged rocks. Fear choked Cousin Rabbit's breath. One crunch of his teeth and she was gone. Cousin Rabbit breathed deeply to draw courage.

She hopped closer. Uncle Tiger was the biggest animal of all. His colors of black, yellow, and white striped as sinister as shadows. His face was as round as the largest moon. Uncle Tiger wore a horsehair hat and smoked his long bamboo pipe.

Cousin Rabbit stood in front of Uncle Tiger. Her fright pounded. Tiger could pounce on her.

"Growwwwllll! Cousin Rabbit, why have you come, alone?"

His breath burned as hot as the summer wind. He smoked his long bamboo pipe. His yellow eyes flashed as bright as the fire. He smelled of the hunt.

Cousin Rabbit bowed. She was in his power, trapped. She crouched unable to run. She thought of her animal cousins. She spoke loud to show bravery. "Uncle Tiger, I ask for all the animal cousins that you not hunt us all day and all night. We have no rest. As Guard of the West, you should honor us."

His stretched and spread his claws sharper than thorns. "What foolishness! I hunt because I am who I am; and I must eat."

To cover the horror of his threat, Cousin Rabbit cautiously hopped closer. With cunning she spoke, "Uncle Tiger, would you like to rest? You must tire of chasing us."

"What do you imply?" He swished his tail back and forth.

Cousin Rabbit swallowed her uneasiness, "Uncle Tiger, have you ever eaten fish?"

Uncle Tiger straightened his horsehair hat. Back and forth he twitched his tail as he puffed his bamboo pipe. "Fish. Fish! I see the fish in the river. I cannot catch them."

"You can! Use your beautiful tail. Fish come to bright colors. Your gorgeous tail is perfect. That beautiful tail will attract many fish."

Uncle Tiger swung his tail. "My tail is attractive. I am tired of chasing my cousins all over the forest. I'll eat fish."

To the river Cousin Rabbit followed Uncle Tiger. She was alert to his strength. She watched and listened for signs of danger. She could run.

"Uncle Tiger, sit here on the edge of the river. Just dip your beautiful tail into the water. My brothers, sisters, and I will wade down the river and chase up many fish. Keep your tail quiet to make a lure. Your tail will feel heavy. When we shout, pull your tail out of the water. Many fish will be ready for you to eat."

The rabbit cousins disappeared down the river. All the other cousins hid in the trees and bushes. They watched Uncle Tiger hang his long tail in the water.

Tiger waited smoking his long pipe and swayed his tail back and forth. "Fish! I wonder how you will taste. Sitting here is so easy."

Unexpectedly, clouds covered the sun. The forest darkened. A bitter wind blew. The river turned to ice around the edges. Tiger's tail felt heavy, cold. He continued to puff his pipe. Snow fell with large wet flakes that put out his pipe and melted his horse hair hat. Although his tail numbed and his fur dripped with water, Uncle Tiger did not move.

The animals cousins watched. They enjoyed seeing Uncle Tiger wet and cold and stubbornly waiting for his meal of fish.

Uncle Tiger shivered; then stopped. He shook the snowflakes from his fur. He removed his horsehair hat. "I will not show any animal cousins my impatience."

The cousins giggled.

Uncle Tiger heard the faint laughing; He twitched his whiskers.

"Someone laughs at me?"

Their laughter got louder. "Ha, ha, ha, he, he, he! Silly Tiger, ha, ha."

He flung his head around and listened.

"Yes, that is laughter in the bushes. Who laughs at Tiger, King of the Beasts and Guard of the West?"

Uncle Tiger jumped up. His tail jerked him down, splat, into the snow. Uncle Tiger yanked on his tail to discover that his tail was frozen in the ice.

"GROOOOWWWLLLLL!"

The animal cousins laughed louder. "Ha, ha, ha, he, he, he! Funny, Funny! Ha, he, he, he, ho, ho! Oh yes! Serves you right! Caught any fish? Ha, ha, ha, he, he, he!"

The animal cousins left Uncle Tiger alone with his tail caught in the river. They ate in the meadows, drank from the river and ponds, walked in the pine and bamboo forests, slept all through the night, and relaxed and rested for days. Uncle Tiger cowered with his tail stuck in ice.

As he waited cold on the river, Uncle Tiger humbled, he lost most of his greed and arrogance in the ice. Finally, the sun warmed the river and the ice melted. Uncle Tiger's tail was released. From that time on Uncle Tiger respected and honored his smaller cousins, who were more clever than he.

As told by Bobbie Kinkead who adapted and re-imaged the story to tell to school children, who come for storytelling tours at the Asian Art Museum in San Francisco, CA

Folktales for Korea, Zong In-Sob, 1952, 1970, 1982 'The old Tiger and the Hare', pp.157-160.

Korea, Land of the Morning Sun, Carol Farley, 'When Tiger Smoked Long Pipes, The Tiger and the Three Wise Rabbits'.

Nearly Bacterial Haiku
by George Staehle

Bachterial Evolution
Pianissimo,
flagella arpeggio into
tiny harpsichords.

Infect You
You should not pick it.
Or it will grow much further
than you might wish it.

Abaku Two
Bead cells reply, "We
think better third line would be:
'Invent cell division.'"

Primordial Soup Ku: Plan B
Human beings take over
cells: weapons, religion,
wrestling on TV.

Bacteria Hai-CHOO!
Filamentously
going, exponentially
growing, in your nose.

Abaku
Early bead-shaped cells
slide up and down filaments.
Multiply quickly.

Primordial Soup Ku: Plan A
Cells become letters
and numerals; write novels;
invent calculus.

Hi Flu
I can't count, and "near-
ly" modifies "bacterial"
because I'm not well.

touches stone

by Ethel Mays

a sooty child
a little girl
dressed in mis-fitting soiled frock
enters the yard on bare feet
she walks through weeds
taller than she
to a thin canted tombstone
taller still
she pauses
nameless weights
shut eyes once bright
as pennies
little mouth sags open
no word escapes
she turns from the marker
as if to leave
but one grubby hand
presses thumb and fingers against it
lightly as if to steady

against a tumble into emptiness
black clouds darken
a bleak sky and the child
looks through weeds
at a tiny light in a window
outside the yard
her hand presses firmly
against the stone now
as if to absorb
all the grittiness
of the stonecutter's soul
heavy rain pelts down
then slows
the child turns
leaving the way she came
away from the light in the window
a wind sighs once
and the child is gone

My Kidney Stone Rocks!
By David Hardiman

Why would anyone voluntarily have a kidney stone removed?

I knew something was wrong when I noticed my urine began resembling Hawaiian Punch and I remembered from writing my name in the snow that it was supposed to be yellow. So I paid a quick visit to my urologist Dr. Young Kang. You all know what a urologist is, don't you? It's an OB GYN for men. The only difference is our stirrups have spurs. Dr. Kang was certain I had a kidney stone. He ordered an inexpensive lab test employing a kidney-specific contrast fluid to highlight any abnormalities. Appropriately enough the test revealed a 7-millimeter kidney-shaped kidney stone happily nestled in the bosom of my nephrons (as opposed to happily nestled in Nora Ephron's bosoms). Dr. Kang solemnly said, "You have about as much chance of passing the stone as a gerbil has of passing a rose bush. But don't worry," Young Kang enthusiastically explained, "We don't cut anything. We only use natural body openings."

"Natural body openings my ass," I erupted. I mean maybe they're natural body openings if you're a salmon going upstream to spawn and die. As far as I'm concerned my internal canals are federally protected waterways and nobody gets in there without an act of Congress or a very influential lobbyist.

Natural body openings, I pondered. Can they even do that? Apparently, they can. So how do they get from the tip of my fountainhead to the nutty nougat of my afflicted kidney? Coarsely stated, the surgeon employs a two-foot long, quarter inch diameter ureteroscope slithered up the urethra, into and through the bladder, bearing right to enter the left ureter and up into the kidney, where a lithroscopic device explodes the stone which is then caught and extracted in a little basket. Tidy enough right? With the removal of the offending stones a stent is then placed along the route of the operation to promote healing by keeping the inflamed tissues open and drained. My stent was about 14-inches long and looked like Siamese seahorses attached at the nose. It's coiled at either end to insure it remains anchored in your urinary tract. I had really hoped to live my entire life without writing "anchored in your urinary tract," and have it refer to my urinary tract. If the stent were to slip from its coiled moorings and poke its spiral tip out through my fountainhead at the wrong time, I'd have an awful lot of explaining to do.

Even though the surgeon uses pre-existing natural openings, the procedure still sounded painful. And in accordance with the Urological Full Employment Act of 1972, Dr. Kang assured me its removal would be only mildly uncomfortable—like when you ask a woman how many months pregnant she is and she says, "I'm not pregnant."

"Don't worry Mr. Hardiman," Young Kang reiterated, "We only use natural body openings."

"I get that," I gritted. "What a drag. Does the possibility of an Immaculate Removal exist?"

"We're surgeons, not saints," Dr. Kang explained. "Besides, your insurance doesn't cover divine intervention."

I tried to find something "zen" about Dr. Kang jamming a 2-foot hose deep into my abdomen. I calmly visualized the procedure and serenely chanted, "AummmOwww!"

On Wednesday January 25th, I arrived at Valley Care Hospital for the 12:30 operation. My fiancée drove and was with me the whole time. I was feeling kind of giddy like the way a prisoner gets just prior to execution, and began nervously reflecting on my life: "When I think about writing my name in the snow, I now realize why men have much better snow penmanship than women."

"Did they drug you already?" my fiancée asked.

"No," I said. "Do you think it's too late to get a surrogate patient? I mean they have surrogate mothers, and this is just a little baby stone."

My suggestion was met with (you may groan now) stony silence.

Of course, due to the enormity of my personal equipment I was told they sent to UC Davis' Veterinarian School for a special 3-foot elongated horse scope, otherwise they wouldn't be able to reach my kidney. They warned me if I got an erection they'd have to scrub the operation entirely because they wouldn't have a scope long enough. I was feeling pretty smug about things until the prep nurse peeked under the sheet and said, "Oh, you're not Mr. Peterson. I've got the wrong chart."

It was now time for the operation. So I gathered all my natural body openings together and had a little pep talk with them about the upcoming event. The sphincters were all puckered up and my penis began crying. At least I hope those were tears. They all knew they were one-way valves. There were no two ways about it. They agreed with me that a surrogate patient was preferable, but if the operation had to be done, heroin would sure be nice. An IV was begun and it took three tries by three different nurses to finally hit my vein. This was a portent of things to come. I kissed my fiancée good-bye and was wheeled into the operating room.

That's where I first got punked. I was hoping the anesthesiologist was going to speak in children's book metaphors and say in comforting tones, "Well hello there David. Are we ready for bye-bye? My name is Dr. Sandman and very soon I'm going to give you some sleepy syrup and then when you wake up everything will be all better."

This was not to be, for they secretly injected me with rhino tranquilizer and I was out like a carp. But as I was going under I thought I heard Dr. Kang say, "Is that my bourbon or yours?" or "Are you sure this is a castration?"

I'd like to report more completely on the operation, but I can't. I wasn't really there. All I know is that when I woke up it felt as if the Indiana Home for the Criminally Insane had played badminton with my shuttlecock.

Evidently the procedure did not go as planned. The stone was more embedded and stubborn than hoped for. A one-hour operation quickly became a three-hour plus operation. This caused enough latent tissue trauma to make the Ali-Frazier bouts look like the Powder Puff Girls having a pillow fight. So I just lay there and took it like the tough guy I'm not.

Let's fast-forward to the aftermath. The offending stone is obliterated and extracted. The ventilator tube is withdrawn from my throat. The ureteroscope is yanked from my shuttlecock and the stent is locked and loaded. The gurney is then rolled into the recovery room, where, irony of ironies, my ex-wife is working, and her familiar face was the first one I saw when I came to. I was so happy I'd made every alimony payment and that she never discovered my chunky peanut butter fetish.

Three hours later I still couldn't pee so it was decided (by others I might add) I'd better get catheterized to relieve the pressure. This is not what you want done (I repeat) after somebody has roto-rootered your delicate urinary membranes for three hours. The recovery nurse Irene was a distant friend of mine, and I don't think I could've presented a more traumatized and visibly retreating penis to her. The thing had actually recoiled like a tape measure. It was nowhere to be found. She professionally took matters in hand, and after a brief search with a magnifying glass and tweezers, found the AWOL member hiding in my abdomen. My usual dangling participle had become a parsed figure of speech. At this point the respective tubes were tip to tip, so in it went and out it came. My fountainhead looked like "Old Faithful," releasing colorful jets of pent up fluid.

That was the easy part. Going home and recovering was the hard part. I don't really know if I have a low or high threshold for pain, but I do know exactly where the threshold is. At some point it's no longer "pain management"—it's just f*cking mercy.

I'm glad I've been a good boy overall because, at the height of my distress, I felt the need to completely bare my soul to my fiancée in the flimsy hope that utter confession would somehow absolve the pain and grant me serenity. Lo and behold, it worked. After my cathartic confession the pain did subside and I felt momentarily restored, but the mental damage was irreparable. Maybe I had said too much to her—especially the part about my chunky peanut butter fetish.

Things continued downhill. My body rejected the Siamese sea horses anchored in my urinary tract. The rejection is termed "stent colic." Imagine that —a colicky 44-year-old. I knew this would happen because generally I do poorly with any 14-inch foreign object buried deep inside me. It was supposed to stay in for three weeks. It didn't last one. So back to Dr. Kang's office I went. I howled all the way there. Of course I howled even more at the office when, without anesthesia, he inserted a port-a-ureteroscope up my shuttlecock and began extracting the Siamese seahorses. This process took about 2 ½ minutes during which time I once again confessed my chunky peanut butter fetish to his little doe-eyed assistant named Mika. Pain is an emotional thing for me, and I tend to testify like a stool pigeon on American Idol.

After the stent was removed, I felt great mental relief. In fact, as Dr. Young Kang had spent more time inside my body than anyone else, I began to develop a peculiar affinity for him—like a hostage feels towards his kidnappers. I wanted the doctor to share in my experience, so I asked Dr. Kang if there was a surgical equivalent of Sadie Hawkins Day whereby I could operate on him?

"C'mon," I cajoled. "I only use natural body openings."

He smiled and said, "Just fork over the co-pay monkey boy."

I felt so much better after the Excalibur was extracted from my body. For a while the tsunami of tsuffering had me beached at Vicodin Resorts. I'm tapering off slowly and should be completely Vicodin-free by 2051 AD.

Three weeks later I was back at work making infantile jokes about the entire episode and writing this cautionary tale to highlight the importance of proper hydration. I celebrated by listening to Jimi Hendrix's "Stone Free" and loading up on chunky peanut butter. My accountant even thought I might be able to depreciate all the hospital bills ($45K) by incorporating my left kidney as a working rock quarry. I'm happy to share with you a window on my bladder. And through it all I can't stop wondering, "Why would anyone voluntarily have a kidney stone removed?"

Death Has Pale Eyes and Greets Me with a Knowing Smile
by Cara Mecozzi

You'd gone over it carefully, and systematically, the pros and the cons. Every option had been explored, bisected, dissected, and fiddled with until it barely resembled the original thought; you'd drawn up charts, put together graphs and decided it would be best just to end it. Nothing too dramatic though, it's not like your mother died in a car crash and your sister was raped and tortured to the brink of insanity or anything. It's not like some soul-crushing depression caused you to smoke a pack a day since you were fourteen. It was nothing as dramatic as your father being an alcoholic and beating you every night; it just seemed like the right thing to do. You'd probably make it look like an accident, make sure you were drunk enough and then throw yourself off of a cliff or something. Nothing too dramatic, not like anyone would see you; you'd float down and become a missing person, but that wouldn't really matter; you'd be legally declared dead within two years, if your body was not discovered.

It's not like all you felt was pain or anything; just happened to be that all you felt was, well, you didn't really feel anything, you just sort of were. You wouldn't go as far as to declare yourself "an empty husk of the person you formerly were." You were, well, never particularly full to begin with. So the gradual emptying that life brought you didn't have much of an effect.

But still you examined every option that life had to offer, and decided after many years of examination, maybe death was the best option. So you'd gone to the liquor store, bought a twelve pack of beer, two packs of cigarettes, because you ran out the day before, and a lighter, for the cigarettes, naturally.

You decided on the night, when fewer people would be around to see you, weighted your coat with as many rocks as you could, then drank and smoked like there was no tomorrow, because for you, you weren't planning on having one. So when you stepped up to the edge and looked down, you smiled. Falling was going to be the fun part, that you could handle, but landing was going to be the worst. Maybe death would be the opposite. Dying would be the hard part, being dead would not be so bad. Well, you'd find out soon enough. But, as you started to step over, someone grabbed you and pulled you back, dragging you away from the cliff, yelling and screaming at you, but all you could understand was someone with a slight English accent and the words "stupid," "never the answer," and "can't be that bad." However, in your drunken haze the only thought you could muster was that now all the options had to be reexamined again.

You woke the next day, alone, with a killer hangover and the sun glaring down on your face. Your pockets had been emptied of the rocks. You managed to stand up, stumbled to the liquor store, bought another pack of cigarettes and went home.

The questions gnawed on you every night and spit you back up every morning.

One question in particular: 'why?' Of course, that was followed by a lesser question such as, 'who?' You continued to live your not-too-particularly-interesting life, reopening and reexamining all the options, trying to decide the best course of action. You decided maybe living was the answer. Maybe offing yourself was a bad idea, and it'd be easier just to do nothing but live. You even got yourself a girlfriend and found yourself thinking of her whenever you let your mind wander. And, you even decided that you were wrong the first time, you'd missed an important part of the equation, because when all of it balanced out, living seemed like a very good option.

Two weeks later you were diagnosed with lung cancer.

A Villanelle
by Harold Gower

How can she know the secrets of my mind?
How can she know the thoughts I've not confessed?
She claims that all her knowledge is divined.

She says that I'm in love and love is blind
(Somehow I'll have to put her to the test)
How can she know the secrets of my mind?

I'll find out what great story she's designed
Perhaps I'll have her as my honored guest
She claims that all her knowledge is divined.

She says my love is gentle, sweet, and kind
The question now a monumental pest...
How can she know the secrets of my mind?

My strategy is firm; I am resigned
She'll dine with me at my engraved request
She claims that all her knowledge is divined.

The feast is done, and she is fully wined.
We retire to the bed at her behest!
How can she know the secrets of my mind?
She claims that all her knowledge is divined.

Kathy
by Pat Coyle

Kathy's dad is with us from Saskatchewan, Canada. Bill is eighty-four and we are lucky he can still visit us, as he has most years since we've been married. We lost Betty, Kathy's mom, over ten years ago.

We drive to the Piatti Locali restaurant in Danville in two vehicles—not enough seat belts for all of us in one. Our daughter, Liz, drives our son Scott and his girlfriend Sylvia in one car. I drive Bill and Kathy. It is her birthday.

I remember when we met. It was the 4th of July, 1975. I'd come into Belize City from the ranch.

I'd been in Belize since October 1974, when I arrived with my family Jay and Jeannie my sister Erin, and brothers Mike and Matt. I'd agreed to help them relocate to Gold Button Ranch to work on Roy Carver's 20,000-acre land development project.

My family had rented a house in Belize City on A Street. Jeannie set up housekeeping there so we had a place in the city.

Jeannie had met a number of people in the city including Jack and Eve Garden. Jack was a retired RAF pilot and ran the USDA certified meat packing plant, an important asset to market beef production from the ranch.

Jeannie told me, "Pat, when I was at the Gardens, I met a really delightful young woman—Kathy Scott. She is a Canadian and works on the Canadian Aid project to bring water and sewage systems to Belize City. I think you'd like her."

I'd already seen Kathy's photo on the cover of *Belize*

magazine. She was featured in a story about the project and her role as the chief administrative officer. She was twenty-three, very accomplished and professional, and extremely attractive. I can see her face: short brown hair, bright eyes, glasses, and pretty smile with a hint of mischief. I was interested in her.

I'd come into Belize City for the 4th of July. It was about ninety miles by dirt roads from the ranch between San Felipe and August Pine Ridge through the villages to Orange Walk Town and then down the Northern Highway to Belize City. When we first got there, it was a three-to-four hour bone-jarring ride that almost always broke something on your vehicle.

Radio Belize, "the voice of the Caribbean Basin," had been advertising for days, ". . . Come on in to the party mon, it 'gwin be the 4th of July and the Bellevue Hotel and Bar 'gwin have one big dance and celebration . . . Not just for the Americans, it'd be fo' all de wan' a party. . . ."

Jack Garden gave me a ride from the A street house to the Bellevue. Jack's face was dark, florid, almost purplish. He was still handsome—an ex-fighter pilot, with a confident assured manner. We stopped at an intersection—no breeze, sticky and humid, the rank, sweet smell of scotch filling the space, as he metabolized it out through every pore of his body as he had every day for years.

Jack drove the yellow Morris Mini-Moke—a jeep-like little open-air vehicle with canvas roof and roll-up side curtains—across Belize City, over the turn bridge across the river and parked by the sea wall facing the harbor. It was still hot and humid, but there was a stiff breeze coming in off the water.

Jack liked to say, "You can fall in love with a rich woman just as easy as a poor one." As near as I could tell, his wife Eve was not rich. She liked to read the Ouija board at her parties.

I walked into the Bellevue and paused in the lobby entrance

area, leaning against the reception counter.

The music was blaring—rock, reggae, country and western, with a Belize local take on all of them. The bar and dance floor were crowded with people for the party.

The British had a six-hundred-person garrison in Belize out by the International Airport, with Harrier jump jets to deter Guatemala's territorial claim to Belize. Lots of RAF guys were on the dance floor. The Harrier pilots were just as you'd expect: young, brash, extremely confident guys.

I looked past the brightly lit lobby into the dance floor. They had cleared the tables from the dining room to make room for the dancing. It was packed. I could see young Belizean guys leaning against the far wall; some were hotel staff, others just checking out the scene.

I spotted Kathy Scott. She was in an animated conversation with a dark-haired, bearded man and a woman with sandy-blond hair. They were gesturing, with lots of facial expressions and body language between them.

"All right. I'm going to finally meet her. I'll wait till there is a chance, then ask her to dance."

Suddenly she turned from them and walked toward me. I watched to see where she went. She kept walking right up to me.

"Hi, do you want to dance?" she asked.

I'm startled, "Sure."

We walked out onto the dance floor and started dancing.

"I'm Pat Coyle. I know you're Kathy Scott. I recognized you from your photo on the cover of *Belize* magazine. I was going to ask you to dance as soon as I got a chance."

She laughed, "My friends, Marten Meadows and Christine Dixon, agreed we would all stick together so I wouldn't have to face the Harrier pilots hitting on me. Then Christine said she was going to go dance with Marten. I needed to do something.

I saw you and thought you look safe, wholesome, like someone from a Methodist Church camp, so I said go ahead. I'll go ask that guy to dance."

We talked. I said, "My mother said she'd met you and thought I'd like you."

Kathy said, "Jeannie is great, it is really nice to be able to talk to her."

We talked and danced. When the party was winding down, she said, "I've got my car. I can drive you home." Marten and Christine had gone their own ways so that worked fine.

We walked out of the Bellevue. The water lapped against the sea wall. The breeze came in across the harbor, cooler now. The music trailed away into the Bellevue as we walked to her car.

We talked as we drove back across the turn bridge and over to the A Street house.

It was late. I said, " Kathy, I am so glad I met you tonight. I've known of you for some time and really wanted to meet you. I want to see you again. I'll call you."

"Good night, Pat. I'm glad I asked you to dance. Do call me."

I did, again and again.

We saw each other more and more, although when I ask her about the transitional details, she says she doesn't recall.

Later on, Kathy considered buying a VW Thing, so she could get up to the ranch more often. I said, "Wait, if you are thinking of that, don't. That road will just tear it up. Let's partner on an airplane."

We bought a used Cessna-172, an older one, the N number was N-2871U. A high-wing, 4-seater, it cruised at 120 mph, with a range of about 4 hours with reserve. Kathy had Lois Young, an attorney in Belize City, draw up papers so it was clear in the event anything happened to us, that it didn't just go to my brother.

It changed our love life dramatically. With the plane, the trip from the ranch to Belize City was 15-20 minutes. I could stay over and go up in the morning to work.

We were in New Orleans, on one of our R&R breaks, sitting in a little room in the French Quarter overlooking a garden courtyard.

"Kathy," I said, "All the people in our lives are going to be a lot more comfortable if we are married. I know I have talked about the issues I have from having been married before, but that just doesn't matter. I love you and I want to be with you. Marry me."

I don't recall just what she said, but the bottom line was yes. We called her folks to let them know.

We flew the plane to Canada from Belize to be married in January of 1977. Flying back to Belize, the paint fell off.

We stayed almost another year, leaving Belize in December of 1977.

We re-entered in Phoenix, back in the USA, then to Livermore in 1980.

Now a family with children grown into young adults, we are looking at retirement.

I called her. I did, again and again. I do now. I will forever. I love you, Kathy.

Bill

by Pat Coyle

Kathy was ready to go into security and on to the gate with her father, Bill Scott. He was headed home to Rosetown, Saskachewan through Calgary, Alberta.

Bill was in a wheelchair—it's the way for him to go in big airports like SFO—it's just not comfortable anymore for him to walk the long distance to the gates in the crowded concourses.

It is quite another story when he is playing golf with his friends, flirting with women, fixing a clock, cleaning out the garage, driving a grain truck at harvest, working outside at his cabin at the lake—or any of the things he does with such vitality and presence.

They'd gotten checked in fast. When I got there from parking the car in the garage, they were ready to roll. An airline staff person had met them with a wheelchair to escort them. I was pleased and surprised that Kathy was able to go to the gate with Bill. Last year we'd said goodbye to him before he went through security. However, the guy said only one person could come with him.

I said, "Kathy, don't worry or cut your time with Bill short. I'll be fine, I'll find a place to wait, maybe read or write."

We always hate to see him go. He is such a pleasure to have with us. I've told Bill, "As much as we hate to see you go, I try to remember there are others who are really looking forward to having you with them too."

I want Kathy to be able to enjoy him right up to the time he has to get on the plane. Bill is an extraordinarily personable man. I've appreciated his friendly outgoing manner for years. He engages people in all kinds of situations, talks with them, and makes them feel comfortable. He is a generous, strikingly handsome man with silver-white hair, sparkling eyes, a quick smile, and a thoroughly charming face that lights up as he connects with you and tells you a story or listens to yours.

I said my goodbye, "See you soon, Bill. We'll hope for better weather the next time, maybe take a trip to Mexico or Nicaragua or San Juan del Sur at Barb and Reine's new place."

It had rained most days for the six weeks Bill had been with us. Bay Area locals were complaining, Seasonal Affective Disorder (SAD) was on the rise and it had kept Bill off the golf course with his buddies.

"All right, Pat. Thanks for everything," he said.

I looked through the viewfinder and taped as they moved away. I went around and up the stairs to see if I could see them in security. I could. They had him take his shoes off, but getting through security went quickly.

I wolf-whistled at Kathy—but didn't think she heard me. A moment later though, she looked up, saw me and waved. As they turned to go on, she told Bill and turned the chair toward me. He looked up my way, waved, pointed his cane at me like it was rifle, and pulled the trigger.

They moved quickly, briefly visible under the wide bank of departure screens, then down the corridor to Gates 76-90 and out of sight.

I paused. I thought how last night I had also said we should see about taking a trip to Mexico or Nicaragua and not wait too many years to do it.

Then and now, I have a heart-filled feeling with tears welling up. Bill is eighty-four. He's not going to be around forever. It is something I think of especially when he's leaving. It is such a reminder to me of how special he is—he is not to be taken for granted.

I'm sipping a Peet's drip coffee, medium with one ice cube. I've got a table at the edge of the food niche; it's not big enough to be a court—with a Burger King, a Subway, and Peet's. The pedestrian bridge from the parking structure comes into this level just to my right, with stairs and an escalator to the level below for check-in.

A nice lady at Bank of America gave me a few sheets of paper to write on, so I'm set. I started writing this.

Looking down the line of tables, I see a blond woman is putting her cat back into its soft carrying case. She's patting its head, zipping up the door, and talking with the man she's sitting with.

I shot a little videotape as we left the house this morning and more here in the terminal, looking through the viewfinder at this slice of our time together.

In the car on the way in to the airport, I'd asked Kathy and Bill about the time I met him and Betty, Kathy's mother, in Santa Fe. "How did we all end up there? I can't recall," I said. It has been about thiry years.

Kathy said, "You and your brother Matt had gone up together, before I did. You were already there with your family. I flew up from Belize to join you. We were going to be able to meet Bill and Betty, who would stop in Santa Fe on their way to Arizona."

We weren't married, but I was ready to meet her parents.

They were driving down from their place in Rosetown, Saskachewan, to visit their other Canadian Snowbird friends in Mesa, near Phoenix.

On that visit, Bill and Betty met me and most of my family. We met at my Grandmother's house at 900 Gildersleeve.

The place on Gildersleeve had always been a base for my family as I grew up along the front range of the Rockies: born in Fort Collins, Colorado, then to Las Cruces, New Mexico while my parents were in university, back to Santa Fe, Tesuque, Cerrillos, Santa Fe again, then ranches in northeastern Wyoming, outside of Gillette and Upton, from fifth grade through high school, college at Colorado School of Mines in Golden, resisted the draft, did seven days in Denver County Jail for an anti-war tax-day demonstration, and worked at National Center for Atmospheric Research (NCAR) in Boulder, Colorado. In 1974, I rejoined my family to help them relocate to Belize.

My Grandmother was called "Granger" by all of us—it started when I called her that as a little boy. Granger's kitchen had always been a place where the family congregated whatever was happening. In addition, they'd usually have a drink there at the end of the day. Some of us would sit on the kitchen counters. Granger and my Grandfather Roy, uncle Jim, aunt Helen, Jeannie, Jay, and other adults would sit around the kitchen table. We'd all visit. Roy liked to snack on sardines on soda crackers and have a drink. He had passed away before we went to Belize.

Bill and Betty were right at home in that kitchen. They were very comfortable just visiting and getting to know this family that their daughter Kathy was getting increasingly involved with.

So that's when I met Bill. When I describe him to others, I hope I convey how much we've enjoyed his visits, first when Betty and he would come. These last years, only him.

I'd told Kathy the night before, "I really appreciate it that Bill made the time to do it. Liz and Scott have grown up really knowing their grandfather Bill. This contrasts with my dad, Jay, who never came."

Part of it was that Bill could. It was his jewelry store until he sold it to his daughter Barbara. He was his own boss and could leave it with his staff for four to six weeks of time away. Bill is a great people person. He'd met the public across the counter for years. He also was a skilled watch repairman and had worked as an aviation electronics technician when he was in the service.

I paused, thinking of my dad Jay. He died young. He worked on other people's ranches, big ones, managed the whole operation for them. I still wonder about why his dad Pat sold the ranch they had outside Newcastle, Wyoming. I wonder what his life would have been like if that ranch had been his base. He also worked for Roy, in the plumbing and heating business, when between ranch jobs.

I'm grateful for the part of my life growing up on ranches in the country, with Jay and all of our family. Jay was a great role model on many fronts: work ethic, competence, and attitude, "making a hand" as he put it. David Davila, who met Jay at the H-V and has been a family friend ever since, said it well: "Jay was a great cheerleader. He somehow just made it fun to work with him—even for the toughest, grinding ranch work."

I remember early one morning, feeding horses with him at the Santa Fe rodeo grounds. It was before he needed to go in to work at Roy's shop. Jay said, "I make it a point to meet the expectations of whoever I am working for. Once I've done that, I have the time before and after work for my things like these horses."

I'm sorry Jay couldn't have had more time with our kids but even the little bit he had meant a lot. Lizzie was little when he died in 1987. Jay saw Scott once when Kathy took him to Santa Fe as a baby and Scott was not quite two when Liz and he picked out a clown doll for Jay at the St. Vincent's gift shop when he was in the hospital with cancer. Scott wanted to give him the doll and Liz let him.

When we came back for Jay's services, Scott said he was going to go see Grandpa Jay in the room where he had been at home. We had to tell him Jay wasn't there anymore.

I pause while writing this. The blonde with the cat in the

carrier comes by. I tell her, "I noticed how you've got your cat there with you—that's pretty neat."

She laughs, "She's great, loves going with me."

As she walks on, with the bag slung over her shoulder, the cat's face presses up against the fabric mesh screen and meows at me.

Kathy just called my cell. She's on her way back. Bill didn't want her to wait with him at the gate any longer.

I push back, "You shouldn't cut your time with him short. I'm fine here."

"Nope. He's fine. He doesn't want me to wait with him," Kathy said.

I finish my coffee, feeling emotions well up again. I'd joked to Kathy about the diamond ad I've seen on television. In it, a woman in a European city square is surprised when her husband gives her a diamond gift. She is overwhelmed and cries out to the whole square, "I love this man."

I feel that way about Bill. He is such a gift. This visit, sometimes I'd pat his back or touch his arm and feel this overwhelming closeness. My eyes filled with tears. Kathy is here.

He Lives Alone, Much Like Unloading a Uhaul

by Mark Cabasino

> *Everywhere is somewhere and nowhere is near*
> *Everybody got somebody with their wine and their beer*
> *But I'm just this tragic figure in the corner over here*
> *Come home to an empty apartment and call a best friend who's a queer.*
> —Moses," Patty Griffin

strain in the calves, heartbreak in a sieve,
blood vessels rush to and fro to the spot,
minus the team of little atomi
and sans girlfriend again, he totes

cumbersome woes and boxes of ache,
seventeen trips down three and up two,
door 410 is the saddest number, no
twenty-ninth bather spies on these shores.

try to maneuver a love seat upstairs.
now try it alone using furniture
no woman has ever loved you on,
and you might know him then—moving man.

he signs the lease and forges a spouse,
crawls on the floor in rhymes of an hour,
watching his opera atop the formica
next to a dishwasher that doesn't rinse.

when the truck is empty, it sounds hollow
like it once held a horse en route to the track,
bucking itself against metal walls.
so he misses sex and hedges his bets.

Dracula traveled with crates of earth
and rats in the hull of an unmanned ship;
just so, moving man began his rebirth,
one by one opening his cargo of...books.

Coyote Laughing

by Ethel Mays

Part I.
Rain came walking
On spindly legs
And heavy feet
With bent head
Trailing blue-black drenching tresses
Onto blistered flats
And shrunken gullies and washes
Until dusty creeks spilled
Over absentminded sands
Forgetful of all
Save immediate wet
While wind fled wailing
Down a nowhere muddy path
With sun and heat
Left far behind
Wet and weary shoulders

Part II.
Wind fled wailing
Down a nowhere muddy path
And Rain reached out
To touch him
While all of Sun's
Vast baying pack
Of golden hounds
Chased both
'Til only Wind
Scorched and parched
Moaning
Stumbled on
With glittering crystal talismans
From a heat-banished lover
Encrusting ragged beard

Part III.

Fog murmured
A misty song
And held wide
Billowing homespun gray
And danced a timeless dance
Of eddying patterns
Borne aloft and beyond
By improbable partner Wind
Now cooled and quenched
By softer waters
Not chosen
But not rebuffed
On this day
Of all

Furious red-faced Sun
Beckons whining hounds
Then hears coyote laughing
And launches
A final petty blast of heat

Red lolling tongue
Retreats behind
Sharp white grin
And desert jester
(But no fool)
Flits beyond reach
And heists his leg
Over inevitable elemental twaddle
Then runs home
To share the gossip

Part IV.

Late afternoon crawled on its hands and knees toward the open arms of waiting sundown and I was as tired as it was. I wanted to take a break from a drive that seemed to be headed to infinity in a California desert I had recently alluded to in casual conversation. Friends had looked at me sideways and now I had to concede to a couple of their concerns about me: easily distracted, doesn't use maps. I didn't think I was lost, but I had no idea where I was. Screw it, I thought. I'm taking a walk.

The day's departing heat almost shoved me back into the car's cool interior when I opened the door. By the time I retrieved my hat and a full water bottle out of the back seat, it had sucked all traces of air conditioning out of the car. I pushed on my shades and stepped onto dense, rocky sand, leaving the locked car on the side of the road. As I skirted scrubby brush, my eyes roved ahead and to each side of me and kept me from disturbing things basking, perched, or coiled. The stark beauty of dark blue sky and impassive Joshua trees upstaged the fact that I carried no gun or even a walking stick to protect myself. I'm not going that far, I thought. What could happen?

Fifteen minutes into my walk something out of the corner of my eye gave me a sudden rush of goose bumps. Fine hairs on my forearms stood up. I stopped walking. When I turned my head, I saw two sharp yellow eyes boring into me. All rational thoughts fled. My mouth opened and I caught my breath with a soft gasp. My heart clenched its fists and tried to beat down the walls of my chest, but I forced myself to breathe slowly and deeply. I stood perfectly still.

A russet coyote sat next to a creosote bush about ten feet away. We stared at each other across a primal chasm and I felt his otherworldly intelligence nudge mine. He flattened his ears. Then he lowered his head a little and extended his nose toward me. He could see that I posed no threat to him. He began gathering information through his fine, sensitive nose – a close-range chance he may never have had before. We studied each other together.

Moments passed. He stood up, poked his nose at me again, and then ambled over to another bush. He took a casual sniff then cocked up a hind leg and peed. Then I knew somewhere in his rusty, wily head he was laughing at me. He moved off with a backward glance as if to say, "Um-hm—caught ya."

I smiled and watched as he loped away and disappeared down into a gully. Under my breath I shot back at him, "Yeah ya did, ya little bastard."

I picked my way back to the car in cooler dusk and heard twilight yips and yaps greeting the approaching night. My coyote had gathered a serenading chorus to make up for having laughed at me.

Hollow, Man.
by Tom Darter

Note: The views expressed herein do not necessarily reflect those of the author.

So when Eliot concocted his cultural brew
that laid us to waste, landed us in the stew,
did he think he was working a common milieu,
or did he pen poems for only the few?

It can't be denied that he did something new,
but if nobody gets it, can it still be true?
When working in riddles, how can one imbue
all the denseness and deepness with thought that gets through?

I've been a part of the puzzlement crew —
those who love being in, being people who knew;
but of late I'm afraid that obscuring the view
throws the bath-water out and the baby goes too.

Decrypting a poem is still fun to do,
and chasing the code keeps us busy in lieu
of the thought that is needed to give us a clue.
Do we untie the knot or just cut it in two?

On Building a Universal Spam Filter
By Peter Bray

I'll build it like an Eiffel Tower
with steel, tenacity, and rivets . . .

Like a castle's moat with
deep and wide black fluids,
burning tar, witches' boils,
hungry predators, glass shard
fragments at the bottom, and fear . . .

Like a sun screen with Joni Mitchell meanings,
Bob Dylan lyrics and many other
state, local, and federal tax codes,
and legislative and tort reforms . . .

Like an immune system with proteins,
antibodies, and all the right
defensive moves . . .

Like a biological clock, booby-trapped
and hog-wire fenced with electrical trip-wire
mechanisms, hormonal changes,
atomic particle explosions,
plastic explosives, and expiration dates
and confusing bar codes,
and a rabbit snare tied to
a bent-over birch or
willow tree sapling . . .

Like an FBI/CIA/Homeland Security
agent-outing memo with no
return address, no point of origin,
but every US columnist's home and
cell phone numbers and their GPS location
and implant codes plus a 24-7 language
reversing and scrambling encryption trigger . . .

Like a Dick Cheney secret agent/
Power & Energy Policy meeting
where all the petroleum moguls
are invited to look at the oil reserve
maps of Iraq but the US press is excluded,
so they fight it with the Freedom of
Information Act, but there's a
Dick Cheney dagger in the door
with a Post-It Note from his desk
saying to the public, written in blood,
"You're NOT invited! Do you get my meaning?"

What I want to know is:
How did you get through
and what password did you use?

Amazing Grace Arrives From Cyberspace
by Karen L. Hogan

"Daemon failure"
   The email announced.

Well, hallelujah and amen! I say.
   The demon has failed
   and it's about time.

He prevailed
way longer than he should,
covering truths with lies.

Like:
  God is a grumpy old man—
        He can never be pleased
  Love is in a vault—
        it's in short supply.
  Life is a sentence—
        it runs on and on.

Well, hallelujah and amen! I say.
    The demon has failed
    and truths have uncovered the lies!

Like:
   God is inside me—
         if I listen I please.
   Love is in the meadow—
         there's plenty to spare.
   Life is a well-crafted sentence—
         it comes to an end.

Well, hallelujah and amen! I say.
    The demon has failed.

The news arrived from cyberspace—
         unsolicited.

Amazing!
Grace.

The Blue Vase
by Diana Carey

The vase stood alone on the shelf, her beautiful blue coat blanketed with dust, a spider web fixing her to the paint chipped surface. She did not remember the last time she had been gently and lovingly lifted from her high perch and set in the center of the large white cloth that had covered the table, the flowers so bright as they poured out from her tall, thin neck.

She used to sit on that table and share in the joyous chaos of the kitchen. The clink of coffee cups on saucers as the mother visited with friends during the day. The smell of baking bread and pies, the clatter of children's shoes running in and out as their owners scurried about finishing their chores for the day. The calm prayer and somewhat less than calm of the family sharing their evening meal together.

She had enjoyed those days, but over the years the kitchen had become quieter and the clatter of shoes and chatter of voices had died away. Now there was just the man and the woman, quiet and slow in their aged steps. How she longed to be taken down and sit gleaming in the center of the table again, the flowers spilling out, bringing the warm glow of the sun back into that dark and silent kitchen.

As she was sitting one day dreaming of those days past a strange woman entered the kitchen, followed by the old man and woman.

"What a terrific kitchen. I think this will be a huge selling point for the right couple. And that view of the backyard with all the bright flowers is fantastic!"

The blue vase was curious. What did this mean? Who was this woman? What was happening? There had not been this much excitement in the kitchen for many years. Even the old copper kettle on the other wall became interested, and he had not roused himself for at least ten years.

There was much gossiping that night after the old man and woman had gone to bed. The silver platter just knew there was going to be a party. "You'll see, I'll be in the center of attention again with all of the cookies."

The big iron pot in the corner was sure there would be a soup for the party. "You just wait. You'll see, I'll have potatoes and onions and carrots."

The old copper kettle chimed in, "There will be tea and I shall boil the water!"

The blue vase was as excited as the rest of them. "And I shall be all clean and shiny with a lovely hat of flowers again!"

Everyone was excited. They could not wait for the party.

The next day more strangers started to come. There were men and women with cameras and business cards, there were families and people who came in and looked and talked and left again. But the party was not to be seen.

One day the first strange woman came back. She pushed open the heavy oak door and lead another young woman into the kitchen.

"Why, this is perfect. I've dreamed of finding a kitchen like this, but I never thought it would be possible to actually see one."

The blue vase was happy to hear the young woman talk like that. She too loved that kitchen. She remembered all the years it had been filled with life and noise and excitement.

"Bob, come in here and look at this kitchen. It's just what I've always wanted!"

A young man opened the door and came in. He looked around at the large old kitchen. The long wooden table standing in the corner, the large, deep sink and the counter spreading out on both sides until it covered the whole wall.

"The stove is a little old, and so is the refrigerator, but I guess we could fix that."

"Oh, it's perfect, Bob. The whole house is perfect. Just the place we need to raise our family."

"There's a lot of work to do around here. Looks like the old man has not been able to do too much for quite a while."

"It's a fixer-upper to be sure, but the price is right and you will not get a better buy anywhere close to town." The real estate woman really wanted to sell this house.

"And all the furnishings come with it?"

"Everything," the woman replied.

"Well, that will give us a good start. We are expecting our first child and we can use all the help we can get to set ourselves up. All right, we can buy it. If you're really sure this is what you want?"

"We can go back to my office and fill out the paperwork if you like." That was the real estate woman. She was happy to hear the old house was going to be off her hands.

They all left the kitchen and the blue vase wondered what was going to happen. Several weeks went by and the house became silent. Even the quiet steps of the old man and woman could no longer be heard.

Then one day the heavy oak door opened and there was the young man and woman. He had a ladder and she had a can of paint. Her hair was in a kerchief and she had on jeans and a plaid shirt. She looked like she was ready for business. The first thing she did was set the ladder up right next to the shelf where blue vase was sitting. The young woman climbed to the top of the ladder and gently lifted the blue vase. She climbed back down and, carrying the vase carefully, moved over to the sink.

The hot sudsy water felt good, and before long all the dust was washed away and the blue vase was sitting upside down in the drainer feeling the warmth of the sun that was shining in through the window. She watched as the young woman busied herself about the kitchen, painting the walls and the shelf the blue vase had been sitting on. When she was done she came back over to the sink and picked up the blue vase.

"I know exactly where you need to be," she told the vase. She set the blue vase down and went out the back door into the garden. In a few minutes she came back in, her arms full of flowers. She filled the vase with cool clear water and started arranging the flowers. Then she gently picked up the vase so as not to disturb the arrangement and carried her over to the table. There was a white cloth on the table. She set the blue vase in the center of the white cloth.

And the blue vase sat, gleaming in the center of the table, the flowers spilling out, bringing the warm glow of the sun into the bright and lively kitchen.

A New Thing Called Television
by Frank Thornburgh

TV was just starting to catch on in 1950 when my Aunt Velma and Uncle Harry bought one. Many weekends they drove over to our farm with the big, new, hunky TV in the back seat of their car. We cleared off a table, plugged in the TV and prepared to put on a TV party by popping corn, frying feed corn, making fudge, mixing Kool Aid, and during winter months gathering fresh snow then sprinkling vanilla extract, sugar, and milk on it.

The experts were constantly working with the rabbit ears antenna or adding aluminum foil to it in an effort to get better reception.

Indianapolis only had two black and white TV stations which were about 40 miles away. Color was years in the future. Just watching the test pattern excited me.

Two other families on our road also had TVs. My brother Donnie and I often rode our bikes down to Jimmy's house about a quarter mile away or another quarter mile farther down to the Bertrum's in the evenings to watch roller derby, wrestling, and variety shows. Normally we stayed past Mom's late limit, always testing the edge of what we could get away with.

Our rural gravel road was treacherous for bicycles even in the daylight. Real skill was needed to stay in the smoother car tracks to avoid the thick gravel areas. Spills and crashes were common, but eleven and twelve year old farm boys were tough.

The one night forever imprinted in my memory was when we had ridden to the Bertrum's. We spent a long summer evening watching TV while playing cards with the two girls and their parents. Later that night we played a game where we sat at a card table, rubbed our hands together until they were hot, lightly placed our finger tips on the table and asked the devil questions with the card table knocking once for yes and two times for no. Our curfew time passed so my little brother and I reset our watches as usual to make an excuse for over-staying our time. Mom never believed that ploy, but we tried anyway.

Donnie and I started riding home in the dark with no lights. We were really scared after all that business with the devil, and wanted to ride fast so nothing could grab us. My need-to-pee signal was maxed out. We got this great idea—get going as fast as we could, then I was to put both feet over to one side and pee while coasting. Well, the first part went OK. I got going as fast as I could, got my little hose out, started putting my foot over, but somehow stuck my foot in the front spokes. The wheel locked instantly, causing me and the bike to do a 180 through the air landing on my back, knocking me unconscious for a few seconds. When I woke up I realized my bladder had started without me. I was peeing up into an arc and down on my face. I almost forgot about being scared.

I called out, "DONNIE!"

No answer.

Either the devil got him or he didn't stop to see what happened to me. He was too busy saving himself.

The next time we went to watch television it didn't include that devil stuff.

Her Last Smile
by Frank Thornburgh

It was a cold winter day. I was parked in a warm sunny spot while on patrol when the radio suddenly broke my trance. "Unit 5 welfare check 2019 Oakhurst, apartment 3." I acknowledged the dispatcher, wrote the address down, started the car and headed in that direction. Calls like that made me wonder what I was going to find. Would it be the usual phone off the hook, someone in trouble, or the worst kind? I concentrated on my driving, trying to get there with the least delay without running code 2.

There was no answer at the locked door. I looked in the mailbox and saw what looked like an accumulation of mail. I kept ringing the doorbell and knocking loudly, calling out who I was; still no response. I looked at the door locks' brand names, then started through my master key rings for that lock brand trying keys until one worked. As I opened the door, calling out who I was, I instinctively sniffed the air. The odor of decaying animal was not present but decaying food was. I went in, looked around, and called out my presence.

As I entered the living room, I saw her sitting in a large upholstered chair. A small, frail old lady with her head slumped to one side. As I examined her, I could see her breathing was short and shallow. I talked to her, asking if she could hear me. She struggled to open her eyes but could not. Finally one eye opened, then the other about half way. I kept trying to get her to answer me, but eye movement was all she could manage. I quickly glanced around and saw the phone off the cradle on the floor beside her. She was cold to the touch. There was one blanket on her lap and one on the floor beside her. I straightened the blankets, wrapped two around her then felt her right foot as I replaced her slipper, which had fallen off. Her foot was cold as ice and dark blue.

Another officer came in with an oxygen resuscitator. We started a light flow of oxygen to her while I kept trying to get a verbal response by telling her who we were and what we were doing. She gave me a faint but definite smile. I reset the phone, dialed my dispatcher, described the situation, and asked to roll the fire rescue plus ambulance. The other officer turned up the furnace thermostat then went out to guide the other emergency units into the correct place. I readjusted her blankets, felt her pulse and skin, continually studying her breathing. As I talked softly to her while holding her hand, she managed another little smile for me. I guessed she was about 90 years old and about 70-80 pounds. She had a little red and white lace hair cover on her head. Her head continued to sag to one side. I could not get her straightened up to a more comfortable position. Her little body seemed to be partially frozen in that position. I saw a pillow nearby, so grabbed it and tried to position it under her head to give some support. She seemed to be a little more comfortable now, no longer struggling to keep her eyes open. I did not know if I should let her rest a little or keep talking to keep her awake. Finally I decided to let her rest. She closed her eyes and appeared to rest. She may have been struggling for days to get her blankets up and use the phone before giving up.

I heard sirens now. The fire rescue guys came in. I gave them the story and stood back to let them take over. I watched as they did the question and response tests again while checking her pulse. She gave them the eye struggle and squeezed their finger for yes and no answers but no smile. I felt sad, privileged, and selfish all together. The little lady near death may have given me her last smile.

I looked around the place for medication containers, mail, personal papers, addresses and personal phone book. The place was not neat and tidy but not too bad. There were lots of bills and papers of all kinds lying around. I found her name on a Medicare statement and told the fire department guys what I had learned for their reports. I also noticed three or four entries on statements, all of which read the same: "amount of home care not covered."

I went back over and asked the fire department guys if they knew what was holding up the ambulance. One got on his radio and inquired. It had been dispatched several minutes ago. The amount of delay was unusual, so I got on my radio and inquired also. The address was hard to find with a tricky entrance so we concluded the ambulance was lost nearby.

Another officer went off searching for the ambulance. I continued looking around the apartment for more information for my report. A half bowl of very cold soup with a cracker was on a living room table. Food was rotting on the kitchen table. There were lots of family pictures on the dining room table sort of scattered around like she had recently looked through them. There was an old-fashioned sewing machine set up on a table in her bedroom with some material on it. The spare bedroom was set up like someone had been using it occasionally to lie there to watch television. On the walls were many framed pictures of a soldier in WWII uniform with a young woman. The many books, papers and receipts could not help me sort out who was living and who was not.

Our community nurse arrived with medical records. The information in the records was sparse and of little help. Finally the ambulance arrived. The paramedics started the whole procedure over again. I sat down in an ornately carved antique chair to study the scene in front of me. This time the medics were getting less response. They administered various drugs then loaded her onto a gurney. I asked how she was doing. One medic looked at me and slowly shook his head no. I knew she had slipped away. I asked which hospital they were going to for my report. The nurse said she would continue to look for the next of kin and notify them.

I checked the stove, lights, doors, and windows then turned down the thermostat. I surveyed the scene once more, picked up the paramedic's debris, went to the front door, turned and looked at all those pictures. Where were all those people when she needed them? I went out and locked the door.

Eating My Way Through India
by Annette Langer

A college anthropology course I was taking when living in Chicago required that I spend five weeks in southern India doing research. The course had all the customary classroom textbook and exam requirements, and these were augmented by films from the India Tourism Board regarding life in India. There also was a class outing to a local Indian restaurant one evening to introduce us to foods to which we may not have been exposed before. Then, the professor informed the class that our studies would culminate with an actual visit to India at the end of the semester. We were expected to write a research paper upon our return to the United States based on our travel experiences, and this would constitute the major portion of the final grade.

About a week before we were to depart the U.S., I received a shocking surprise. I learned that no one else in the class would be going. Everyone seemed to have an excuse for not making the trip—couldn't afford it, couldn't get the time off work, didn't want to go, etc. I was disappointed but had no intentions of canceling myself, so it was just me, the professor, and his wife. She had preceded us to India by a few weeks, to get "the lay of the land," I presumed. It wasn't explained why, and I didn't ask. The three of us were to meet in Bombay and then travel together for the balance of the trip.

But, my adventure began even before reaching India. The professor and I departed from Chicago and flew directly to London, England, where we were informed that we had no confirmed reservations for the rest of the journey. One of my classmates, a travel and tourism student, had made the arrangements for us, but didn't notice that the remaining portion of the trip after the London stop was "on request." That's airline lingo for "standby only," rather than confirmed reservations. We were placed on the waiting list for each of the remaining segments of our flight: London to Rome, Italy, Rome to Karachi, Pakistan, and finally, Karachi to Bombay, India—taking almost three days in total.

Each of us carried only a large backpack and nothing more. We intended to travel as cheaply as possible in order to really get into the experience and not "view it from afar" (from a first-class section point of view, that is). When we arrived in Bombay finally well after midnight, the professor retrieved his backpack from the luggage carousel, and that's when we discovered that mine was missing. Of course, the Lost and Found Department was closed at that time of night, so we'd have to wait until morning to either locate my backpack or file a lost baggage claim.

Our accommodations for the first night also had been arranged by my classmate (God help him!), but after that, we were on our own. We took a taxi to the YWCA guest house in Bombay, where the professor joined his wife in the "for-couples-only" section. I secured shared lodging with two female students in the building next door in the young-women-only dormitory-style hostel.

I had breakfast with my new roomies in the morning and learned all about their lives as students in India. They spoke very good English and proceeded to tell me all about their Home Economics classes. One animated girl chatted on about their teacher who was trying to instruct them on how to use a sewing machine. The teacher's favorite expression when something didn't work right on the machine was, "It's all haywire" (much the same feeling that I had about how my trip had begun).

I met up with the professor and his wife after breakfast, and we attempted to locate my missing backpack. A trip back to the airport proved unsuccessful as there was still no sign of my bag, nor any airplanes landing at that time of day. We decided to do a bit of sightseeing to pass the time after learning that the next plane would not arrive until the middle of the night. After a dinner of Chinese food, I left the professor and his wife and returned to the airport myself to keep the vigil for my lost bag. In the end, it was worth the wait and happily, my backpack and I were reunited at long last.

It was so late when I got back to the youth hostel that I had to awaken our security guard to gain entry. (The students had a strict 10:30 P.M. curfew, which I missed by a mile.) The security guard was at his post doing what he was supposed to do at that time of night—sleep in the doorway of the hostel to prevent anyone from getting past him. I awakened him, apologized, carefully stepped over him, apologized again and went inside. I trudged up the stairs to my room, changed into clean clothes, shoved the backpack under my bed and got a few hours' blessed sleep.

After breakfast and bidding my roommates farewell, I joined the professor and his wife for the official beginning of the adventure we were about to experience. At each place we visited, they would introduce themselves to people first and then introduce me as "the class." (That got old pretty fast.) We stayed in other hostels and cheapie hotels along the way, and ate primarily Chinese food—lots and lots of Chinese food. Contrary to what the professor had been stressing all semester long about savoring the new and different experiences we would have, I guess curry-spiced Indian food was not on his "to do" list.

After several days of sightseeing and exploring our new environment, we finally left Bombay and headed further south. We booked first-class passage for ourselves on an overnight steamer cruise to Goa, where I shared a cabin with the professor, his wife, and his filthy cigar. Second-class accommodations were supposed to be worse.

At Goa, I decided to find out just how much worse, and secured second-class passage for myself on a local train to take us the final leg to Bangalore. "Second class" is exactly what you might imagine. Absent were the padded railway seats, and in their place were only hard, wooden benches. If I opened the window to get some air inside the stifling train car, I had to do battle with the constant onslaught of coal dust from the engine. Wipe off perspiration or wipe off soot—those were my choices.

We were met at the railway station in Bangalore by another academic, a friend of my professor. Paul, originally from Great Britain, was there on sabbatical from the University of Illinois, writing a book about the life of the hill tribes in the south of India. He taught anthropology at the University back home and used filmmaking as his primary medium of instruction. He became our instant guide (and my instant friend!), and got us into places normally not visited by tourists.

Wherever we went, the strong scent of eucalyptus hung in the air. At first, it assaulted my senses because I wasn't used to such a constant, heady aroma. But, by the end of our journey, I inhaled great lungs full, welcoming the pungent ever-present scent. To this day, I find the smell of eucalyptus in the air a pleasant one, easily transporting me back in time (*a la* Pavlov's dogs) to the weeks I spent there.

The car traffic in India was unusual, at best. At night, drivers didn't turn on their headlights, whether in or outside the towns, except to flash an oncoming car in warning. It's a wonder anyone survived that system—including sparing me so I could live to tell this story.

It was difficult, as well, getting used to crossing the streets on foot in the city. One always had to be mindful of traffic passing on the "wrong side" of the street, as in England. One street in Bangalore completely mystified me. When crossing over on the striped, pedestrian crosswalk to the opposite side of the street, I was met at the curb by an iron railing barring my path. Then, I had to walk about twenty feet in the street before being able to step up onto the curb where the "safety" railing ended.

I found the city markets fascinating, though. Everything imaginable seemed to be for sale, from booths where vendors sold lace tablecloths to family planning tents where vasectomies were performed on the spot. (Talk about acquiring "seedless grapes" at the marketplace!)

We had been in Bangalore for just a short time when Paul introduced us to a restaurant called "The Only Place" for one of the most delicious (and cheapest) steak dinners I've ever eaten. It became a regular haunt, and after dinner, we'd go to "The Milk Bar" for what was to become a dessert favorite with us— vanilla ice cream topped with fruit salad and whipped cream. Cruelly, there was a scale on the street corner just outside "The Milk Bar." We'd weigh ourselves, and then the machine would dispense a fortune-telling card. It beckoned me, and guiltily, I let myself be drawn to it each and every time we ate there.

Before leaving the U.S., I had secured an "All-India Liquor Permit" from the Indian Consulate in order to obtain liquor legally during our stay. Once in India, my name would be recorded, the permit would be used to purchase "six units" of liquor per month and would expire after three months' time (the permit, not me). The six units denoted various quantities, depending upon whether you purchased beer, wine or "spirits" (hard liquor).

One day, Paul and I went into town to purchase liquor. Most of it would be used for gifts we'd present to the various tribal leaders that we planned to visit in the Nilgiri Hills of southern India, but some would be for our own personal use. I underwent the lengthy registration process in Bangalore so my name could be logged into the registry as a bona fide purchaser of "spirits."

My passport, my tourist visa, the liquor permit and the liquor order form I had filled out were carefully checked by the local authority. Surreptitiously, Paul and I lifted several blank order forms from the counter so that I could sign my name and turn them over to him for his later use. (Once this initial registration is completed, the order blank holder need not present any identification for future purchases.) Paul cautioned me in advance to sign only my first and last names on the registration form without the title of "Ms." In short order, my title would become "Mr." once he began using my permit after I departed for the U.S.

Before long, my professor and his wife informed us that they'd had enough of our itinerary. They decided to leave us and travel to a resort area in the south of the country but would rejoin me in Bombay a couple days before our return to the U.S. Left to our own devices, Paul decided that he would continue doing research on his book and that I would help him. Oh, I almost forgot to mention our mode of transportation for the balance of the trip—Paul's motorcycle.

Our first stop was at a French Catholic mission where the only person living there was a French priest who spoke no English. This was no problem for Paul who is multi-lingual, and he chatted away with the priest for quite some time. (I was very bored.) The priest gave us access to the library there at the mission, and we pored over dusty tomes for hours, locating several important references for the book Paul was writing.

We declined an invitation to stay for lunch, because we did not want to be late for a fire-walking ceremony Paul wanted me to see. He apologized to the priest for cutting our visit short, but said we only had time to stay for a drink. Imagine my surprise when a box of crackers and a bottle of Red Knight Whiskey appeared from the priest's desk drawer, especially at 11:00 A.M. on a Sunday morning!

"*Je suis desolee que je ne peux pas offrir le* Johnny Walker," he apologized. ("I'm sorry I can't offer you any Johnny Walker.")

He explained that the isolated mission is a good place for meditation, but that's about all.

We visited several of the tribes in the Nilgiri Hills during those next two weeks, finding lodging at a missionary tourist home run by a charming, elderly New Zealand woman. She had emigrated from her homeland many years before and now offered room and board at reasonable rates to traveling missionaries and others. We were served sumptuous European-style meals, each of which was preceded by a prayer of thanksgiving led by our gracious hostess.

Each morning a servant would quietly slip in through my unlocked back door (sometimes while I was still asleep in the other room) to bring pots of hot water to fill my nineteenth century cast-iron bathtub. After bathing, I'd dress as fast as possible in order that my body might retain some of the heat from the bath water's temperature. Our rooms weren't heated, so I learned quickly to bathe and dress as hurriedly as possible. Then, after having our breakfast, we'd hop on the motorcycle and leave the tourist home to begin the adventure *du jour*.

Over the days that passed, we paid a visit to many of the tribes in the area, obtaining interviews from the elders for Paul's research (and mine). If we were lucky enough to find a ritual ceremony of some kind going on nearby, we'd make it a point to attend. During the day, we'd be offered something to eat and drink at every place we stopped. To refuse the hospitality would be taken as a personal insult to the host. And each evening, of course, we'd have a big dinner at home to look forward to. Many times we'd have to stop in the forest between tribal visits to give up our last meal, just in order to make room for the next one.

I know. Yuck.

At the various festivals and ceremonies we attended, Paul filmed the activities, and I took on the role as his assistant. My job was to follow him around and capture the background music and crowd sounds for later dubbing into the film he was shooting. I toted a tape recorder slung over one shoulder while pointing a three-foot-long directional microphone at the crowd to capture the audio portion. I wore headphones and walked a couple paces behind him, careful to not get distracted from my duties in case he stopped suddenly. I even remembered to hit "Record" (most of the time) as he filmed.

The male-female gender roles were still quite separate and distinct at that point in time. A woman "knew her place" and accepted it without question. But, if she were a foreign woman, it was an entirely different story—the second-class citizen status did not apply. I was accorded every courtesy and consideration that men were given, including being invited to sit on the "men's side" of an arena at festival celebrations. My status was elevated even more by being in the company of Paul, who was very well known and well liked by many of the tribal leaders. He was known to them as "King" (which totally impressed me at the time until he explained later that the word simply meant "white man").

The local women occupied a separate, subordinated place

there and did not directly take part in the festivities as the men did. They just observed from the sidelines. A prime example of this occurred at a village ceremony we attended to celebrate the cleansing and reopening of a temple previously "defiled by an unclean woman" (someone who had entered the temple during her menstrual cycle).

Musicians began to play, and the men moved from the perimeter of the outdoor arena to the center. They formed a large circle and moved to the music of horns and drums, maintaining the circle as they danced. And then, I was invited to join in the dancing—just me and the guys. The women watched from the outer edge of the grassy field, and no one, male or female, voiced any complaint about my participation. It was simply an accepted fact that a foreign woman enjoyed the same status as the men. Everyone just appeared happy to have their temple back in use again. (I smiled, too, and then tucked my spare Tampax down a little further inside my pocket).

After a couple weeks of traveling around the southern hills of India, Paul and I finally returned to the "big city" of Bangalore. All I craved was a long, hot shower and a pillow on which to rest my sore butt after spending too many hours on the back of a motorcycle, especially while wearing my oversized backpack. One of the places where we found lodging on the way back was a rest house in the town of Mysore. It was at a railway station by the name of Mysore Junction. (How appropriate!)

A final visit to "The Only Place" for one last, delectable steak dinner with an ice cream and fruit salad chaser, and I was ready for my trip home. Despite all the walking I had done throughout my stay, the meals had outpaced the exercise, and that damnable scale on the street corner by "The Milk Bar" showed I'd gained eleven pounds! Even the message on the fortune card spit out by the scale was a disappointment.

We returned to the U.S. after five weeks, and I wrote a brilliant (I thought) seventy-eight page paper detailing my experiences. I walked into the old professor's office, beaming my exuberance, and presented my masterpiece to him with a flourish.

He looked up from his work, took the paper from me and said, "Oh, yeah. I turned in the grades already. I gave you an A."

Sol
by J.D. Blair

He relinquished the sky
to a rabble of fog
choking the mouth of Carquinez Strait.
Spinnakers whipping capricious winds
whitecaps dancing above the prows of
tonnage inching toward dockside respite
in the shallows.
He waits in the pre-dusk
glowing low below the mist
that holds the narrows.

    He will warm us tomorrow.

Sometimes I Just

by Selene Steese

want a view of the sky
unobstructed by wire, unmarred
by antenae, just wide
and just blue.

As each season
shifts, I let soak into my skin winds
ripe with scents of blossoms,
of waterfalls, of apples, of frost.

Sometimes I just want the winds
to shift without the smell
of dumpsters, of smokestacks,
of smog, of exhaust.

Sometimes I just want the feel
of cool green grass between
my naked toes, without fear
of broken bottles, rusted nails,
hypodermic needles
or razor blades.

This is the world I live in.

I write this poem
to the wide, blue sky
and the cool, green grass;
to the changing seasons
and the fragrant winds.

The Monologue of Rainsworth, the One-Eared Cat

by Mark L. Cabasino

*modeled after an exercise in sestina by Mary Kinzie,
inspired in part by a Red House Painters song called "Three-Legged Cat"*

Evening and we proceed with our different labors:
I lick my whiskers flat; he fixes student
papers with a highlighter. Why he takes the trouble
is less clear—caressing each page like a missing
child flyer, not finding them. He's gothic—
that must be it—a glutton. I wash my earlobe.

I'm compulsive when it comes to bathing my earlobe:
my arm makes sweeping convulsions, like a woman in labor
trying to dislodge what's stuck. Meanwhile my gothic
master spears his pen and screams some student's
name, like sex only nothing like that. He's missing
the growing years a proud father has. The trouble

with his job is that every teenager in trouble
becomes his trouble. Again I lick my earlobe.
Sometimes it's a blessing my left ear is missing.
Sometimes he contemplates manual labor,
a harvest or assembly line: anything but some student
talking behind his back about how that gothic

teacher sucks, that class is so gay, that wannabe goth
dude thinks he's like 18 again, I sooo got in trouble
from that one gothic teacher for cheating. Yet students
get fed before I do! I twitch my earlobe.
Master, I hate to be the one to belabor
the obvious, but don't you think something is missing

from your life? He shakes like a dog, dismissing
my mew—the cat-and-dog version of American Gothic.
Oh master, set down your pitchfork, your demon! Labor
no more! Oh, and I hate to be too much trouble,
but can I get some kibbles? I perk my earlobe
when his mouth moves, but it's not my name—another student

probably. Sometimes I wish I was his student.
I'd never be tardy. I'd never have any missing
assignments. I'd always point my one earlobe
in his direction to listen, like some rusty Gothic
weathervane. I'd take notes. I'd never trouble
him with stupid questions. I'd perform hard labor.

But I'm not gothic and I'm not a trouble-
maker. I won't do labor and I'm not a student.
I'm just a goddamn hungry cat with a missing earlobe.

Again
by K E Froeschner

O, might I walk with thee again,
      take thy hand and be thy man again,

O, might we walk our hills again,
    feel the clouds and drifting mists again,

O, let us fly among our dreams again,
      roll in our lovely beds again,

O, might we live our lives again,
      knowing how it ends again,

O, might I just kiss you again,
    yes, once more,
        yet again.

O, may we go and dance again
    a lovely pas de deux,

O, might I hold your hand again
    and feel you spin
      your lithe waist in
        my arms again.

O, might the world be new again,
        might it be just us two again,

O, the years ahead are too few,
        yet I would know you anew.

So, might we please begin again ?
        May I tempt you with sin again ?

O, could we hear the din again
        of children, friends and kin again,
              with kegs and beer, live rock and roll
                      and bon-fires in our woods.

May old friends wake upon our humble floors again.

And might I hold your hand again
        and would you take me there again,

And could we go together, then
        for ever more.

Doctor Visit
by Thomas Darter

I had a ringing in my ear, so I went to see the doctor.

"Doctor," I said, "it sounds like water running over rocks in a stream. It's like white noise. It's there all the time."

"Well," said the doctor, "we'll have to do some tests."

He looked, poked, prodded; collected samples, sent them out. After he got the test results, he had me come back to his office. "Have you noticed any moisture in your ears?" he asked.

"Yes, recently I have."

"Well, I have some bad news. I don't know what's causing the ringing, exactly, but I know what's causing the moisture: Your brains have started leaking out your ears."

I was stunned. "How is that possible? How does anything get past the eardrum?"

"Look, we don't really know how everything works, but I do know what the moisture is: It's melted brains. Have you been doing any particularly heavy thinking lately?"

"Well, I have been thinking a lot about death—about whether I would continue in some way after my body failed."

"That's your problem right there. We all think that somehow the brain houses 'us'—I think it happens because it's located behind our eyes. We spend most of our time dealing with visual stuff, so we think that 'we' are back there behind what we see. But the brain is just the brain—it's just matter. And for matter, matter is all that matters. You got your brain worked up. You got it wondering about what it was supposed to do when it was no longer there, and it was just too much. The damn thing overheated."

"Now wait a minute," I said. "How can the brain have its own thoughts? It has my thoughts, doesn't it?"

"Look, you're just a conglomeration of stuff. What makes you think that the stuff doesn't want to take care of itself? Your brain, of course, knows what you're thinking, and sometimes it has its own reactions to that. You know, if you're going to keep thinking about stuff like this, you might want to move to a colder climate. Use ice packs. Might help some."

"Is there anything else I can do?"

"I guess you could put corks in your ears, to make sure the stuff doesn't evaporate away; but even if you collect it, it won't do you much good. Once it's liquefied, it isn't really brains anymore."

I thanked the doctor and left. Needless to say, I have stopped worrying about my ears ringing. The problem is that I can't stop thinking about dying, especially now that I know my organs are just in it for themselves. I save some of the liquid every once in a while, and stare at it. But see, it no longer knows. And because it's in a little dish looking up at me, neither do I.

The Loch
by Diana Carey

Jinny sat on a patch of moss, the tree-covered hill overlooking the cool grey of the loch. The water extended east and west as far as she could see. The ruins of Castle Urquart stood stark on the uncluttered northern rim of the loch.

She was alone as usual; this was not a place Jinny liked to share. She had found the clearing when she was a young girl. Her family lived in a small cottage on the other side of this hill and she had spent many an hour scouting the rough, forested hills. This had been the place she ran to whenever she felt troubled or if she simply wanted to get away from the turmoil of two brothers and a sister in that ancient little home.

Today she had driven up from the city and climbed the once familiar hill to the comfort of her sanctuary. Jinny hated the city. So many people and nothing but buildings to look at. She missed the trees and the quiet of the Highlands. Here on her hill she could sit for hours and hear nothing but the wind and the birds.

Not that she didn't enjoy the cultural life in Edinburgh. There was always something to see or do there. It's just that sometimes she needed to escape back to her roots. She needed to ground herself again and feed her spirit. That is what she was doing today, just drinking in the peace and opening herself up to communicate with her inner being.

So she sat, the wind kissing her cheek, as she watched the birds soaring through the air. Feeling their freedom and the loch's calm.

Suddenly, as she was watching a bird swoop down and glide over the loch something leaped up, breaking the surface of the water and grabbing the bird. Then it disappeared again leaving behind an ever expanding ring of ripples. Jinny had never seen anything like the giant shape that had just burst into her solitude. It had a small head and a very long neck. And it was larger than any animal she had ever seen before.

Jinny was curious; in all the years she had been coming here this creature had never shown itself. She had always suspected the old tales were true, but she had never had any proof. Now she had seen it herself. There really was a Loch Ness Monster. And she had seen it. Jinny wished she had her camera with her. But really, there would have been no time to snap a photo, it had happened so fast.

Standing up and moving slowly downhill she worked her way to the edge of the water. The surface was calm again, the ripples gone, along with the creature that made them. She stood a while wondering what to do. She wanted to see the creature again, but how could she call for it? How could she let it know she would not hurt it?

As Jinny was standing and thinking she remembered her grandfather and the many talks they had had together. He had spent much time out on the loch and he knew it well. He was the one who had first told Jinny about the creature in the loch. Grandfather had told her many stories of when he was younger and how he had seen 'Nessie' gliding along, looking like a Viking ship sailing to Valhalla. He had told her something else too. He had taught her a secret call, if only she could remember it, that would bring the creature to her. She had tried it when she was young, but her small voice did not carry far and it had never worked. Her brother had teased her telling her that grandfather was cracked and she was cracked for listening to him. But she didn't care, she was sure it would work.

She stood a few moments in quiet thought, casting her mind back twenty years, trying to remember. How did that go? What were the words? They were Gaelic, she knew that. It had been so many years, how could she remember? Gradually she began to hear her grandfather talking to her, quietly repeating the words. "An do cluas."

That was it! Jinny brought herself up straight and called in a clear strong voice. Nothing happened. She tried it again. Still nothing happened. She was beginning to feel a little foolish now. Perhaps her brother had been right. But no, she would not believe that. She took a deep breath and tried one more time.

"An do cluas."

The water began to stir, just a little at first, but gradually it grew stronger and very agitated. Jinny could see a head slowly rise out of the water just a few yards away from her. It rose higher and higher, until it stood quite tall, perhaps ten feet. And there she was, Nessie!

Jinny stood, aghast, quite unable to speak or move. Now that the creature was there, what would she do about it?

Actually, the creature was wondering the same thing. It cleared it's throat "A-hum. Excuse me, but why precisely have you called me?"

Jinny's knees buckled and she was no longer standing. The creature merely looked at her.

"P-P-Pardon me, I-I do hope I'm not disturbing you."

"Well, not really. There isn't a whole lot to do out here in the loch you know. Swimming of course, but one gets tired of swimming all day every day and longs for something more entertaining you know. I do take the occasional nip at a tourist boat of course, but even that gets old.

"I've seen you before you know. Up on your hill. You used to go there quite a lot, didn't you? I have wondered what happened to you."

172

"Well, my family moved away and I got a job in the city and . . . and. . . . You saw me? How come I never saw you before?"

"Oh, I don't like to show myself to just everyone you know."

"Did you hear me calling when I was younger? I never saw you then, but maybe you heard me. My brother told me I was cracked because I kept calling you and you never came and he said it was because you didn't exist and I was just being silly and. . . ."

"My goodness, you do carry on, don't you? Yes I heard you calling, you were such a cute little girl. Very shy."

Jinny could hardly believe she was holding a conversation with the creature. She realized she had not asked the creature if it had a name. I mean, she couldn't just keep calling it Creature.

"Excuse me, but do you have a name? I mean people call you Nessie, but what is your real name?"

"Well, my real name is Agnes, but all of my friends call me Aggie."

"Friends? Are there more like you?"

"Of course! You don't think I would stay here in this loch all by myself with no one to talk to do you? I mean, where is the mental stimulation in that?"

Jinny had to agree that it would be a pretty dismal life if there was no one to talk with ever, although sometimes it is nice to get away.

"We have our retreats you know. Sometimes I swim over to the next loch and spend a week just watching the fish go by. Very relaxing. But I can only take so much of that and then I need to get back to some company."

"How many of you are there?"

"Well, at last count there were about fifty of us down here. Although there are other clans all over the world. I guess there are about one thousand all told. I went on a lovely trip to Norway a few years ago and visited with some distant relations there. Very nice they were."

"I'm sure they were. It would be nice to meet your friends and family."

"Do you think so? Would you like to?"

"Well, yes, but how? It would be pretty crowded if they all came up here to this little inlet."

"Oh, they don't have to. You could go see them!"

"Go see them! But how? I can not go underwater for very long, I have to breath you know."

"Well, so do I, but I spend most of my time underwater. Here, eat some of the grass, there, sticking out of the water. Just a bit will do the trick, don't need much. That will allow you to stay underwater for hours."

Jinny looked at the grass doubtfully. It seemed impossible that something like grass could keep you alive underwater, and for hours? Was it a trick on Agnes's part? Maybe she was trying to coax her into the water and then drown her.

Jinny took a handful of the grass and nibbled on it. Actually it didn't taste bad, sort of a cross between spinach and celery. She ate the handful and looked doubtfully at Agnes.

Agnes looked friendly enough, for a "monster" that is. Jinny slipped out of her shoes and took a tentative step out into the water. It was cool, but not cold so she waded out further. Finally she was up to her neck and it was time to either take a plunge or turn around and go back to the shore. Jinny closed her eyes, took a deep breath and sank under the water.

She waited there for two minutes. She felt no discomfort, nor did she feel as if she needed air. Jinny opened her eyes. There was Agnes watching her. She seemed to hear Agnes talking to her.

"See, I told you. It is a little scary at first, I know, but you'll get used to it."

How can I hear her? Her mouth isn't moving and I couldn't hear her underwater anyway.

"Telepathy. We use telepathy to converse."

"Oh. So you will be able to hear everything I think?"

"That's right, so you had better be careful what you think."

"Whoa! Got that right."

"Come on, I'll show you my home and introduce you around. Hold onto my neck. I swim faster than you and you would have a hard time keeping up. I don't want you to get lost out here in the loch."

Jinny swam over and grabbed onto Agnes's neck, close to her head where it was narrowest. Agnes turned and started swiftly swimming down and toward the center of the loch. They went deeper and deeper. The water became darker and darker. It became difficult for Jinny to see clearly. Finally they reached the bottom. Agnes turned south and Jinny began to notice a change in her surroundings. The water became easier to see in and the bottom of the loch began to look as if it were paved with large flat stones.

Then Jinny saw it, the town under the water. This is where Agnes lived with her friends and relations.

"It's beautiful!"

"Yes it is, isn't it? I always think it looks like fairies made it."

The buildings were all a coral pink color and had spires and minarets. There was grass growing all about, deep lush and green. There were statues of, one might presume, famous "monsters."

"You know Agnes, people call you 'monster.' I can see that is not so. Could you please tell me what exactly you are?"

"Well, I am a kelpie."

Jinny knew what a kelpie was. "But that is a water demon in the shape of a horse that lures people to their deaths! Are you going to kill me now?"

"No, no, NO! Don't be silly. Why would I do that? I have brought you here to meet my family. I don't want to kill you!

"There are some kelpies who have turned evil and would do

harm, but they are really few and far between. We don't have them in our society, we shun them."

Jinny still felt a little shaky, but she didn't think any more for a while. They swam in toward the center of town. There Jinny saw about fifteen kelpies. She had expected them to all look the same, but she was surprised to find that they were as different as one type of flower is from another. They were all large, but some of them had very slender bodies so that they almost looked like snakes. Some had large bulbous bodies with shorter necks and scales (they looked like dragons). Some looked like Agnes with a long neck and a large body.

Agnes swam right up into the middle of them.

"Look everyone, we have a visitor. This is Jinny, you know her. She is the one who sits up on the hill all alone."

They all crowded round to get a better view of her. Jinny felt a little nervous, being surrounded by all the huge kelpies. She held on tight to Agnes. Everyone was very kind to her. They all thought to her how they had watched her over the years and how she seemed to be a very nice girl. It was strange talking (if that is what you called it) with all of them. They seemed to know her quite well. She soon relaxed and began to enjoy the visit, even laughing at their jokes and talking quite a while with one of the kelpies who had known her grandfather.

After a while Agnes thought to Jinny that it was time to go. She was sorry to leave such wonderful friends, but Agnes said she could come back again some other day. Jinny again clung to Agnes's neck and up they went, swimming toward the southern shore where they had met.

Agnes swam right up to the shore and let Jinny climb down.

"Thank you so very much for taking me to visit with your family and friends. They are wonderful."

"Thank you for coming. And please feel free to come visit us any time you want. We are always happy to have visitors, although most people are too scared of us. Goodbye, and may the fairies guide your footsteps."

"Goodbye Agnes. Take care of yourself."

Agnes turned and slowly swam out into the deeper water, gradually sinking as she swam, until she was completely out of sight.

Jinny climbed back up the hill the way she had come down. She could hardly believe she had not been dreaming. If her clothes were not so wet she wouldn't believe it. She mounted the top of the hill and went down to her car, parked by the old cottage she had grown up in.

Driving back to Edinburgh she tried to think of who she could tell about what had happened and decided that no one would believe her. She knew her brother would tease her about it if she told him. Most everyone else would just look at her as if she were joking. She decided she could not tell anyone.

So Jinny returned to her flat in the city and kept the secret of the kelpies to herself. But every once in a while she would drive back up to the old cottage, climb over the hill and visit with her new friends.

Mono Tome
by Jason Hambrecht

Heavy and dark your eyebrows are
You look good in hats

Sleeveless dress, your hair's a mess
Let go of my hand

Away you'll walk, if you must
You've got less to lose

Unlock the door and then you're gone
I watch you from the street

Headache on my steering wheel
Think I'll start the car

Cannot say that I'm lost
I just don't know where to go

Math Attack
by Phil K. Mitchell

Although mathematics lies at the heart of advances in science, engineering, medicine, communications and business, people with the requisite mathematical qualifications are at a premium. Unfortunately, studies indicate, and our experience tends to confirm, that all too frequently our young people are not very good at simple arithmetic. I suspect that, like many of us, today's students tend to look upon math as something that has to be taken—like medicine—because it's supposed to be good for you rather than as something that can be enjoyed.

I believe that learning math, or any subject, is most efficient—most effective—when it is motivated by the pleasure and excitement associated with the hard work, challenge and exploration that awakens curiosity and stretches the imagination. Learning must be a lifetime process if we are continuously to acquire the new knowledge and skills needed to cope with a rapidly changing world. Perhaps the most important lesson to learn in these changing times is that learning can be fun and exciting. Play and excitement enhances, rather than diminishes, the learning process.

I hope all of us, from time to time, have been sparked by teachers and instructors who adhered to that belief. Teachers who had the skill to capture our interest and stretch our imaginations so that, in their classes, we learned and accomplished more than we would ever have thought possible. In this regard I was fortunate in that—before I had a chance to learn that arithmetic was the equivalent of medicine—I attended a small rural grammar school presided over by Clyde Simpson, an outstanding principal and teacher with a knack for making any subject, even math, interesting. He believed that learning should excite curiosity, promote logical thinking, expand horizons and set the stage for a lifetime learning experience.

He liked kids, he liked to teach, and he was good at it. Reading, writing or arithmetic—his students were never bored.

In arithmetic, for example, you might say he was master of the math attack. On the spur of the moment, he could invent all kinds of exercises in mental arithmetic. He had many of us believing that he was endowed with some kind of prescience. Starting with an unknown number, or the change in our pockets, he would guide us through a series of multiplications, additions and divisions concluding with a request for our answers which appeared to have no bearing on anything. But from those answers, he could tell us how rich we were, what our secret numbers were and, it seemed to us, almost any secret he wished to know. We had fun with our introduction to the world of numbers—odd numbers, even numbers, whole numbers, fractions. We were learning too—addition, subtraction, multiplication, division, and also curious properties of numbers. For example, we learned that nine is a remarkably persistent number. Any whole number multiplied by nine will provide an answer having the seeds of nine within it. For instance, 183 x 9 = 1647. How that answer relates to nine did not seem all that obvious to us. But the sum of the digits 1, 6, 4 and 7 is 18 and 1+8 is 9. Nine is the digital root of 1,647 or any number that is a multiple of nine. This proved to be a great springboard for creating our own puzzles.

Our curiosity grew as we progressed and became adept at arithmetic operations. Could we come up with our own exercises and puzzles? From mental arithmetic, it was but a step to the introduction of algebra. In due time, Mr. Simpson taught us the connections so that we could invent our own exercises. He explained that we if ask someone to think of a number, that number is unknown to us, so call it "x" and use what we have learned of algebra to invent our own exercises. Or he might run us through a mental arithmetic exercise and ask us to explain the underlying algebra.

He might challenge us to think of any multiple digit number, rearrange the digits in any order to form a new number, subtract the smaller from the larger, and using what we knew of the decimal numbering system, explain why the answer will always be divisible by nine. We found that we could create all kinds of interesting puzzles based on this fact.

Following our introductory experience with algebra, we were introduced to geometry associated with familiar and not so familiar objects. For example, after we became familiar with the two- and three-dimensional properties of everyday objects, he introduced us to one-sided surfaces. We all knew that a sheet of paper was two-sided, and if you joined the ends of a two-sided strip you created a three-dimensional figure—a cylinder—with an inside and an outside that could be painted one color on the inside and another on the outside. We found it hard to imagine any object with only one side, whereupon he distributed strips of paper to each of us with instructions on how to give a half twist to the strip, and join the ends together to make a rather odd-looking figure. He then challenged us to color all of one side red and the other green. Of course when we colored all of one side red, there was no side left to paint green for a Mobius strip has only one side and one edge.

There wasn't a lot of rote memory work in Clyde Simpson's classes. We were all too busy finding out things for ourselves. We were encouraged to experiment and ask "what if" questions. It didn't cost much—pencil, paper, scissors, and glue. It was challenging and exciting to use what we knew to dream up new puzzles and experiments which in turn provided new insights and opened doors to still other worlds.

By the time we had graduated from our small country school, we had become adept at mental arithmetic and acquired some understanding and interest in algebra and geometry. But more important, we found that it was fun to use our imaginations to explore real and imaginary worlds. We had been taught to open doors—a skill that applied to the many worlds of numbers and mathematics and to any other world we might wish to explore. We were ready not only for high school, but a lifetime of learning. Clyde Simpson taught us to enjoy using our curiosity and imagination to explore real and fanciful worlds, and in the process, we found that not even math was to be taken like medicine.

Calculus
by Charan Sue Wollard

What if
2 plus 2 really does equal 5
What if we scan the line of
X plus Y to infinity
and the numbers turn inside themselves
round, around
until the truth of their nature
bursts forth as suns

What if
X times Y equals 0
What if everything always equals 0
endless lines of 0s
circles of emptiness
amid noiseless chaos
And 0 isn't nothing
but is the secret shape
of All

3 of 9: Can't Wait!
by sandra kay

    -so- wrote a fourth poem inspired by the same mystery, and was interrupted by the thought (intuition, whatever.), that this fourth poem is one of ten inspired by this mystery. at the completion of the 10th poem, the mystery will go away.

    oh my goodness. the sadness. the sadnes that swept over and through me. for hours.. (not really. but for at least ten minutes) i walked slowly around my house, shoulders falling down like teardrops (maya angelou). "No! Please No! NO! Don't take my mystery away from me!" and just as i was about to let grief get the best of me, i was interrupted by this thought:

Hey Stupid   -Write Nine Poems. Stop At Nine!

and then i smiled and skipped to my office to blog.

3 of 9: can't wait!

i want to thank you
and spank you
and SWALLOW you whole

baste you
and taste you
LOVE not cajole

abuse you
confuse you
tear down your walls

tie your shoe-strings together
then cushion your fall

I will

seize you
and tease you
then please you some more

poke you
provoke you
even the score

attract you
distract you
reveal all your flaws

undress you
caress you
hold all your calls

I will

disarm you
alarm you
trip up your step

reduce you
seduce you
make you my pet

I will

derail you
unveil you
see who you are

intimately
KISS
your incredulous scars

i can't wait

to conquer you
unarmed
then let you defeat me

engage you
outrage you
surprise! you completely

tempt you
and starve you
ration your meals

repay you
x-ray you
lick wounds til they heal

it's my greatest pleasure

to unnerve you
and serve you
withhold, enter-rupt
baptize your memories
blind-side and corrupt

I am

the kick in your ass
the thorn in your side

the glorious meal
the car you must drive

that unanswered question
the tag on your wings

your reason for living
your every ~ your thing

i like to

make you so angry
then comfort and calm

excite you
ignite you
write all your wrongs

blame you
untame you
intrude on your space

cost you
exhaust you
wipe the SMILE from your face

I am

who you need
who you want
who you can't live without

who you TRUST
who you LOVE
who exploits all your doubts

I WILL

unrest in your arms
break in to your castle
fuck up your day
be worth the hassle

rob you of freedom
but give you your way
spoil your limited silence
with nothing to say

I am

your right arm
your lucky charm
your upside down
your sideways

your twist of fate
your altered state
your I CAN'T WAIT
your always

I AM THE ONE who makes you

change your mind
then change it back
look twice in both directions

your stupid fool
your broken tool
your live wire, your connection

I am

your four leaf clover
shooting star
lucky number
two

the splinter in your finger
the pebble in your shoe

I am

your best friend
your enemy
your mess
and your temptation

the typo on your final draft
your lies and your creation

I AM

your conflict
resolution
your ending
and your sequel

your irritant
your peace; content
your lesser, more
and equal

I will

ignore you
but store you
in the front part of my mind

irrate you
sedate you
fast-forward, then rewind

I CAN'T WAIT!

for you to JUMP!
to fall up
in the sky

to clip your wings
blow your mind
teach you how
to fly

i so totally adore you
live to learn
how to
unbore you

I'M THE ONE
YOU CAN'T
LET SLIP AWAY

you so totally adore me
find such clever
ways to floor me

YOU ARE
I AM
WE WILL

CAN'T WAIT!

think TODAY
just might be

our
LucKy dAY?

Shooting Moon Rocks
by Charan Sue Wollard

Rachel had only been half listening, being polite really, trying not to give too much encouragement to the toady little bald man sitting next to her in coach. When he'd asked if she was heading home, she'd told him no, this was her first trip to Houston. Her husband was training at Flight Safety and she was flying in to spend a few days with him. One half of the perfect couple. From her seat in 18C, she'd gazed down the aisle, wondering when the flight attendant would come with drinks.

She had succeeded in shutting him out almost entirely—until he started talking about Buzz Aldrin playing with moon rocks.

"It was on the return leg," he said. "Ole Buzz was cuttin' up, jugglin' those moon rocks in zero gravity like they were balloons. Smuggled a few of 'em down, too. I was over at his house one day when he set 'em on the pool table. Yes sir, racked 'em up."

"You played pool with moon rocks?" Rachel couldn't help herself. His story was too astonishing to ignore. "How do you know Buzz Aldrin? Do you work for NASA?"

"Yes, ma'am, I do. Flew on STS-9 back in '83. Jim Logan," he introduced himself. Rachel studied his quaggy features, the too-wide striped tie, the cowboy boots now crossed at his ankles. Jim Logan didn't look like her idea of an astronaut, but what did she know?

"Rachel McBride."

"What's your hubby fly?" he asked.

"Challenger." Usually the next question was something like, "Is that a Lear?"

Instead he asked, "601 or 604?"

"'01." Well, he knew something about aviation.

The flight attendant arrived with the drink cart. While Rachel ordered a Bloody Mary—with a twist, no ice—the lanky brunette in the window seat pounced on Jim Logan like the celebrity he was. "What's it like to fly on a rocket ship?" the brunette cooed.

"Actually, ma'am, it's a shuttle. That's a rocket that tries to act like an airplane."

Let her have him, Rachel thought, gulping rather than sipping her cocktail. In a couple of hours, Robert would meet her at the airport, whisk her off to the hotel room where he'd been staying all week. She twisted the dainty platinum ring on her left hand until it almost spun off her finger.

The plane hit a patch of turbulence and the seatbelt light flashed on. The plastic cup with the remains of Rachel's Bloody Mary lurched across her tray. A hirsute hand darted from across the aisle to rescue the cup before it landed on her lap.

She glanced up. A man in a fisherman's sweater held out the plastic cup to her. Rachel noticed broad shoulders, white teeth, flecks of gray softening jet black hair. His dark eyes glimmered; he launched a crooked smile. Rachel straightened in her seat.

"Are you traveling alone?" he asked.

Rachel was tempted to say yes.

Instead she said: "I'm meeting my husband. Tomorrow's our tenth anniversary."

Sweater Man's smile ratcheted down a notch. "Ten years," he said. "Takes guts to hold a marriage together these days."

Guts—is that it? she wondered.

Rachel could hear Jim Logan regaling the brunette with more legends of space travel. And not just the brunette. The family in the row ahead of them had turned around and was peppering him with questions, comments, oohs and ahhs. He seemed to have an endless supply of stories.

Rachel leaned toward Sweater Man and whispered: "That guy's an astronaut."

He seemed impressed. "Yeah?"

"Jim Logan."

By now Sweater Man was standing in the aisle, leaning across Rachel like she was part of the furniture, turning that crooked, toothy grin on the man beside her.

"Hey, buddy," he said. "You look familiar. Do I know you?"

Jim Logan stopped midway through his description of life on the Spacelab to look up. He shook his head. Sweater Man leaned in closer, hand outstretched.

"Blackie Maselli," he said. Jim Logan shook Blackie's hand.

"Jim Logan," he responded. At that point Blackie uttered a big, overblown gasp of surprise.

"Jim Logan the astronaut?!" he exclaimed, pumping the smaller man's arm mercilessly. "I am honored to meet you, sir."

Rachel could not believe what she was hearing. Five minutes ago he'd never heard of Jim Logan the astronaut, now he was president of his damn fan club. She wriggled out of her seat past Blackie and headed for the rest room. She knew when she got back Blackie would have taken her seat, monopolized the astronaut. No matter. She would sit across the aisle. At least she would have a good story to tell Robert. They would be together all weekend; it would be useful to have something to talk about.

The plane touched down at Hobby Airport ten minutes ahead of schedule. By then, half the passengers on board knew they were in the presence of a real American hero. Jim shook hands with every one of them, even signed a few autographs. Blackie clutched his, rushed out past her, giddy as a schoolgirl. Rachel waited until the crowd thinned out a little before retrieving her carry-on from the overhead bin. As she pulled it down, she turned and found herself eye-to-eye with Jim Logan. He looked rumpled and goofy, just as he had when she first sat down next to him, but now that she knew who he was, he seemed different.

"It was nice to meet you, Jim" she said, startling him.

"Really?"

"Yeah, sure. Of course."

He rocked back on his heels and smiled at her.

"I could give you a tour of the Space Center sometime," he said. "Sections the public can't get into."

"Sounds interesting, but I'm only here for the weekend."

He nodded and turned, then both of them slipped into the line heading down the aisle to the exit.

Once in the terminal, Rachel checked her cell phone for messages. One from Robert. She hoped he wouldn't be late this time, wouldn't leave her pacing the pavement waiting for him. But it wasn't that. His message said he couldn't pick her up at all. Training was running late. He'd meet her in the hotel restaurant at seven for dinner.

The hotel offered shuttle service, so she wheeled her suitcase outside to wait for the van, which circled through the airport every half hour. The air was heavy with humidity and Rachel was weary from a long day of travel, but the stone benches didn't look very clean, so she stood, shifting her weight from foot to foot, twisting at the heels, peering up the roadway for signs of the shuttle. Taxis and Metro buses cruised by, but no shuttle. A Yellow cab pulled to the curb. Rachel felt a tap at her elbow. It was Jim Logan.

"Waiting on your hubby?"

"No. The Marriott shuttle."

"We could share the taxi." He started piling his suitcases into the cab's open trunk. "I'm headed in the same direction."

Why not? She'd get to the hotel faster, maybe even have time to shower and change before dinner.

"Sure. Thank you."

Rachel wheeled her bag to the curb and let Jim haul it into the trunk beside his. Jim gave the driver instructions and they climbed into the back seat of the taxi, sitting neither close nor too far apart. Rachel was nervous, although she could not have said why.

"Robert—my husband—his training is running late. Otherwise he would have been here to pick me up."

Jim nodded.

"I really appreciate the lift."

"No problem. Hey, if his training runs late tomorrow, I could give you that tour," he said. "I'll call you at your hotel."

"I don't think that's a good idea."

He looked uncertain for a minute, then he said, "You can call me." He fumbled in his jacket, pulled a Bic pen and an old Walmart receipt from one of the pockets, and scribbled something. "I don't have a business card on me. Anyway, it's hard to reach me at the center. But here's my cell phone number." He handed her the receipt with his name and a number written on it.

She stared at the number, not sure how to respond. He took it from her hands and tucked it into the side pouch of her purse.

The cab was pulling through the porte cochere to the Marriott's front doors. She opened her purse to give Jim her share of the taxi fare, but he put his hand over hers and wouldn't take it.

The driver set her bag on the curb, and Rachel climbed out.

"Thanks again," she said, pushing the door shut. She watched the taxis as it pulled away. Jim was twisted around in his seat, grinning at her through the rear window.

An astronaut. She rolled her bag around and went inside.

Dinner at the hotel was not how Rachel liked to spend her first evening in a new city, but Robert was here on business. He had been in training all day—a long day—and he would be worn out. Besides, they had the whole weekend. There would be plenty of time to explore the town, see the sights, discover whatever delights Houston might have to offer. She wouldn't complain about this evening. Would not complain about having to find her own way from the airport. Would not mention that he had seemed less than enthusiastic about her even coming to Houston. Would not complain about a single thing. No, she would concentrate on making the evening enjoyable for both of them.

Their room was on the ninth floor, with a decent view of the city. The maids had cleaned—trash cans were empty, cellophane-covered glasses waited undisturbed on the reading table. But the queen-sized bed was not as tidy as Rachel's specifications. Robert's clothes and papers were strewn about the room, a habit of his that never failed to annoy Rachel. She set her things down, and remade the bed, carefully tucking the sheets under the mattress and pulling the spread across the length and width of the bed, folding it back over the pillows. Then she gathered Robert's papers into a tidy stack on the desk in the corner. She picked up his clothes, folded each item neatly, and tucked them into the wood-veneer dresser. He had tossed things into every drawer, so Rachel spent a few moments rearranging his things, clearing space for her own, before she unpacked her bag. She would be settled in soon enough, with time for a warm soak before she dressed for dinner.

She ran the water and added bath salts she had brought from home. The water was soothing against her skin, and soon she had settled back into the curve of the tub, her eyes closed, the steam from the bath filling the room. What would she wear this evening? Maybe her blue knit dress. Robert liked that one. She would eat lightly – perhaps a salad – and no more than two glasses of wine with dinner. Maybe she would tell him about her flight, about meeting a real live astronaut. Robert would get a kick out of that. She might even tell him that she'd shared a cab with Jim Logan. Maybe he would laugh about Buzz Aldrin and the moon rocks. Maybe he would be impressed. Maybe the story would break the ice so they could talk about them, about what wasn't working, about how to rescue their free fall of a marriage. If not, it would at least pass the time.

By 6:30, Rachel was dressed in the blue knit and sling-back sandals. Her hair and her makeup were done. She had spritzed a little cologne behind her ears and in the crooks of her elbows. She would have preferred to meet Robert in the room so they could go downstairs together, but he was expecting to meet her in the restaurant. She sat on the edge of the bed and waited.

At 6:55, she took the elevator downstairs to the lobby and found her way to the restaurant. The maitre d' had no reservation for McBride, but seating was not a problem. Rachel waited in the foyer for Robert. By 7:15, when he still had not arrived, she had the maitre d' seat her, at a lovely booth by the window. If Robert was running really late, he would phone. She thought about calling him, but she didn't want to be too demanding, did not want to make him angry before their weekend had even started. Certainly he would be here any moment. She thought about the afternoon, practiced in her mind how she would tell Robert the story of meeting Jim Logan.

The waiter came, set out silverware for two, lit the candles, brought her ice water, bread and oil, and a vodka and orange juice. She checked her cell phone. It was on, but there were no messages. She straightened the silverware until every piece lined up. Sipped her drink until even the ice was gone.

By the time Robert arrived, it was 7:42. Rachel was halfway through her second screwdriver. She could hear him talking, laughing with the maitre d', before she saw him stride across the room in his jeans and sweatshirt.

"There's the prettiest girl in the room!" he hollered.

He bent down and kissed her full on the mouth before sliding into the booth across from her. She gave him her best smile.

"You're making a scene," she whispered, but he ignored that.

"Hey, sugar." He glanced at her glass. "Looks like you managed to keep yourself entertained."

"It's orange juice."

"You order yet?"

"I was waiting for you."

"It wasn't my fault. It was the idiot instructor. OK?"

Rachel nodded. This was a good start.

The waiter brought Robert a menu.

"I recommend the Jambalaya. Tres magnifique! I'll bring more bread while you decide. Monsieur, ma'mselle."

Rachel leaned across the table. "I love that Cajun accent."

"Cajun, my ass. He just talks that way so the tourists will tip him better."

"Not you."

"Hell, no. I may just dock him for that shit."

That was one of his more creative justifications for miserliness, Rachel thought. When the waiter returned, Rachel studied him, trying to discern if this was what an accent forger might look like.

"Will monsieur try the jambalaya?"

"You talked me into it."

"And for the lady?"

"I'll have the lobster," Rachel said, daring Robert to object.

As soon as the waiter left, Robert twisted in his seat, his eyes darting in every corner, as though he were searching for something.

"It's a nice hotel," she said.

He just picked up his fork, tapped it nervously against the side of his water glass.

"Bad day?"

"That goddam sim is a piece of crap if I ever saw one."

"Never the pilot, always the plane." As soon as the old adage was out of her mouth, she knew it was mistake.

"You're so smart. It's a simulator."

Never the pilot, always the imaginary plane, she thought.

Robert let the fork rattle to the table top, shifted to settle himself against the leather of the seat. "So how was your flight? Smooth?"

"Yeah, fine."

Robert nodded, still distracted and edgy.

"Actually—something interesting happened. You'll never guess who I met."

Just then Robert's cell phone interrupted.

"I gotta take this. It's Michelle."

Michelle was the other pilot in training this week. She and Robert had worked together for a long time. At first, Robert had resented her. He would not admit it, but Rachel was pretty sure Robert had trouble with the idea of a woman in the cockpit. Rachel had leapt to Michelle's defense, to the defense of their entire gender. Eventually Robert had gotten comfortable flying with Michelle, and now he was as big a supporter of women pilots as anyone. Rachel and Robert even socialized occasionally with Michelle and her boyfriend *du jour*, although it had been a while.

"Are you sure, Michelle? That is bullshit. . . . You know, if we stick together, make it clear to those assholes that none of this divide and conquer shit is gonna fly. . . . Exactly." He was still on the phone when the waiter arrived with their dinners, a steaming bowl of rice and spicy meat for Robert, and a plate heaped with lobster, Cajun rice, and little side dishes of melted butter and sour cream for Rachel.

"Will there be anything else?"

Robert shook his head.

"A refill," Rachel said, holding up her glass. Then she whispered, "A little less OJ this time."

Robert finally signed off with Michelle, put the phone away, even took a few bites of his dinner. But his mind was elsewhere. At one point, Rachel reached across the table to take his hand. He looked startled, then patted her on the arm. Rachel asked what was wrong, but he didn't want to talk about it. She wouldn't have understood anyway.

"I'm really sorry, sugar. If those fuckers weren't so goddamned incompetent, we'd have wrapped things up today, but it looks like I'll be back in the sim tomorrow. You can take the rental car so you're not stuck hanging around the hotel all day. I'll ride over with Michelle."

Rachel stared at him. "Tomorrow's our anniversary."

"Oh, shit! That's right." He closed his eyes, shook his head. "Look, we'll go out for a nice dinner."

"Like tonight?"

"Champagne and everything. OK?"

Rachel nodded. "That would be great."

By the time they got back to the hotel room, Robert was exhausted. He kissed her on the cheek and fell into bed. The vodka was buzzing around Rachel's head, but she wasn't ready to go to sleep yet. She checked her watch. It was barely eight-thirty on the West Coast. She could call her sister. But what could they talk about that would not lead to questions Rachel didn't want to answer? So Rachel turned on the TV, volume down low. She flicked around the channels. The Right Stuff was playing on AMC. The coincidence made her smile, and she settled down to watch it, falling asleep before the credits rolled.

Robert got up early the next morning. Before he left, he set the key to the rental car on the nightstand.

"There's a shopping mall not far from here," he told her. "I'm sure you'll find something to do. I'll meet you in the lobby at six."

Alone in Houston with a whole day to kill. She didn't need to see the inside of another shopping mall. She had Macy's, Starbucks, and Banana Republic at home. She was in a brand new city. She wanted to see something that distinguished it from every other big city in the world. She got up, got dressed and drove to Johnson Space Center.

Rachel didn't call Jim Logan. Did not want to give him the wrong idea. But while she was at the Space Center she would look up his name, read about his exploits, know that she had actually met face-to-face a man whose life was more daring and true than her petty existence.

She parked the rental car in the lot and walked inside.

The visitor's hall was a sweeping vestibule of light, sound, computer images, and space icons. Even on a weekday, the place was crowded. Eager sightseers, schoolchildren on field trips, obvious foreigners with cameras around their necks, gray-haired veterans and young soldiers home on leave, grandmothers, sweethearts, all viewed the displays, climbed into the space craft, paid homage to valor.

There was so much to see, so much to learn. The displays about the exploration of space and the brave men and women who had pioneered such distant mysteries gave her goose bumps. It might be corny, but she was filled with awe. She had been there several hours before she made her way to the kiosks with computers where one could look up the details of the astronauts' careers. Every astronaut who had ever served in the program, retired or active, was included in the database.

Rachel typed in: J-o-h-n G-l-e-n-n. The space hero-turned-senator's name and career synopsis appeared on the screen in bright blue.

Next she tried: B-u-z-z A-l-d-r-i-n. The highlights of his two space expeditions, including the historic first lunar landing in 1969, popped up. No mention of juggling moon rocks, Rachel noticed with a smile.

She was ready now to do what she had come for. She was ready to learn more about the hero in 18B, Jim Logan, a man who was honest, brave and true. Tingling a little with anticipation, she typed in the letters J-a-m-e-s L-o-g-a-n. The screen flickered briefly, then a message flashed: No such entry. Okay. She typed in J-i-m L-o-g-a-n. No such entry. She dug the Walmart receipt out of her purse and checked the name scrawled on it. Jim Logan. No mistake there. Maybe Jim was his middle name, she thought. Or he could be a Jamison or even a Jaime.

The computer program offered alphabetical searches — Rachel clicked on L. She scrolled down the names of astronauts whose last names started with L-o. Lockhart. Lopez-Alegria. Loria. Lounge. Lousma. Lovell. Low. This could not be. They had left Jim out. Surely this was some egregious misunderstanding.

She pulled her cell phone out and punched in 4-1-1. "Johnson Space Center, main switchboard."

"Johnson Space Center, where may I direct your call?"

"Space Flight. Jim Logan, please."

"I'm sorry, ma'am. There is no Logan listed."

No Logan listed. He was a fraud? If you couldn't trust an astronaut, then nothing was true anymore.

Angry now, she punched in the number Jim Logan had scribbled down.

"This is Rachel, from the plane."

"Rachel."

"You lied to me."

"Rachel, I—"

"Some hotshot. You don't even work at NASA."

"Yeah, I do—"

"The switchboard operator says you don't."

Silence. And then: "Facilities maintenance personnel don't have phone mail," he muttered. Rachel was dumbfounded.

"You're a janitor?!"

"Rachel, meet me somewhere."

"This was—what? An elaborate pickup line?"

"Let me explain—"

"Because I'm a happily married woman," she said righteously. "Buzz Aldrin and the moon rocks?" She heard him chuckle.

"I guess that was a pretty wild tale."

"Why?" she demanded. The voice on the other end of the line sighed deeply.

"Haven't you ever wanted something so bad?"

"Poor baby," she shot back. "Poor, pathetic middle—age astro—wannabe with a Walter Mitty complex."

Silence. When Jim continued, his voice was softer, thick and a bit wistful.

"You pretend, ya know. Just pretend that you're it. Like maybe that would do the trick."

"I don't lie," Rachel said. "And I don't need people who do."

Rachel snapped the phone shut and jammed it back into her purse. What the hell was she doing here anyway?

The overhead clock in the crowded hall read nearly 3 o'clock. Suddenly, she wanted to get away. She fumbled for her keys; hurried out of the building, out to the rental car, back to the hotel, where she would meet Robert, where they would celebrate their anniversary.

NanoFiction: One Billionth of an *Oeuvre*

by Jason Hambrecht

Erika
She was Erika. What can I say?

Blackleg the Squirrel
His portside front leg is black. I can see his scrotum.

Batman Married
Holy Matrimony, Batman! You just fucked Catwoman.

The Zoo
I went to the zoo today. The animals were nice to me but I was sad.

I Dove You
Doves aren't smart. Neither am I. I've always wanted to be a bird.

Ask Your Mother
"Can we build a bat house?" No, her mother said.

The Sunrise Ritual

by Cara Mecozzi

"McGregor." He gave the slightest inclination with his head in acknowledgment. It would have gone unnoticed, if she had not spent much of her school career trying to better understand the enigmatic boy.

"Lev." It was bad enough having the first name Levianth, he did not need unintelligent nicknames from immature girls. His upper lip curled into the most subtle of sneers, but this did not discourage her, she was a McGregor for God's sake. They were known specifically for their idioc—their bravery, yes, they were known for their bravery.

"It's time," she finally said, after deciding that Lev was not about to say anything, even after using one of the many disliked pet names she had invented for him.

"Already?" It was more of a statement than a question, but she nodded in the affirmative for a reply anyway.

"All right," he began tucking a strand of black hair, which, contrary to popular belief, was not dyed, behind his ear with his bony fingers. "Let me just get my coat."

"Come off it, Lev. How many times have we done this?" The red-head, whose hair really was dyed, was grinning a rather attractive lop-sided smile that reached her hazel eyes and made them seem like they were dancing with laughter.

The calculations were simple enough. It had started near the end of sixth grade, and now they were nearing the end of tenth grade, and it happened once a month every month.

"About fifty-three times," he replied dryly, dark brown eyes trying and succeeding to appear bored.

"And, how many times have you needed a coat?" Her dark eyebrows were raised, and it was quite obvious she was trying to egg him on; he just rolled his dark brown eyes and shut the door behind him.

He was unsure how she always managed to find him; he was rarely, if ever, in the same place whenever it was 'time,' but she always managed to find him. Even during the summer and winter holidays, if need be. He had asked her once in eighth grade how she did it, how she found him. There had been a glint in her eyes that had been a bit hard to characterize, which, years later, he would say had been 'playful,' for lack of a better word.

She had grinned, the one that reached her eyes, and stated it simply, "It's magic." The novelty of trying to uncover her secret wore off very quickly, and he hoped one day she would just tell him.

The cement felt frigid under their bare feet, but they proceeded on anyway, without complaint. Well, Levianth complained a little bit, but that is to be expected from any sixteen-year-old boy; it was somewhat of a mumble peppered with a few curse words and "Remind me why I do this?"

Lilianna (call her by that and she might just have to punch you in the face, Lily would do just fine) McGregor's good-natured smirk only broadened, and in the grayish-green light still pouring out from the streetlamps they passed, she managed to look positively breathtaking.

"Because you love me."

"Of course," the sarcasm in his voice may have been a bit more biting and scathing than usual. "There is nothing I enjoy more than being dragged off on the third Wednesday of every month before the sun is even awake to accompany you out into the freezing morning."

Lily seemed to ignore the derisive comment, but after some time responded, "And yet, you still follow."

It was raining by the time they finally made it outside the campus grounds. Not drizzling. Not showering lightly. No, it was like some god was completely bawling and the heavens were dumping down buckets full of tears.

Lily's hair, now a lovely shade of dark auburn, was plastered against her fair-skinned face and shielding her eyes from the view of everything.

She tilted her chin up to the clouded sky, extending her pink tongue out of her mouth in an attempt to catch raindrops. Levianth watched her; he had always prided himself in being able to think of the right words for any situation, but right now, they were eluding him. Lily appeared to be . . . lost. Content, like nothing in the world mattered more than the raindrops pounding against her flushed face.

Levianth did not look so bad in the rain either. Though far from an attractive youth, the water made his greasy hair give way to a much more socially acceptable wet look. His eyes reflected what was around him, and right now, that was her happiness. His eyes, characteristically cold, were a tad bit warmer.

"Let's dance!" Levianth looked so confused by her sudden exclamation that he did not even bother to tell her there was no music. She would probably just give him a cryptic string of verbs, nouns, and subjects anyway.

Lily was skipping over to him, and suddenly he found his eyes straying down to their bare feet. Her toenails were painted a rather vivid shade of hot pink, which clashed wonderfully with the dark mud and her pallid skin.

Soon she was in his arms and they were dancing, though

Levianth really had no idea why. He didn't know why he was nervous either; it was not like anyone would catch them. The sun was only slowly beginning to creep into existence, extending long fingers of light over the grounds. Splotches reflected on the lake, shimmering like freshly melted batches of molten gold.

It happened every time, but he was always a little shocked when she broke away from his hold and began to truly dance. She looked free and wild and so very pure. She appeared as if she was in a trance. Vaguely he was reminded of the ancient druids they had been forced to study in history.

Mud from the ground had splattered up to her knees. Levianth was grinning, because he knew what would come next—she began singing. And not some ancient hymn or chant that would have been expected from the way she was moving, nope, just an old Beatles song, "Here Comes the Sun."

True, she did not have the best singing voice, but it was sweet and enjoyable. It was a voice that would be perfect for bedtime lullabies.

He knew what was supposed to happen. He knew what he was supposed to do next. He was supposed to laugh sardonically, then she was supposed to feign anger and together they were supposed to welcome the sun over the hills. But always, always, he could leave exactly when it completely cleared the mountains.

Maybe it had to do with truly watching her. Truly watching her—with her soggy clothes and her wet hair plastered against her skin. He knew what he was supposed to do, but he did not do it. He just moved closer to her, the support from the ground somewhat giving way and squishing beneath his frozen feet.

She had almost finished the song, but stopped singing and watched him curiously with her shining green eyes. His long fingers, which would have probably been called elegant, if they were not so emaciated, reached for her and rested against either side of her face. And he did something that was not part of the plan. He did something that was not part of the ritual.

He leaned in and kissed her. He was careful not to let his nose bump into hers, wanting what was already a rather awkward moment, not to be any worse. Surprisingly enough, she leaned into the kiss, wrapping her arms behind the nape of his neck. He was unsure how long it was before they broke apart. He was unsure whether it was nothing, or an eternity, because it felt like both, with her warm lips and the frigid drops of rain pouring down from the sky.

The sun had fully cleared the hills when they broke apart.

They met every third Wednesday of every month and watched the sun ascend into the heavens. But that was it; that was their time together. They could only meet during the in-betweens, neither was ready to fully step into the other's world.

The meetings continued, but the kissing stopped.

She was one day married to a man who had humiliated and ridiculed him all through high school. The meetings continued well after graduation, even long after her wedding had taken place, until her husband finally learned where she went on those Wednesday mornings. The last time they met, she kissed him, and she smiled

The smile had not reached her eyes.

Atlas of the World
by Calvin Roberts

Your postcard arrived yesterday and with nothing better to do I decided to find out just exactly where Nyìregyhaza Sosto is. I have this awesome Oxford Atlas of the World ("Extraordinary"—*The New York Times*); satellite images of Earth, the gazetteer of nations, world statistics, city maps, world maps, the Universe, the Solar system, Landforms, climate, population.... well, everything.

In the "Index to World Maps" I have found Nyìregyhaza but not Nyìregyhaza Sosto. What is it, a village, a suburb? Anyway, I decided that Nyìregyhaza would do and found it on page 52, grid square C6. The Index even gave the co-ordinates, down to the minutes. So, I opened the Atlas at page 52 and there, under the heading "Hungary, Romania and the Lower Danube," which also includes page 53, I found the place where you are enjoying the lazy days of summer. The postcard doesn't show much; an old, well taken care of, white-washed building, with tiled roof and big windows; a wooden sign that says "..m.y.. Restaurant," the first word obscured by a leafy branch. I looked at it for a long time, trying to imagine what is beyond the edges of the card. I see the Great Hungarian Plain (*Nagyalföld*) stretching in all directions, green with corn, golden with wheat, straight country roads lined with white poplars, clusters of weeping willows near ponds, creeks and rivers.

This is how I travel now—leafing though this beautiful book, exercising my imagination and burrowing through my increasingly unreliable memory. As I was looking at the map of Hungary I stated remembering my experiences with your "old country" and its people—they go back, way back.

On the bottom half of page 52 is a part of my "old country," now actually parts of three different countries. Just below the middle and very near the left margin of the map, in Crotia, is Koprivnica, a small town where I was born, just a few miles from the Hungarian border. In the first four grades I sat two rows behind, a Zoltan who looked and spoke just like the rest of us kids but, I am sure, did not get his distinctly Hungarian name just because his parents thought it fashionable. In Geography class neighboring countries got a lot of time and we learned quite a bit about Hungary. In History class we learned that our peoples fought, formed uneasy alliances, were thrown together or used against each other by the powers that were, since the first of our tribes wandered into this part of the world. My grandmother made goulash with paprika and according to her all bad weather came from Hungary. In the late 70s and throughout the 80s we took trips to Csurgo, Nagyatad or Nagykanizsa, exchanged some of our hard currency (*Lire, Marks, Schillings*) for Forints—half legally in a bank the other half clandestinely in back alleys—and bought cheese, sausages, paprika and leather gloves. The unwritten rule was to cross the border driving on fumes and then fill'er up on "your" side where gas was cheaper. We drove Yugos, Yugoslavian-made Fiats, under the name Zastava, and used Peugeots, VW Golfs and Audis, which drew the attention of local girls. They were approachable and friendly but chatting them up required a lot of sign language. Croatian and Hungarian, notwithstanding the centuries of close existence, are as alien to each other as two languages can be. The goods moved in both directions and on a Saturday morning one could hear Hungarian spoken in stores all over the town. Hungarians bought coffee, cooking oil, VEGETA seasoning, cans of PODRAVKA Liver-pâte, pocket transistor radios, occasionally a bicycle, a washing machine or a refrigerator. They crammed the stuff into their Ladas, Skodas and Trabants (two cylinders, hard plastic body), and were gone by early afternoon. The last time I saw a Trabant, in 1994 I think, it was suspended high above the stage, next to a giant martini glass with a beach-ball sized plastic olive in it, at a U2 concert in Oakland, California (page 160).

The two lane road connecting Koprivnica and villages north of the town, and then crossing the Drava river into Hungary, did not rate even the thinnest red line on the map. A gray line, the railway, is there, straight as an arrow all the way to the border, and then just one bend before Csurgo. Koprivnica was an important railway junction and freight trains rumbled through at all hours. In the evening, at six o'clock when on time, an international express from Budapest, dubbed Magyar (the Hungarian), arrived in town. After a brief stay, during which passengers' passports were checked and a few people embarked, the train—only five or six cars long—continued its journey to Zagreb, and, ultimately, Rijeka. In summertime, especially in July, the Hungarian was a lot longer, on some evenings fifteen or even twenty cars long. Some of the cars bore plates with the name of the cities where they came from: Warszawa (page 55), Krakow (page 55), Praha (page 34), Debrecen, Budapest . . .. While the passport checking crew worked its way from the middle toward the ends of the train, passengers came out to stretch their legs, buy refreshments and cigarettes and for a short while, our small-town train station became truly international, echoing with chatter of excited travelers speaking Polish, Czech, Slovakian, and Hungarian. On occasion, when a large group of workers from the factory went on vacation with their families, or when Scouts went to their camp on the Adriatic Coast another car was added to the train in Koprivnica and our town's name found itself in this unlikely procession of country capitals and big cities. In Ogulin—just off page 52 and with most of the rest of Croatia on page 45—the Hungarian was dismembered, groups of cars attached to different locomotives and, under the same name, pulled toward their final destinations: Rijeka, Zadar, Sibenik, and Split. Many of my trips have started, and some were entirely done on board the Hungarian. At the end of the summer after we graduated from high school, a bunch of us boys were called to serve our compulsory twelve or fifteen months in the army. It was, for most of us, the first extended period of time away from home, and was supposed to turn us into men. From the platform crowded with proud and tearful families, girlfriends and friends, it was the Hungarian that carried us to Zagreb, from where, on some other trains, we scattered all over the country. I ended up in Bitola, Macedonia, just a few miles from the Greek border (page 50).

In my college years, at the end of a weekend at home when my small town started to suffocate me, I would suddenly remember an early Monday morning class, catch the Hungarian at the last minute, anxious to see my friends and lights of the big city. My most affectionate memory of the Hungarian is as the place of my first kiss. The kiss—twice frustrated in its early stages of heads tilting and eyes closing—was the culmination of long hours of hand-holding and numerous promising glances. It was awkward, inquiring and uncertain at first, but it became the most beautiful experience of my young life. It happened the day after my thirteenth birthday, in a dark, cool compartment, under a blanket in a seat by the window, with her parents and my mother asleep so dangerously near, as the train meandered cautiously through the mountains between Plavno and Knin.

The Electric Lady
by Vanitha Sankaran

Janine plopped into her seat at the front as the bus doors hissed shut. She fanned her sweaty face with a folded section from the daily funnies.

"Anyone know the time?" she asked loudly, looking at the watch on her wrist. Damn thing was broken, stuck in place. She tapped on it with her finger. The second hand just wouldn't move. Caught on the five, twitching in place like a preying mantis jerking in the throes of sex. Janine had seen that once, quivering sticks on the edge of the sidewalk. It'd looked like one fat knobby stick, till the two had split apart. One stick leapt away nimbly, her poor lover left in pieces. His body gone, a delicious meal, only a puddle of slime and guts left behind.

Life can be dangerous.

She tapped harder on the watch. Piece of junk. Kept zapping out, just like her hearing aid.

"Excuse me?" she said to the passenger across the aisle. His bald head poked over his newspaper. "Excuse me, do you have the time?"

There was no answer, so she jabbed at the center of the sports page. "Excuse me," she said again, "I asked, do you have the time?"

The man slowly lowered his paper, stared at her up and down. One corner of his lips curled upwards, sending a chill spilling down her spine. What was he looking at anyway? He went back to reading his paper. And still she felt him, his gaze caressing her flesh. Good Lord, the realization hit her.

X-ray vision was his power.

He could stare at her skin right through her clothes. She folded her arms over her chest, glared at him in anger. Filthy pervert.

The woman sitting next to her chuckled and swayed back and forth. "Right on, right on."

Janine whipped her head around to look. What was that lady laughing at, nasty old bat? Was she listening to all of Janine's thoughts? Dear God, they were all around her! Superheroes, freaks, call them what you will.

Janine was one too.

At first she'd thought no one would believe her. Turned out she just hadn't known where to look. Her power was a simple one, barely even noticed it at the start. Oh, little things were going wrong, but little things always were. Soon, though, they started adding up. Clocks blinking twelve midnight, coffeemaker burning with a flash, the television fading out right in the middle of her soap. It'd seemed like odd coincidences. Till Charlie died anyway.

Police said it was suicide. Janine didn't bother to tell them otherwise. Who committed suicide by dropping a hairdryer into the bath? Now suicide, that was a bullet in the brain, maybe wrists slashed wide open. What did they call it, electrocution? Left him like a waffle sitting too long in the pan.

She'd always had a spark about her. How many men had told her that in bed?

What other explanation could there be anyway? Things only broke after she touched them, and Charlie, well, he deserved it. A right cross straight to his nose while he was soaping his belly. Served him right, whoring old drunk.

"I zapped him," she'd giggled at his funeral. "Bzzz, just like a microwave." Just call her the Electric Lady.

Now Joey, there'd been a keeper. Too bad he'd already had

a wife. Shouldn't have been having affairs then, leaving his complications all around town. Public service, that one had been, a gift to all single women. Just a wish and a whisper, and the spark had flown from her fingers. He'd keeled over on her toaster, burned his face onto the metal.

She never told anyone, not that anyone would believe her anyway. Only slipped once in fifteen years, and then on account that she'd been drinking.

"I got something to tell you," she remembered saying, motioning her friend Marta closer with one hand. Marta was like a sister, known her for twenty years. Janine had sipped her margarita in thought, licked the salt from the rim of her glass.

"I'm different from all of you," she blurted, "got powers you wouldn't believe."

Marta laughed, played along like she was drunk. "What kind of powers, Janie?" she teased. "The kind that make men drool all over you, or the kind that make them come back for more?" She purred a naughty growl.

"Superhero powers," Janine answered. "Ever heard how my first husband died? I zapped him to death with my electric personality." She tittered at her own cleverness.

Marta looked at her oddly so Janine just had to continue.

"They said it was suicide, but I know it was all my fault."

Marta still didn't believe so Janine kept talking. "They don't know about Joey, he was the next. And then Luke, and Alex, my favorite."

"I know someone you can go to," Marta whispered after an hour of talk. "Don't worry, it's just between us girls." She scribbled a name on a paper, pushed the crumpled scrap into Janine's hand. "Go to him and tell him what you told me. He'll understand. He'll be able to help."

Oh he helped all right, only man worth the salt in his blood. Brought her here, to this sanctuary. He was the only one who'd believed her.

The bus stopped with a lurch, and the doors slid wide open. Janine waited for the others to leave, watching as they passed her. The attendant stood over them like a vulture, only he was dressed in seraphic white. Goodbye, Pervert, goodbye Bat. See you later, Smelly Lady in Blue.

Her fingers itched with months of disuse. The charge was building inside her. But how to dispel it, what could she do? Wasn't polite to zap other superheroes. Her gaze turned to Cody, the angelic assistant who always helped her off the bus.

"C'mon, Ms. Evans," he urged, offering her his hand. "Time to go back. Did you enjoy the trip? Must be nice to get off the grounds once in a while."

Janine stared at him, the chubby cheeks and sleepy brown eyes. The white shirts were here to help her, she thought. Well, she needed some help now.

"Why, thank you, sir," she murmured demurely, reaching her fingers for his. The cold metal of her hearing aid controller brushed against his hand. Oh Cody, sweet darling boy. He hiccuped once, then fell silent.

The exhilaration skimmed along her body.

Such a pity, she thought sadly, walking off the bus in dainty steps. What a man he might have been.

destiny's token
by Ethel Mays

nut-brown woman
sits in thick spring grass
on mountain slope

paint pony crops nearby

ankles cross
forearms rest on upright knees

dark eyes gaze
on creek-crossed valley

cool breezes groom
slow-to-silver long black hair

high-wind hawk
slows flight
then streaks unerringly

too-slow rabbit
dies on valley floor

breezes halt

One feather
floats down

slim brown hand
reaches
plucks

The Trilogy of DEATH!*

by Tom Darter

*When this poem is read aloud, the reader should use low-budget hand reverb** when saying "*DEATH!*" in the title.
Low-budget hand reverb is actually closer to tremolo. *
***Well, it's not tremolo, either; just a low-budget sound effect: Cover and uncover your mouth three or four times with your cupped hand, quickly, while saying "*DEATH!*"

1. Death
I hate death.

Not the bald, sepulchral,
skin-wrapped skeleton
in *The Seventh Seal*,

nor the bald, albino,
minstrel-faced parody
in *Bill and Ted's Bogus Journey*,

and certainly not the tarot card Death —
which is, of course, not about death
(but that's another story).

No, I simply hate
the fact of death.

The impending end,
the winking out,
the soon to be
    of having been.

Most gifts are given,
but life is a loan.

We're not even asked
if we want to offer collateral —
we are it, and the damage is done
    before it is known.

Yes, I know the jokes and homilies —

Life is a terminal disease.

Life is what happens while you're making other plans.

Life sucks, but it's better than the alternative.

— but I reject them.
They are paths of avoidance.
They are about
    not seeing the truth.
If it's a disease,
    why do I want it?

If it's just what happens,
    what do my plans
    have to do with it?

If it's better than the alternative,
    why isn't it simply
    an alternative?
Why is it a fact?

I hate death.

Still, I don't fight it
by trying to look younger.

The grim reaper is a glam reader:
He sees through
    the lack of lines,
    the frozen face,
    the puffed-up lips.

And why would I want
    to freeze my face
    before it's done
    for me
    forever?

No, fighting doesn't work.

Death is just a loss waiting to happen,
a loss of which I am already aware.

And I can't beat it.
And I hate that.

But—I know it,
    and so won't waste time
    pretending that I don't.

How about acceptance?

No, that's crap. Spare me!
(But, of course, I wish I could be
    so set aside
    by not being set aside.)

All of those five stages —
    fine if you have the time.

But does the soldier
have time to pass through
those layers of understanding
in the short time between
the sharp report and the instant it takes
    for the shell to pass through
    the brittle shell that housed
    his understanding?

And did my twin brother
    (who lived for one day)
have time to deal with his life,
let alone his death,
let alone the never-ending grief
    of our mother?

I hate death.

But it's there.

Beyond my paltry ability
>to understand,
>to accept,
>to get used to.

I guess the only thing
>that might make it easier
>is knowing that,
>after my death happens
>(after I wink out),
I won't be around to notice
>how much it sucked.

Still, I hate death.

And will,
>until I'm not.

2. Death on the Half Shell
You watch it.
You know you want to watch it.

Not your death, but death delivered,
in movies, TV shows, and news.

Most of all in news,
>because every time
>someone real dies
>you win, because
>you are still here.

Still here. Still able to
    see death elsewhere.

And as long as you keep
your mind focused on
    those others,

        you don't see it
        in your vicinity.

Still, death *will* rise out of the ocean,
    seemingly modest,
until it stretches out its arms
    to enfold you,
and reveals how it really looks.

When you see it naked for yourself,
it will not be pretty. Or ugly.

It will not be summarized
or encapsulated on
the nightly news.

It will be, simply,
the last thing you know.

And you'll discover you
didn't learn much about it
by watching others go.

3. So?
And is that it?

Since death is the end,
is that all?

No. In *The Gem of the Ocean*,
a dying character's last words,
uttered mantra-like,
are: "So, live."

Well, why not?

Death is the end,
but all this is not.

Until we run, headlong, into
the final, immovable,
son-of-a-bitching brick wall,

we might as well enjoy
whatever this is, as we
move on down the road to
that final collision.

No, not *carpe diem*.
    Too simple.
I think search is better
    than seizure.

And not the *grave's a fine
    and private place.*
I plan to be cremated.

I will, I hope, defeat
the worms at least.

But, before I deny them
the remnants of my succulent self,
I shall strive to live.

Good Daughter
by Camille Thompson

I open the door to the bright, expansive common room. Warm autumn sun beams in from windows on the opposite wall high above the door that leads out to the tidy garden patio. I steel my churning stomach against the smell of disinfectant poorly masking the urine odor. Bent bodies barely supporting lonely, vacant faces are scattered about at the round tables that fill the large room. Reminding myself to smile, I greet those whose expressions flicker with comprehension. Weaving through the wheelchairs and shuffling slippers, my steps are quick and light. I am ashamed of my forty-something agility.

I ascend the staircase and find my mother's room. The bathroom door is propped open, nearly blocking the entry doorway. This is undoubtedly to ensure some privacy from the nosy residents who stroll up and down the hall and peer in at her.

I nudge the door and squeeze through the narrow space silently so as not to startle her. She is dozing in the recliner my brother Gary and I bought her two weeks after we moved her here. She insisted we find her a recliner that didn't rock. Most of them rock, we learned, but this one didn't, and it was on sale. We hoped she would like it. She almost did. The color is too light—she keeps a crocheted afghan spread out over it—and, she says, it's too hard to push back into the reclining position. Gary offered to WD40 the recline mechanism. I don't know if he ever did. I do know my mother never reclines in her recliner.

Mom awakens to my soft touch on her shoulder and gets up

to offer me her seat. It's the only chair in her half of the shared room, so she sits on the end of her twin bed. The flowered coverlet does little to cheer up the dormitory setting.

I offer her a piece of the raspberry scone I bought on the way over. She spreads open a Kleenex and lays it across her trembling outstretched hand. I set her portion of the treat in it. Mom nibbles the scone and comments that she doesn't get sweets much here. I notice that her tremor is not bad this morning. It may be the hour, I tell myself. Her Parkinson's medication causes noticeable peaks and valleys of effectiveness over the course of the day.

"Did you pay my bills?" she asks.

"Yes, Mom. I paid them."

"Well, do you have the receipt for the rent?"

"They don't give me a receipt." I know this answer will not satisfy her.

"Then how do you know if they got it?"

I stifle a sigh of exasperation. "I bring the check when I come to visit you the week it's due. I hand it to them in person."

She asks nothing more; her eyes register uncertainty. I wonder if I'll trust my daughter to pay my bills when I'm too ill to pay them myself.

We engage in small talk for a time. She asks about Kristen, my twenty-two-year-old daughter. I tell her she's fine, still dating the same guy. I don't tell her that Kristen is considering a move to Oregon next year. We have learned to keep the real family news from Mom. She sees only the dark side. Only how it will impact her, or how she is in some way the reason for the decision.

"Oh my God. Now I'll have to worry about that," she would say of Kristen's impending move. Never mind that Kristen views it as an exciting adventure. Never mind that I am perfectly capable of worrying about my only child moving 500 miles away.

After awhile she comments that it's really not so bad here. That she doesn't really mind staying here.

"That's good," I reply, unable to think of anything else to say. I am relieved she's not unhappy. I think maybe she has accepted the change as permanent.

It was a difficult decision to move her, one that my brothers and I put off too long. The first sign of her failing health was in April 1996. One night, she inadvertently locked herself outside the security apartment building where she lived at the time, became irrational, and started shouting obscenities and tipping over the benches in the entryway. Paramedics took her to the hospital where she stayed two days.

Her doctor blamed the outburst on an adverse reaction to medication.

After the incident, she was so humiliated she seldom left her apartment. Never a social person, she became increasingly reclusive and paranoid. She began losing weight and failing to take her medications on schedule.

When my brothers and I finally accepted the fact that she needed more care than we could provide her on a drop-in basis, we convinced each other it was time to relocate her to a facility that provided twenty-four-hour care.

We never convinced Mom. She didn't go willingly. Wouldn't let go of the notion that one of us could care for her in our home. Looking back, the day we moved her was an intervention of sorts. Like the kind people stage for alcoholics. We gathered at her tiny studio apartment and talked with her, reassured her, but wouldn't allow her any other choice but to move.

I don't tell her that I've begged Kristen never to put me in a place like this, just as Mom begged my brothers and me. I temper my pleas with reassurances that I will trust Kristen's judgment, and go quietly if there is no other option. I won't be difficult.

Still, I can't imagine being bathed and fed by strangers, however friendly and pleasant they seem. I can't imagine sharing a bedroom and a bathroom with a woman who wets and soils herself, whose expressionless face is the last thing I see when the lights go out.

I glance down at Mom's bare feet and notice that her nails need clipping. I wonder if other daughters take care of these personal needs for their mothers. Mine doesn't ask, and I don't offer.

A young woman with a caring smile, dressed in a white uniform, looks in on us and reminds Mom that it's time to go downstairs for lunch. I thank the woman and gather my things together, grateful that the awkward visit is over.

I descend the stairs slowly, so as not to get too far ahead of Mom. At the bottom, I kiss her soft cheek, tell her I love her and that I'll see her next week.

"Love you," she replies, then turns to make her way haltingly to her assigned seat.

Again I remind myself to smile and nod at the other residents as I glide toward the door to freedom.

Riding home in the car, I cannot erase the image of my mother and her lonely existence. I resolve to take nail clippers with me when I visit next week.

The Island
by Ben Jones

After the ceremony, instead of finding my parents, I go into the auditorium. Everyone else is out front with cameras, setting up family groupings to be inserted into scrapbooks. The auditorium doubles as a gymnasium, and doubles again as a church for the most crowded Sunday masses. It could double yet again as a cafeteria except we always eat lunch at our desks in the classrooms. It has a kitchen used only for cooking food during the annual carnival and storing the daily deliveries of milk. That was my job once, accepting the milk crates full of little cartons from the same milkman who delivers quart bottles to my home. I would count out the right number of cartons of milk for the different classes. I was always at the school early anyway, and it was a good way to get inside on cold days, when my feet would be painfully cold. But more that that it was a job I did for the honor of it, like clapping the blackboard erasers at the end of the day. The kitchen has a homey, familiar feel. I am saying goodbye to it.

The tables in the auditorium are laden with empty cardboard boxes, waiting to be refilled with blue graduation robes. I take my robe off and put it in its box, and pick up my Sunday jacket. Two tables away I spot Marianne's coat where I saw her lay it down earlier. When I go to public school in the fall I won't see her anymore. A few months ago I discovered she's pretty. That seemed odd at the time. Why was it suddenly so interesting that she's pretty? Didn't I know that already? It doesn't matter anymore, though, after what happened last month. She hates me. She and Matt both hate me. And it's not fair. I didn't do anything to them, but now I can't even look at either of them without my face getting hot. So I stay away from them.

Matt and I have played together since first grade, but it was always at his house or my house. We never just wandered off into the woods like I do when I'm playing alone. It wasn't until last month that I showed him my secret hideouts. I took him to the pond at the very end of the swamp, where there is a huge rock rising out of the water, covered with moss and tiny wildflowers and a thin sapling squeezing out of a long crack. On one side of the pond the hillside rises dry and safe. On the other the swamp stretches dark and brooding for miles. We have to circle around the pond jumping from rock to stump to mossy, treacherous hummock, and then walk across a fallen tree and two half-submerged logs to get to the rock. If we aren't careful the moss on the logs will rip and our shoes will plunge into the muck, but we make it OK. It is a mysterious, dark, quiet pool with sunlight only in the center, making the rock and its sapling a refuge of light and warmth. Time waits here, waits for something to happen. Perhaps the call of a bird or the splash of a frog. Perhaps the rise of a dinosaur's head and long neck out of the thick green water. Surely the pond has been here, will be here forever.

Once I found a duck egg perched delicately at the foot of a tree on a tiny tongue of roots and moss overhanging the pond, and there were often deer droppings among the bushes on the hillside. Their appearance seemed as mysterious as the pond itself, because I never saw ducks nor deer here. The droppings were piles of pellets each about half an inch in diameter. When they were months old they were tiny bundles of fiber washed by the rain, still retaining their shape. On this visit with Matt, when I pointed them out to him, I suddenly saw them differently. The deer were leaf and grass processors. They remove the nutrients and eject the remaining fibers. I had never done this before, but I picked one up. It was mostly air, light and feathery. I tore it open, revealing only more fibers.

The next day during recess a laughing Marianne came to find me on the playground. I was smiling too at the idea that she wanted to talk to me, when she said, "I hear you pick up deer droppings in the woods," and I gasped, and turned to escape, to run, from the ridicule in her smile.

Once I was far away, but hardly safe, I could only wonder why Matt had told her about that. Did he think she was pretty too? Had he done this on purpose because of her? Had they laughed together about me and how stupid I was to touch such stuff? Could I face either of them again? The only answer I had was to the last question.

Ned is another friend I won't see in public high school. He was the first person I had met at the school, on the first day of first grade. Our mothers had dropped us off early in the deserted schoolyard to wait for the doors to open, and we waited nervously together in the cold while hundreds of other children gradually appeared. We were best friends until sixth grade, when he joined Little League. All the boys that tormented me on the playground were in Little League. I felt Ned had made a choice, and he had chosen them instead of me.

I would also be leaving Simon. He had been adopted by the in-crowd when they discovered how far he could throw a ball. They named him Condor because of his nose, in their mocking friendly way that they never used for me. Simon and I remained friends even though we spent less time together, until the day on the playground I stood listening to a group exchanging insults. Simon was in the middle of the group, holding his own. I didn't understand most of the words they used, but I liked puns. A Condor was a bird, and birds peck with their beaks. Lots of the boys joked about peckers, whatever they were.

"So if you're a condor, does that make you a pecker?"

Simon looked at me and said, "I expected somebody to say that, but not YOU!" I backed away from a dozen silent stares, not knowing what I had said.

Simon and Matt and Marianne and the others will be going on to the Catholic high school up the street, but I won't. I won't have to face them. I will be free. Free of my friends.

I look at the tables laden with coats and boxes. I will be leaving all of them. Everything will be different when I go to public high school. I won't know anybody. That was the point, of course. When my parents had offered me the choice of following my brother and sister into Catholic High School or switching to public school I had thought of their stories of mean teachers and bullying athletes. Nuns whose idea of self-sacrifice was to give up teaching what they were good at and instead teach subjects they didn't know. But the real reason was to escape from the betrayals, theirs and mine.

In public school there won't be recess, so there won't be any more fights on the playground. It just wasn't fair when someone took our ball to force us to play keepaway with them, in order to get the ball back. In public school we would have gym class instead, and the teachers would prevent the bullies from picking on everyone. No more crying silently in class because I think nobody likes me. I won't be so sensitive. I won't be lonely, or at least not at school. I won't feel guilty or ashamed. This is a completely new life. It won't happen again. Will it?

What if it does happen?

But it couldn't happen. It can't happen.

But it might.

Back in my school jacket, I cross the auditorium toward the parking lot door. It must not happen. I glance up at the stage as I cross the center aisle. Auditorium or not, the altar contains the sacred hosts, so this is a church. I sign myself as I cross in front of it.

I ponder as I walk toward the door. I need a guarantee. I need a promise. I've never broken a promise. A sudden wave of determination breaks over me. I say, out loud, "I'm never going to cry again."

The words flash, startling me. They light up the inside of my skull like silent lightning. My mind is blinded by them. The world blinks. It seems that time stops and then starts again an instant later. Not just here in this auditorium but the whole universe.

This is a promise with power, with magic. I said it, and now it is true. I suddenly understand what a vow is, what an oath is. It is not just words, but a real thing. I wonder what it is that I have done. Whatever it was, my determination has not ebbed. I repeat, "Never again."

I suddenly have a picture in my mind. I see fields and forests and hills and houses, and a black road that winds among them into the distance. The ground at my feet rises and falls as a wave starts there and speeds away from me like a wave on the ocean. It rolls across the landscape with an effect like an earthquake, destroying everything in its path. But behind it there is not destruction but a different landscape, with different forests and houses and fields. With a different road among different hills.

Somehow I know that it is my future I see. Two futures. I have destroyed one, and created a new one.

As the vision fades, I realize I am still walking across the auditorium. As I pass through the door into the bright June sunlight, I can feel myself changing, inside. I am becoming strong, self-sufficient, a rock, an island.

Poor Claude du Bois
by Leslie Flannery

Larry Williams picked up his daughter at his ex-wife's house nearly four hours after the slated time. Geraldine had been waiting, bags packed, for all four hours. Juliet was furious with Larry but it was all for naught because to chastise him only created a scene, which was sure to embarrass and hurt her daughter. Larry had been drinking but he always had a little in him so it was difficult to tell if he was newly drunk, drunk from the night before, just starting to get drunk, or pretending to be drunk just to irritate her. Nothing was out of the realm of possibility with Larry.

"Have you been drinking?" Juliet pressed at the doorway while Gerry went out to the car to put her bags in the trunk.

"When have you known me to drink?" he stated with a shit-eating grin.

"Your daughter is going to be in the car with you—get it together," she demanded, knowing full well that it was all a routine, their pattern. Juliet hadn't been able to affect Larry and his drinking while they were married so there was surely not going to be a transformation after the fact.

Juliet did the best thing she could do, and that was to save herself and rescue as much of Gerry's life as custody would allow. The break was nice too; weekends to herself without spills, questions, projects or child rearing hassles.

"Well, I wasn't going to let her ride in the car, I was going to put her in the trunk where it's safer. If that's what you mean?"

"You're a bastard!" Juliet whispered.

"I'm ready Dad," Gerry called from inside the car with the impatience of someone that wanted to hurry up and leave. Juliet always felt that Gerry was excited to spend the weekends with her Dad, or at least that was the impression Gerry liked to give. Whatever the case it was what the judge had declared; it was what it was.

The pick-ups were difficult for Gerry so she liked the meetings to be as brief as possible. Her mom and dad made her nervous together. Just the thought of them talking made her anxious and sick. Something bad was sure to happen if too much time passed between the two. Gerry figured early on that it was best to keep all of the information separated between households. Since no one ever asked about the details when she was away, it made good sense not to rock the dinghy. The arrangement appeared to be mutually agreeable, as evidenced by her parents' lack of initiative to change anything.

It wasn't that she was necessarily hiding anything, after all, her mom had lived with her dad; she knew how he was, didn't she?

"How's Dollbaby?" he said with a big kiss and a warm scruffy snuggle to the top of Gerry's brown mop. Her dad always smelled good; Aqua Velva, cigarettes and vodka permeated the car to make a manly dad smell. "Where do you want to go this weekend?" Larry lit a cigarette, slipped in an eight-track tape of Elvis Presley and then eased the long sleek Cadillac into gear and away they went.

"Like where can we go?"

"We can go to the movies, we can go to a basketball game down at the stadium, we can go to the lake and we can call up the President and see the White Hou . . .."

"Dad!" Gerry interrupted once she detected that he was teasing her. "Let's go to the movies," she said as she caressed his tan hand, petting his arm hair, taking in all the glory of her father-daughter moment. These were the good days when Dad picked her up, he was happy, and as far as she could tell completely sober. Today there was promise for a grand weekend full of activities and good things.

"All right, what do you want to see?" he asked.

"I don't know."

"We'll pull in and get a paper at Tom's Tavern and you can pick one," he suggested. That was a danger sign to Gerry, but he seemed so confident and so eager to go to the movies that it was hard to tell if her radar was off. It was the gradual decay of instinct.

"Well, how long are we going to stay there?" she asked cautiously.

"Not long, just long enough to figure out the movie situation," he promised with the scouts honor pledge.

They entered the dingy premises and there wasn't even one patron in the bar. The only sound in the room came from a TV up in the ceiling's corner. The bartender poured Larry a drink of scotch and soda before he had reached the end stool. Larry took a long suck from his glass, draining half of its contents in one gulp. He was immediately quenched, like a marathon runner guzzling a bottle of Gatorade. Gerry gave her dad "the look," as if to say, "Okay where's the paper?"

"Stan, you got today's paper?" Larry called to the bartender.

"Yeah, here." Stan produced a rolled up paper he had stashed behind the cash register. "She want anything?"

"No!" Gerry blurted out with a little too much enthusiasm. "I mean, no thank you." Every extra minute, every extra comfort was a red flag screaming, "Danger. Code three. Batman come quick." There was imminent danger of staying and staying and staying.

The man handed the paper to Larry and continued to watch the TV. "Suit yourself."

Larry handed the paper to Gerry and she understood that it was her job to figure out the movie. After looking through the pages for a few minutes she found the movie section but was unable to decipher the theater times and locations. "Dad, I can't figure it out."

"Stan, one more would ya?" He asked as he lit a cigarette and studied the TV up in the air.

"Dad, I can't understand it."

"What? Wait till the commercial," he commanded with his scotch scepter.

Gerry looked up at the TV and noticed that there was now a football game on the screen and the tiny beveled panes of glass that had channled sunlight onto the wall were beginning to go dark. Her anxiety began to build as her dad started his second drink.

"Dad, you said we wouldn't stay long."

"We'll go. Be patient. Stan get her a Coke, would ya?" he called to the bartender.

Gerry watched the clock tick and followed the second hand around and around. She did her best to pass the time. Her eyes went open and close, open and close as she counted seconds to see if she could accurately see the time on the clock. She counted minutes, then sets of minutes, later played tic tac toe, and finally she counted hours with toothpicks. Her napkin asked, "What's your sign?" Four toothpicks in a shot glass proved Einsteins theory to the ten-year-old girl; Time + Time = Longer.

A man came into the bar at some point and sat next to Larry and they began to enjoy the football game together. The man tried to make fake pleasantries to Gerry but she was not interested. Showing interest in anything would only add to the time. Time went on and so did the commercials. Each time a commercial came on, Gerry would poke and prod her dad to take her to the movies and each time he rebuffed her with another stall. Anxiety was eventually replaced with sadness as she settled into the reality that her dad was not going to take her to the movies. There was always hope, but it was the kind of hope that even a child knew was hollow.

Her dad had become slower now and had lost the excitement he had first displayed when he picked her up. He was starting to put the cigarette to his mouth in a funny way and he wasn't drinking his drink very much either. Gerry laid her head on the bar and closed her eyes trying to rest her sorrow and despair. She wanted to cry but was afraid that a show of emotion would upset her dad and cause him to become angry.

Larry had three ways of being; sober, primed, and drunk. He was preparing to enter the drunk stage, and it was just as well Gerry thought.

Sober required serious management, as Larry was easily aggravated by things that upset his own pattern of comfort. It went without saying that Gerry should try extra hard not to spill her milk, but other than something obvious like that, Gerry found it hard to figure out how to avoid getting yelled at in that stage. Drunk was easier because there was more of a system; so long as her dad was free to drink or watch his movies or talk with his friends, he seemed to have a much larger scope of tolerance. The good times were in the middle, between sober and drunk and they had passed the middle over six commercials ago.

Gerry did her best not to become overwhelmed during her dad's spells. Her dad was confounded by his daughter's tears and it enraged him to see her that way. Once she figured out that there was no one available to hug her, she decided early on that it was best to avoid that situation if at all possible. Larry's tantrums in front of her friends were also difficult times for her to manage; the secrets threatened to leak out. It was a prospect worse than death to a ten-year old. She felt bad for anyone who didn't know her dad like she did, because she was certain they didn't understand the good part of her dad.

Her dad had once bought her a puppy—one of the most pleasant memories of her childhood. The dog gave her purpose and friendship during her weekends with Larry. The puppy needed her, slept with her and was cute as well. Her mother would never let her have a dog, which she suspected was why her dad had gotten Meathead in the first place, but now she had something special at her dad's house. The dog was all hers and she loved it. Her dad gave her money to buy it a few items, and when the money ran out, Gerry brought items from her room at her mom's house: blankets, a ball—she even snuck a spatula out of the house to make cleaning up the poo easier.

The puppy was named Claude du Bois after a type of wine that Frizzy Clyde drank down at the Seashore Cove. When she had heard the name, Gerry felt that it rolled off the tongue nicely, "Claude du Bois," she would say over and over to pass the time at the bar. It sounded regal until you said it too many times and it became, "Clod boob wa." Even so, her dad called the puppy Meathead, and he made no attempt to call him by his proper name. One day Gerry was watching TV, not paying attention to her dad or Claude, when out on the patio he began beating and screaming at the dog. The dog yelped and squealed in an effort to get away from Larry but there was nowhere to go. The dog was as deep into the fence corner as he could fit. Larry kicked the little dog as it shivered and cowered, yelling, "You fucking meathead!" over and over. Gerry ran outside to save him, screaming at her dad to quit while being mindful not to get in the cross fire herself. Cowering and keeping her head low and her eyes pointing down towards the pavement, she sidewaysed into the space and grabbed Claude. Gerry quickly shuttled her dog to safety about twelve feet from Larry's range. Larry was red faced and angry. Gerry had eventually surmised that Meathead had peed somewhere bad.

Gerry stayed next to the puppy the rest of the weekend trying to soothe and comfort it. She was immersed in shame for not having protected her baby and then it came time to return to her mother's house; she felt a sickness in her stomach that she did not know how to quell. Leaving Claude du Bois alone with her dad for the next two weeks was wrong. He would be subject to unspeakable tortures.

"What kind of mother are you?" she asked herself.

How could she leave a puppy with her dad after knowing how he was? Who in their right mind would let Larry have access to an innocent dog? She begged to take the dog with her, but her dad was adamant that the animal was hers to enjoy only when she came to his house to visit. She reluctantly left the dog but remained sick to her stomach for the two weeks until her next visit.

Claude du Bois was innocent and he did not understand her dad the way she did. He didn't know how to be very careful when Larry was sober and to save his playing until Larry was in the middle phase. He didn't know where to play when Larry was in the drunk stage and he didn't know not to spill his water during the sober stage. He didn't know enough yet. It was easy if you knew how, but if you didn't, bad things happened. How could he learn any of this without her?

On Gerry's next visit, she woke herself up in the middle of the night and crept out to the back patio, and cracked the fence open, and kissed her puppy goodbye. Scampering back upstairs in her nightgown and bare feet, she didn't even notice that Claude had turned away from the fence and was pressing his nose up against the glass hoping that she would return to let him in.

Praying into the darkness of the room Gerry asked God to make sure her dog would "please find a family before it was time to eat again." Politely she prefaced every request with "please," hoping that proper manners would increase the chance that God would care for the dog.

"Please, God, let him find food by dinner time, and please let him be with a girl, like me, who loves him and please remind her to brush him often . . . and please tell her not to forget about him when it's cold . . . and please, God, let him be with a fine family like he deserves. Dear God, if you gave him a family I would promise to give..."

Gerry sobbed into the pillow at her predicament. She wished to give up herself, as she had nothing else to give, but she knew that God didn't want a damaged girl from a damaged family. With nothing to give, Gerry knew that she could not get God's attention. God, like her parents, was busy. Now her little dog would have to suffer . . . all because of her.

Invisible tears streamed down Gerry's face as one more toothpick filled the glass.

My First Enterprise
by Frank Thornburgh

Tony was one of my junior high school classmates. He was a tall, fun-loving bean pole with premature big feet, long nose, and stooped posture, which reminded me of Icabod Crane.

Between classes at school, Tony ran up to me in the hallway all excited, talking so fast I couldn't quite keep up with what he was saying, so I asked him to say it again . . . slower. He said, "I just shit a two-foot turd there in the boys' restroom. How about helping me manage it? We can charge the kids a dime to see it. But you gotta help keep anyone from flushing it."

I said, "Ok, but I wanna see it first."

Some other guys tried to crowd around to get in on the action, but we pushed them back telling them they had to pay to see it. As I looked down there in the toilet at that-all-time-record-breaking brown snake, I was having a hard time believing all that came out of Tony at one time. But since it was in one piece there was no denying it.

We quickly pushed everybody away from the stall and started trying to collect the dimes. The guys were whining they barely had lunch money and a dime was too high a price. So we lowered the price to a nickel, collected a few, which by now thinned the crowd enough to get everyone back out into the hallway away from the trophy. We said emphatically, "that particular restroom is off limits." No one can go in there without paying a nickel." Up and down through the crowd we hawked our enterprise in a not-so-subtle way resulting in some of the girls hearing what was going on. I realized this was the wrong way to get female attention so toned it down. The bell rang so it was back into the class rooms. Concentration and close attention to lecture was impossible. I just had to find a way to protect our golden egg and get out there quick to guard the door. Mr. Stucky's class went on forever—completely unnoticed, even though he was the one that wielded the two-handed paddle for the women teachers. (The paddle had holes drilled in it to prevent wind resistance.) Stucky wore thick glasses, continually made a false smile and reminded me of a Nazi doctor anxious to do "experiments." Finally back out into the hall, quick! into the bathroom to check on the core of our business. Tony rushed in. Our attraction was dissolving. We quickly put on a final push for customers, but the initial interest had faded. Our market was tapped out. The bell rang so off to class with old Mrs. Williams with the big hands, who thhpit with her llithhp. During her class my business enthusiasm faded. At the next bell we went back to check on the snake, it was gone. Someone had flushed the all-time record breaking trophy that made Tony famous . . . to this day.

Buckarooing
by Harold Gower

In dreams I'll go buckarooing
My horse is ready to ride
With bridle and saddle and lasso,
Stamps his hooves with spirited stride.

I'm ready to go buckarooing
Following cows through the knee high sage
Chasing them down from the canyons
For only a cowboy's wage.

The deserts of Northern Nevada
Have beauty that very few see
For some it's a job, buckarooing,
But it's always a pleasure to me.

The cooky will bring the chuck wagon
And rustle up three squares a day
We always eat good on the roundup
Hooray for the cooky hooray.

We bed down ourselves and the cattle
The sky is starry and clear
In dreams I'll go buckarooing
The moment that day-break is near.

Kiss Dancing
by Selene Steese

Whenever the mood takes us,
we can be found touching
lips, giving each other a little
mouth-to-mouth, bodies
swaying, hips swinging
to some lustful melody
only we can hear.

Together we are this quiet
miracle—two people who still lust
after each other
twenty-three years
beyond the first meeting
of their lips.

Two people who still
love each other
after twenty-three years
of life's indifferent battering
and unexpected beauty.

Whenever the mood takes us,
you will find us
kiss dancing, giving each other
a little bliss.

In all this world, there is nothing
sweeter than the taste
of you.

Hoppe's #9
by Frank Thornburgh

Hoppe's is a bore cleaner for firearm. (Usually pronounced "hoppies.") It has a very distinctive odor. Some might think it smells good. I am one of those. The smell of Hoppe's brings 50-year-old images back to me like it was just last year.

I grew up in Indiana. The family clan would usually gather at our farm around Thanksgiving time for the traditional rabbit hunt. The visiting group would be my aunt, uncle and their kids plus my grandparents and sometimes step brothers and Mr. Rogers.

One main rule was: we went hunting rain, shine, sleet, snow, or slight blizzard. (A big blizzard did count.) Story telling, reminders, admonitions, bragging, and general excitement preceded the latest quest.

My stepfather raised and trained beagle hounds as a hobby. The most I remember having at the same time was 70, counting all puppies. Normally we had about 30 in dog runs that were 8-10 feet wide by 40-50 feet long with some 10 dogs to a run.

Beagles become focused when hunting and especially on a hot trail. I have seen them run in front of cars, trains, careless hunters, and other dangers. We lost a few that way.

Well, it was a big decision to determine which dogs to take and they knew it. Imagine the begging noise accompanying the extreme show of enthusiasm. Some six-ten would be sorted out and not let go until we started across the fields.

My brother and I would put on two pair of pants, two pair of socks, 3-4 shirts, coats and heavy caps with earflaps. We multi-layered gloves so the holes in each pair did not line up. We were very poor farmers and wore hand-me-down clothing and often the wrong size shoes or boots.

When we finally went to the fields with 2-3 cartridges each, we would spread out in a straight line abreast left and right for safety. Two of us would be on a fence row and two to three others across the fields and two on the next fence row and so on, always staying abreast. The dogs would be everywhere in between and all around and very busy wagging their white tail tips like little flags. We had quite a chore to keep yelling to them by name to keep them close and not jump game too far away. This would continue for two to five hours depending on the weather.

I think we only got skunked once. Our bag was usually two to eight cottontails and one to two bobwhite.

One thing we always got was cold. I mean cold cold. Toes got numb first, then slowly all the feet, then up the lower leg. When numbness got up to the knees someone would start complaining, and eventually we would all agree to head back to the house.

The house could be one to three miles away. It always seemed farther going back frozen and wet. The coal cook stove in the kitchen and the second coal heating stove in the living room could not be hot enough for us. (The bedrooms were never heated.) We would peel off our wet or frozen clothes and put them right on the living room stove for a few seconds to watch them sizzle and steam. Clothes were hung on chairs, wire hooks, clothes lines, spread on the floor or anywhere to dry out. One or two low ranking kids would have to stay out to skin the frozen rabbits and put them to soak in saltwater. We must have eaten hundreds of rabbits as I was growing up.

All the time we were out hunting, the family women would be cooking turkeys, potatoes, beans, gravy, biscuits, pies and other nasal-torturing delights. We might have been poor, but we ate well. All the hunters would be spread out around the living room trying to dry out, change clothes, and clean guns. The smell of Hoppe's #9 would permeate the air and compete with the kitchen smells. Colorful stories also filled the air about the ones that got away or something the dogs did or who froze out first or who missed an easy shot.

This ritual and many in between went on for nearly 10 years. There were many hunts day and night. There were many dog-training outings on full moon nights when the snow was not too deep. There were many numb feet.

It has been fifty-plus years now and all those people have passed away but me. I have told my remaining family and close friends to sprinkle some Hoppe's #9 around my grave so I can take those memories with me.

Red Wing Shoes
By Frank Thornburgh

My grandfather was not a very sophisticated person in a lot of ways, but he did appreciate quality.

From 1947 to 1954 my little brother and I were poor but healthy farm boys in Indiana. We were hard on clothes and shoes when we had them. Every Christmas we could depend on receiving certain things from Grandpa and Grandma. Usually we received two out of four of their special gifts. Those gifts might be: Oshkosh-By-Gosh Overalls, Mackinaw coats, Karo corn syrup, (it came in a one-gallon type paint can), or Red Wing high top work shoes we called Clod Hoppers. Those Clod Hoppers prevented a lot of cuts and abrasions from the dangers of farm life. Grandpa bought what he thought was best, even if it did not fit in with the current fashion at school. Unfortunately the high quality clothes and shoes he bought for us wore a lot longer than my brother and I would have liked as far as school trends were concerned.

In the 1960s, while I was a police officer, I bought black Red Wing boots that I could spit shine to stand out and "shine." There was a newspaper article printed about my devotion to and care of polished boots.

For about the last 13 years my Red Wing high-heeled cowboy boots saw it all visiting and working on my cousin's cattle ranch in Oregon. By "all," I mean being submerged hours at a time in water, snow, rain, mud, horse manure, cow manure and unmentionables from my cousin's custom slaughter business. No doubt they are form fitted by now.

I can tell you from first hand experience how tough those boots were when a German Sheppard was trying to bite through them to get to my good stuff. That was not the only dog bite they survived. One of my cousin's Blue Heeler males is wildly sensitive to having anyone stick their boot under his private parts. He goes into a crazy biting fit. My cousin Ambers likes to annoy his sister. One day she was standing next to me talking to Ambers. Rocky, the sensitive Blue Heeler, was sitting between us. I stuck my Red Wing cowboy boot in Rockies private parts knowing what he would do. While he was frantically chewing on my boot with a lot of fanfare, Amber's wild-eyed sister went straight up for the rafters.

Those boots receive one or two affectionate preservative rubdowns each year and are still going strong.

Flight Path
by Mary Druce

Sitting on the green lawn
beneath the SFO flight path
I see a graceful silver dolphin
appear from the north-west corner
of the placid blue ocean sky.

Swimming easily, gliding through
the scattered white-cap clouds,
quietly heading south, its deep
throaty rumble gradually insinuates
the quiet as it comes overhead.

Sure and persistent, it banks left
inscribing a circle in the ocean sky,
heading north again, steadily
descending from the ocean depths,
intent on its destination.

On final approach, its red-tipped tail
now apparent, it is joined by another
giant silver dolphin, rushing in from the west.
The blue-finned dolphin falls in line behind,
like the water ballet of a master choreographer.

Discarded Things
By Judy Clement Wall

He can't be sure what it is—the silence, maybe, or the waiting, the sunlight slanting through the window just so—but it stirs in him something unfamiliar, a yearning, sorrowful and low, and for a few ridiculous seconds, Arthur believes he might actually cry. Right here, alone in his kitchen on an ordinary Tuesday afternoon, a grown man, ambushed by rogue emotions.

Unnerved, embarrassed, he jokes to no one: "Why shouldn't I cry?" he says aloud. "It's a sensitive thing, this business of making tea in the afternoon. Not a task for the faint of heart." And then, for good measure, he chuckles.

He pours water over the teabag in his cup, sits down at the table, picks up the latest issue of *Newsweek*. He doesn't notice when his mind begins to wander. He's half way through the second page when it dawns on him that he has no idea what he's read.

Glancing across the table, he imagines for an instant Elle sitting there, as had been their custom when he'd first retired, when he was still the center of her everything, he with his *Newsweek* and she with her *Good Housekeeping*. She had a habit of humming tunelessly as she read, and of announcing things —the title of a story, recipe ingredients, helpful household hints. Eventually, she would look up, notice his expression, his finger holding his place on the page. "Oh I'm sorry," she would say, "you go ahead." And then a few minutes later they would do it all again.

But now the quiet disquiets him, and he wonders where she is, when she'll be home because it's so hard to keep straight the details of her busy schedule. When he finishes his tea, he wanders, restless, room to room, averting his eyes as he passes the coffee table, the monstrosity that sits upon it vying for his attention.

When Elle pulls up, hours later, Arthur's in the garden. He hears her car and, brushing the dirt from his pants, goes inside and finds her in the kitchen.

"Did you eat?" she asks, pulling TV dinners from the freezer, popping them into the microwave, carrying lettuce, tomatoes and mushrooms to the sink. Her book bag, fluorescent green, sits on the floor beside the table. "I met an amazing woman, today," she says. "Della Langston—Brown, an author, came to speak at the college." Elle pauses to inspect a mushroom, tosses it down the disposal. "It was a seminar for women returning to school. Older women, like me, only Della calls us life—experienced. You've got to love that. I bought one of her books. . . ."

Elle shreds the lettuce into bowls. Standing in the doorway, Arthur watches her, all movement, sound, purpose. He tries to remember the last time he held her, the last time they kissed or laughed or looked into each other's eyes, and suddenly the distance between them, much greater than the space of a kitchen, seems vast and unbearable.

He takes a step toward her, hears himself blurt, "I miss you," but Elle keeps on talking, so happy, so enthusiastic, that her voice approaches song, and Arthur falters, uncertain in the end if he's even spoken the words aloud.

Elle sets the salads on the table. "Della says if we believe in ourselves, our inner strength is limitless. Isn't that wonderful?. . . Arthur?"

"Yes."

"Are you all right?"

He wants to tell her he isn't. He wants to stride across the room, take her in his arms, feel her embrace, his salvation. But when he opens his mouth, no words come. His feet refuse to move.

Elle laughs. "Arthur?"

Seconds drag by, and then, like a game show buzzer signaling the end of his turn, the microwave beeps. Elle retrieves the dinners, sits down, motions for Arthur to join her. She rummages through her bag, sets a paperback book, entitled *The Power of You: Applying Your Inner Strength*, on the table between them

"It's signed," she announces, showing him the inside cover, where in bold red script it says:

Elle, Don't look back!

— *Della Langston Brown*

Reading it, Arthur feels a twinge of panic. Don't look back. He wants to ask Elle what it means, but it's too late. She's already picked up the book and is a million miles away from him, humming tunelessly as she reads.

He has come to think of it as the turning point, that morning, months before, standing in line at the pharmacy. He remembers the man behind them, his cough, oddly rhythmic, musical. An illness in three-quarter time. He remembers trying out tunes in his head, tapping his foot to the coughing beat. And he remembers Rita, of course, every detail, from the little purple flowers on her dress, to the lilt of her voice, to the sweet, unassuming look on her face as she turned and spoke to his wife for the very first time.

"It's eerie, isn't it?" she said. "Look at this line. Little automatons, we are, all in a row." She was still a stranger then, but when she lowered her voice and leaned in closer, so did Elle, like schoolgirls in the back of the class. "All these people waiting to get their prescriptions filled. It's a good thing I'm not into conspiracy theories."

Elle nodded gravely. Arthur wondered if he'd missed something.

"I mean, what if we're not being given what we think we're being given?" she said. "What if the pills we pop have nothing to do with our hearts or joints or cholesterol levels? What if they're . . . something else entirely?"

"Something sinister," Elle suggested, her voice uncharacteristically playful.

"Exactly."

"Mind altering?"

"Maybe."

"How would we know?"

"How indeed?" The woman smiled, nodding, then shrugged her shoulders and held out her hand. "My name is Rita Bonwell."

"Elle," his wife said, and then, as an afterthought, "this is Arthur."

Rita beamed at Elle, then turned to Arthur, her eyes traveling slowly from his head to his feet and back again—so slowly that Arthur began to believe somehow that the measure of his worth rested finally, and irrevocably, in the appraisal of this stranger. When she looked away, he breathed again and wondered if he'd only imagined the disappointment in her eyes. Or the sparkle in Elle's.

He sensed it almost immediately, the change in his wife, like something awakening—a readiness, an enthusiasm —as if all along she'd been waiting for this, for something different. For something new. For Rita.

In the parking lot, Rita said, "You know, there's a group of us. Every morning we meet at the mall to walk. And talk," she laughed. "We solve the world's problems, daily. Exercise for the body and mind. We meet at the west entrance in front of Starbucks at nine. You should come," she said, her hand on Elle's arm. Arthur cleared his throat, took a few steps toward the car. No one noticed.

On the ride home, he said, "So, that was kind of strange, don't you think?"

Elle didn't answer.

"Rita and The Mall Walkers," he tried again. "Sounds like a rock group, doesn't it? Or a horror movie?"

Elle smiled then, a smile unrelated to his words, a distant, forward-looking smile that made Arthur uneasy, afraid of being left behind.

In the middle of the night, he sits bolt upright in bed, sweating, heart pounding, blood rushing in his ears. He remembers running – it's all he can do to catch his breath – but when he tries to recall the rest of his dream, it's gone. Unable to fall back to sleep, he gets out of bed, careful not to wake Elle. He'll go outside, he thinks, out into the garden, the cool night air. He pulls his robe on, pads through the hall and into the living room, where he freezes.

It sits, majestic and imposing, in a shaft of silver cast down from the moon and shot through the window like a spotlight. It sits, as if in waiting, like a vision, a gift. A horrible, ominous warning. "It's only a sculpture," Arthur whispers, but this time his self reassurance cannot break the spell.

Elle made the statue in her first class after deciding to return to school (a decision encouraged and applauded by Rita and the Mall Walkers). The figure is nearly two feet high and in the daylight, loosely resembles a woman with wild, flowing hair, long, twisted arms. Her upturned head has no face, a fact Arthur finds vaguely disturbing, and one he asked Elle about the day she brought it home.

"You ran out of time?"

"I named it Growing Woman," she said, as if that somehow explained the missing face. Centering it on the coffee table, she beamed. "My first piece," she said, and Arthur could tell from her voice that there would be more, maybe a lot more, and he tried to conceal his alarm.

Now, in the moonlight, the sculpture looks strange, shadowy. Alive. He steps back, and it leans toward him, reaching. He closes his eyes, tells himself it's a trick of the light, that the statue cannot, in fact, be moving. Or reaching. Or sneering, because sneering, Arthur reasons, is a feat that simply cannot be accomplished without a face. Still, he retreats, backing into the hallway, into the bedroom where Elle's soft, rhythmic breathing holds no comfort. He climbs into bed half hoping she'll awaken, but instead she rolls away, sighs deeply and begins to snore.

In the morning Arthur wakes to kitchen sounds, the smell of coffee, music on the radio. He keeps his eyes closed, pretending, imagining he'll get up, put on his green bathrobe, go into the kitchen and there Elle will be sitting at the table working the daily crossword, sipping coffee. She'll look beautiful in her bathrobe just like his.

But when he opens his eyes, she's only a few feet away, pulling her running shoes from the closet, sitting down on the edge of the bed, smiling absently when she notices Arthur watching her.

"Would you like to join us this morning?" she asks, just like she does every morning, and Arthur says no, just like he does every morning.

Except for once.

"Would you like to join us this morning," Elle had asked him, and even though he could hear the reluctance in her voice (and maybe because he could hear it), he said yes.

In his worn sneakers and wrinkle-free trousers, he'd found

himself in sharp contrast with the coordinated jogging suits and high-tech running shoes of Rita and her Mall Walkers. They were serious, fast, efficient, walking in formation, arms swinging, hips swaying—a synchronized, geriatric, mall-walking machine. Within minutes, Arthur had fallen behind, the group smiling politely as they passed him, one after another. In the distance, he could just make out Elle, taking the lead, blazing trails, Rita by her side.

Approaching an escalator, Arthur felt relief, then terror. He would never make it through another floor. He called out, louder, more panicky than he intended, and the whole procession stopped to watch him as he struggled for breath, sweating profusely.

His words came in fitful spurts. "I'm a little . . . tired . . . think I'll just sit . . . " he motioned toward a bench. "I'll wait," he said.

They stared at him. No one spoke. He found Elle's face in the crowd, heard himself reassuring first her and then all of them, that he was fine, that they should go on ahead without him. With his eyes, though, he tried to implore her: Rescue me. When she smiled, his heart leapt, until she turned away, offering her smile to the others, an embarrassed apology. He watched her board the escalator, watched her wave goodbye, mid-ascension, wondrous and fleeting, like an angel in flight.

He watches her now, standing up, stretching her fingers toward the ceiling, bending slowly to the left and to the right, so graceful she takes his breath away.

She tells him there's coffee in the kitchen on her way out the door.

He is dusting, his cloth moving across the coffee table, pushing her to the edge, little by little, an inch at a time. He hasn't really formed the thought, not in words, but it's there, translating itself into the movement of his hands, the rollercoaster giddiness that twists in his belly. And then it's done, a flick of his wrist, a swipe of the cloth and the sculpture topples over the edge, shattering the stillness of the room, the day, his life, pieces skimming off in every direction across the hardwood floor.

Arthur is stunned by the absolute silence that follows, the tremble of adrenaline, the unexpected relief, irrational and overwhelming, as if he's just escaped some horrible fate. It's done, he thinks, and in the quiet, even his thoughts feel loud. The Growing Woman is dead.

He is cleaning up the mess when he hears Elle on the porch calling to Rita, Rita's car pulling away. With a broom in one hand and a dustpan in the other, he watches his wife come through the door.

"Arthur, I think we should take a line-dancing class," she says. "It's—" But her eyes find the coffee table, the broom in Arthur's hand, the trashcan at his feet. Arthur watches her face, her slow comprehension, his guilt tempered by a strange, reckless excitement.

"It broke," she says finally, not a question, but a statement of fact.

Arthur nods, and for several moments, they stand there, Elle staring down at the trashcan, Arthur staring at Elle, feeling inexplicably alive. Finally she sighs, straightening her shoulders, managing a smile. "I'll make another one," she says.

"What?"

"I'll make another one. I did it once, I can do it again."

"You can?"

"Don't you think so?"

Arthur nods, his head spinning.

"My inner strength is limitless," she says. A declaration. A mantra. An unalterable truth. "I'll make something even better this time."

"Yes," Arthur says, "of course, you will."

"I'll check the class schedule right after I take a shower." And Arthur watches her turn away, walk to the bedroom, slip her T-shirt over her head and drop it to the floor—a simple act that makes his heart ache.

Over her shoulder, she says, "Oh, Arthur, the charity truck will be here any minute. I put a box of old clothes by the front door. Can you set it out on the porch?" and kicking off her shoes, she disappears into the bathroom.

Dazed, Arthur drops the last few pieces of clay from his dustpan into the trash. The shower comes on, Elle begins to sing, and Arthur trudges to the foyer, to the carton marked CHARITY, where Elle's bathrobe, just like his, sits neatly on top like an announcement. As soon as he sees it, he steps back, leaves the box of discarded things and returns to the bedroom, to the sound of her voice. He sits on the bed to listen, stares down at her running shoes, imagines, suddenly, the floor beneath him opening up, a great, gaping chasm where seconds before his life had been.

A knock on the door brings him to his feet. Outside the window, he can see the large white truck—Williamson Youth Ranch painted on the side. Turning toward the door, he trips over Elle's shoes and, swearing, kicks one across the room. The passion of the assault startles him and Arthur has to steady himself before picking the shoes up, heading to the foyer. When he reaches the box, he hesitates, just an instant, then lifts the bathrobe and places the shoes underneath.

He opens the door and a gravelly voiced man says, "We're here to pick up."

Arthur glances at the box.

"I'll get that," the man says, reaching inside. His partner

hands Arthur a receipt, tells him his donation is tax-deductible, and Arthur nods, his eyes on the box being carried down his driveway, loaded onto the truck. The men move in slow motion, like a dream, closing the back, consulting over a clipboard, getting back into the cab. It isn't until the truck is pulling away that Arthur comes to, crying out, springing from the porch, waving his hands, chasing them down the street until finally one of the men leans out his window. "You all right?"

Arthur points to the back of the truck. It slows.

"You need something off the truck?"

"Please."

The man ducks back inside, the truck stops and the driver gets out, eyeing Arthur suspiciously.

"I'm sorry," Arthur pants. "I made a mistake."

"A mistake?"

"Yes. I wanted . . . I thought . . . " Fumbling for the words, and then, finally, "It won't work," he says softly, hoping it's enough, knowing it isn't. Still, he wants the driver to smile, to understand, to offer him absolution right here in the street, in the middle of the day, in the shadow of the Williamson Youth Ranch truck. He waits, but the driver cares more about his schedule than Arthur's soul.

"What the hell?"

"I just need to grab something off the truck," Arthur says. "It'll only take a second."

He hesitates.

"Please," Arthur says again, aware of the sweat trickling down his back. The man shakes his head, opens the back, watches Arthur reach into the box and retrieve the hidden shoes. "Just these," Arthur says, holding them out. "I shouldn't have given you these. They're . . . still good."

Uninterested, the driver pulls the cargo door closed. Arthur thanks him, waits for the truck to start, waves as it rolls down the street. When they are gone, he goes home, stands in the living room staring down at the shoes in his hands.

He hears the shower turn off, Elle, nearing the end of her song. She sings the last note triumphantly, as if she were on stage, drawing it out, running it up and down the scales, opera-style. Arthur can't help but smile. He sets the shoes on the coffee table and walks back through the bedroom, applauding.

Elle sticks her head out the door. "Thank you, thank you," she says.

In her voice Arthur can still hear the music. In her smile he thinks he glimpses the future, and he quickens his pace in an effort to close the distance between them.

The Ladder

by Mary Druce

Then I stopped.
My head empty.
My heart grew numb,
My legs heavy.
My arms grew tired,
I climbed to climb.
The more I climbed, the faster I climbed.
I climbed for life.
Where was I going? Or why?
I could not see where I started.
The higher the ladder seemed,
The more I climbed.
Higher and higher.
Up I went
I clung on for life.
On, then on. Another foot,
Another rung, and I hung.
I put my foot on the
Sky, ground, birds, flowers, heart,
You.

Stop.
I could not.
I climbed because,
I climbed because I could.
I climbed to stretch;
I climbed to get ahead;
I climbed to get away.
In the sky
Somewhere high above
The top was obscured
So tall it was, that
Ladder I climbed.

Moon Ride
by Ethel Mays

Summer sings around me like the local chorus warming up for a concert. It sounds like every cricket and frog in the county is trying out for a solo spot. They don't want to go to bed yet because it's a warm, sultry night—perfect for serenading and courting. There are so many stars out! You can read a book by their light. But I can see a glow behind Cougar Hill from where I'm sitting on the creek bank. Pretty soon, the moon will come up and the whole world will light up like daytime. Except all the colors will turn silvery, like they've been touched by a magic wand. We'll ride out into all this mysterious beauty and the horses will be our silent witnesses and partners.

I'm sitting with my knees up to my chin when Mick rides up to the creek bank. He's on Champ and leading Spaniard. We're going on a moon ride before he takes off again for the rodeo. It's supposed to be sort of a birthday present. Yesterday was my sixteenth. I still haven't told him I'm pregnant.

"Hey, girl," he calls, "Y' ready to go?"

I can't answer around the lump in my throat. Then I can't control anything. I bury my face in my arms and bawl like there's no tomorrow. Mick's off Champ like a shot and then I feel his hand between my shoulders.

"Hey, hey—what's all this?" he asks softly.

"Mick, I'm in trouble," I choke out. "Me an' Dan Reno . . ."

I don't even finish before Mick growls, "Dan Reno..." Then

he pulls me up to my feet and says, "C'mere." We wrap ourselves around each other and I cry into his chest until my stomach's sore and I can't cry anymore.

"Where's he at now?" Mick wants to know.

"I don't know," I say, "Nevada, maybe Utah."

Dan's in the pro rodeo like Mick. I only know his circuit's heading east before cutting north to Montana. He and Mick hate each other and always have. Mick thinks Dan is lying, cheating scum and says he's seen and heard the proof. Dan is three years older than Mick and acts superior. He thinks Mick is "just a 'breed" that should "take himself back to the rez where he belongs." Both are experts with horses and know it. But neither will ever admit it about the other. Two months ago, Mick beat Dan at calf roping. Dan was so mad he kicked a dent in his own horse trailer. Some people laughed but not Mick. He left the way he came—quiet—and I left with him. A week or so later, Dan started acting nice and polite to me, sweet even. I thought that maybe if we talked I could convince him that Mick's Indian side was as good as his Scots-Irish side.

Mick had a fit when he found out about these "talks," and Dan made sure he found out. Mick told me to stay away from Dan and started telling my parents all my whereabouts, at least all the ones he knew of. That made me really mad, so I started sneaking out of the house to go see Dan and spite Mick. Then Mick went on the road and I thought I was glad. But I didn't know how fast things could move and Dan Reno was like a coiled-up rattler. He had an ugly smile on his face when he finally got what he wanted. He pushed himself off me and said, "There—let's see your 'breed fix that." The next day, he was gone.

At first, I tried to hide how awful I felt by holing up in my room and pretending to read. But when I figured out I was late, I couldn't act like nothing was wrong every day. Dad and

Mama would catch on after a while. So I started getting out of bed early, before the sun came up, and went walking in the hills around our house. I stayed gone all day, even when it got hot as little blue blazes. My dog, Prince, and I always found a tree to flop ourselves under when it got like that. Whenever Dad and Mama asked me about my day, it was easy to tell them about it because I really had gone places and seen things. I told them about finding spring-fed livestock troughs in the hollows where hills meet and flatten out. One even had an old windmill that still worked. A cave only a couple of miles away from the house was high enough up the hill to become one of my secret lookout spots. Sometimes I'd see cattle being worked from up there.

Mama let me borrow her twenty-two, for "luck," she said, even though I'm not as good a shot as she is. And I took it, too, because there was always something else in the back of my mind. It would be so easy to just end everything, I thought. All it would take was a shot into the eye.... But Prince and I always made it back home before dark, just in time for dinner. Then I had to work my way through that because I wasn't hungry. Prince ended up eating really well under the table. He was lucky our hikes kept him from getting fat. But when I started losing too much weight, I had to make myself eat to keep from being taken to the doctor. That was a visit I really didn't want.

After dinner, I'd walk over to "our spot" on the creek bank, about a quarter-mile away from the house. It's where Mick and I swore we were "bestest friends forever and ever" when I was seven. I threw a tantrum there, too, when I was nine when he told me about a girl he'd met. Three years later, he teased me at that very same spot about my first "for reallies" boyfriend. It's where we go to wrap ourselves up in dreams—pro rodeo for Mick, four-year college for me. Mick is on his way and then some at twenty-three. But my dream's hit a real rough spot and the only person in the world that I can talk to about it isn't here.

One evening, when I came in from the hills, Mama gave me a funny little smile and I wondered what was up. After I put her gun away, I went into my room and found an envelope with a Wyoming postmark on it lying on my pillow. Big sprawling handwriting invited me on a moon ride for my birthday. There was an apology, too, because it would have to be a day late. Better late than never, I figured.

The chorus of bugs and frogs is almost deafening now that I've stopped crying. Mick pulls a handkerchief out of his pocket and says, "Here—blow." He holds the cloth for me like he did when I was four. I let go a big honk and he folds away the wet part, and then scrubs my face dry.

"Know how far along y'are?" he asks quietly.

I hiccup and nod my head. My face is sore and swollen and I'm having a hard time catching my breath. But there's no need for any of the figuring my mother ever taught me. "Six weeks," I say.

He puts the handkerchief back in his pocket then leans over to take my face between his hands. "Listen to me, girl," he says softly, "you have some hard thinkin' to do. No matter which way y' cut it, it ain't gonna be easy." He stops and puts one hand on my shoulder and looks away. He has a look on his face I only see when something goes bad with one of the horses. He takes a deep breath and looks me in the eyes before going on. "Push comes to shove," he says, "I'll talk to Nate. He knows someone up north." He stops again, then puts his arms around me and pulls my head back into his chest. "But, girl," he says in a harder voice, "it will take one damned big shove."

It's the first time I've ever heard Mick use a swear word. He's hinting at the "trouble" his older brother Nate "fixed" a few years back. The girl and her family eventually moved away, but she wasn't carrying Randall offspring when she left the Valley. Then Nate went to work cattle up in Alberta for a while.

When he came back, the scandal had died down and things were almost normal again.

I can hear and feel Mick's heart beating in my ear. I turn my head. "I haven't told Dad or Mama yet," I say into his chest.

Mick heaves a sigh. "That might be the hardest one," he says, real low. Then he puts both his hands on my shoulders and pushes me back a little so he can look into my face. "Look," he says, "right now, let's go for that ride, okay? We'll get this worked out."

"But Mick . . . " I start.

"C'mon—let's ride," he says.

He's all gruff now so I turn and walk over to the horses. They're standing, ground-tied, almost as if someone's holding them for us. Spaniard nuzzles my cheek and whickers softly. Mick smiles and says, "That horse is crazy about you, girl — only lick o' sense he's ever had."

I know he's trying to make me feel better so I grit my teeth and smile, too. He gives me a one-handed leg up into Spaniard's saddle, then swings up on Champ in one easy move. "Let's cross the creek and go run Miller's field," he says once we're up. We won't have to worry about finding our way. The moon has climbed on top of the hill and it's so bright you could pour it into a glass and drink some. Mick leads and we start across the creek in front of where I've been sitting. The summer has taken the water level down so low that it's only up to the horses' ankles. Their hooves make loud clunking sounds on the smooth stones of the creek bed. Mick looks back and gives me a small smile. I smile back. We know the horses' hooves are practically shouting out where we are. Except for the bugs and frogs and the trickling creek, nothing else is moving around except us. There isn't even a breeze rustling in the skinny trees along the bank. But even if the sound of our crossing carries for miles, we don't care. Miller's field is only a quick scramble up the creek bank.

We burst through the trees on the other side of the creek and all of Miller's field rushes out in front of us. Cougar Hill sweeps away and up, off to our left. About a mile away on our right, we see the tiny lights of a car out on the one-lane road going through our narrow valley. The lights disappear around a bend in the road and my feeling of what's real goes with them. The moon laughs at the long-gone sun because it's made the night as light as day. But all the colors are pale and magic cracks through the air like electricity. Rocks in the field look like creatures from fantasy picture books. An owl flies out of the trees behind us and a small whoosh touches our ears. His wings are so quiet we would have missed him if he hadn't dipped once above us before going on with his hunt. This time we have no trouble grinning at each other. We know this fellow. He's a friend.

We nudge Champ and Spaniard forward and let them pick their way through grass dyed frost by the moon. A smell of skunk hits our noses. Somewhere, somebody's made one mad and is probably paying the price. We look at each other and laugh out loud. Then we find the dirt road that runs through Miller's field and around the bottom of Cougar Hill. Ranch trucks come out often enough to keep it smooth and there's a rough strip of grass between the tire tracks. We walk at a good clip on either side of it, but Champ and Spaniard snort and toss their heads up and down. They act like they know something's up. They want to run.

Mick leans his forearm on his saddle horn. He turns to me and says, "All right, girl—race y'around the hill to the first gate."

I look at him like he's out of his mind. Champ's strong and fast but a little heavier than Spaniard is, and tonight, he's carrying some weight. From where we are, it'll be a good run and both horses will do it just fine. But Spaniard will fly.

The horses are jigging now and want to go. Mick's eyes are

two pools of moonlight and when he smiles at me this time, I shiver. He goads me a little bit with my college dream. "C'mon, girl," he whispers, "run for that sheepskin."

I narrow my eyes at him and hiss back, "Let's go, cowboy."

There's no ready-set-go. We're off and pounding in one stride. I lean as far forward as I can and Spaniard moves like smooth thunder beneath me. There is only the silvery stretch of a single path in front of us. The air blowing past me smells like earth and wild oats. I taste the rush of wind passing through the tops of pines, and spray from a stream crashing onto boulders is bitter and sweet and cold. My heart ignites and scatters embers. I look over my shoulder once and see my childhood burning far behind me. Ages have passed since we bolted up the creek bank and onto Miller's field. Then I hear Champ's hooves pounding behind me and know I've won the race. I slow Spaniard to a canter, wheel him at the gate, and tag up.

Mick slows Champ. "Camilla," he calls, "did you taste that wind?"

I call back to him. "Yes, Mick, I did."

We face each other and the breeze that was missing earlier floats down from the top of Cougar Hill and wraps around our shoulders. I let him come to me. He steps Champ forward and stops him close to Spaniard's right side. We still quiver from the race but the horses stand quietly now. Mick reaches out and I lean my cheek into his hand.

Mick's gone back on the road by the time my girlfriend Bonnie pulls up to the house two days later. It's 4:30 in the morning. I've told my parents we're going to Springville to the horse auctions. We won't be back until after dark. Bonnie's seventeen and already drives her dad's big, smooth-riding pickup. When we get to the one-lane road at the end of my driveway, we take a right instead of a left and head out for Highway 198. She hands me a small deerskin pouch. Inside are a roll of money and a piece of paper with directions and a name and number on it. Underneath the money and note are an owl's feather and a smooth white pebble. We head west on 198 to Highway 99 and take another right. We drive until we see the signs pointing to San Francisco. We don't take time to sightsee once we get there. We take care of our business and head back home to the Valley. Later, I talk to my mother on the phone from Bonnie's house and let her know I'm spending the night. I might stay a few days to help move stock. She wants to know how the horse auctions went. I don't lie. I tell her Bonnie picked out a pair of nice-looking yearlings. After we hang up, I go into the bathroom and take painkillers with a glass of water.

Jihad American Style
by Joy Montgomery

Ahmed reviewed the plan. It was an elegant solution. The device was small enough to go unnoticed, except by the most technical experts, and the technical experts on this project were all his people. It would respond to a remote signal. The initial reaction would be so tiny that people would be unaware of it. The beauty of the plan was that each tiny reaction would be multiplied hundreds of thousands of times in crowded areas and be too scattered to effectively combat. This tiny attack would grow into a nation-wide victory for Islam that would make the World Trade Center seem like child's play. The potential destruction would be thousands of times what his heroes had accomplished on that day—maybe hundreds of thousands of times that victory if all went well.

The real beauty of it was that every day the company he worked for installed more of the devices without even knowing that their endless greed was going to be the most effective weapon against tyranny in world history. There were already hundreds of thousands of them in use and the more concentrated the population, the more concentrated the devices were and the more difficult it would be to put out the resulting fires, ensuring a maximum impact.

He laughed as he pictured people eagerly welcoming his little treasures into their lives, demanding them, in fact. He was a constant joy to the sales staff with his stream of excellent ideas to promote the product. How could they know how many experts were feeding him ideas to help sell the product. Ed Murphy, the Vice President of Sales and Marketing, tried, after every management meeting, to convince him to leave engineering and join marketing. He pointed out the more luxurious offices and raved about the potential for more income. Ahmed, of course, could not leave his position as the Director of Engineering Design. It was his signature that approved every little refinement that came in from cells in Germany.

He told Ed, every time, that he loved his work and felt that he could make a real difference where he was. He regularly overheard the conversations about his brilliant ideas and his rejection of promotions and the resulting rewards. He knew that people talked about how they could never understand engineers and agreed that they just seemed to lack the ambition to go for power and rewards. He knew, too, that they agreed that he did seem to be very happy in the job he had and seemed to be completely satisfied with the rut he was in.

Ahmed smiled and waited. He waited for the day when he could let the technicians know to start setting off their tiny weapons of mass destruction. It delighted him so that he laughed out loud, again. Marian, the buyer/planner, in her customary revealing whore-like outfit, looked in the door and smiled. She made some ridiculous comment about how happy Ahmed always seemed to be and tossed her head, trying to distract him with her unclean thoughts. He smiled and she winked. Ahmed scribbled a quick note to start up an employee appreciation award and make sure that Marian received a two-night stay at a first class American hotel of her own choosing.

He returned to his pleasant thoughts of Americans scurrying across Afghanistan and Iraq, looking for weapons of mass destruction. He savored the vision of American soldiers and inspectors, looking like fools and killers to the world. He grew dizzy from his delight in their frustration while minuscule weapons of mass destruction grew in numbers and spread more pervasively than any bio-weapon every day in their own country, financed and endlessly promoted by American greed and American lust for luxury and unclean entertainment.

Chuck came in with a stack of requisitions for more components. Ahmed signed each one of the "reqs" with a flourish and Chuck hurried off to place the orders. That batch of signatures would put another thousand remote controls into luxurious hotel rooms. That would add another thousand tiny explosives to the mix. There would be another thousand devices that would join those already in the field, ready to start tiny fires simultaneously in hundreds of thousands of hotel rooms in tens of thousands of hotels in thousands of American cities. All the while, American soldiers would be scouring Afghanistan and Iraq, hunting for weapons that didn't exist and would never be needed.

America's Rising Heart

by Karen L. Hogan

Overcome any bitterness because you were not up to the magnitude of the pain entrusted to you.
Like the mother of the world, you are carrying the pain of the world in your heart.
Sufi quote
"Why should we hear about body bags and death. Oh, I mean, it's not relevant.
So why should I waste my beautiful mind on something like that?"
Barbara Bush

As the sons of the embittered mothers
Shield their hearts
With "died for a noble cause,"

A woman,
Fresh from shoveling dirt onto
The grave of her sacrificed son,
Endures the heat of the Texas sun
So our beautiful minds can receive
The magnitude of her pain.

As the embittered sons
Conserve their compassion
For white-skinned cronies,

A young black woman,
Laboring under the pain of a new life emerging,
Swims past corpses in the water swollen streets
To save her asthmatic son
So our beautiful minds can receive
The magnitude of her pain.

America,
We are entrusted with this pain.
Let us lead the embittered sons from the
Sound of their faintly-beating hearts,
To the symphony of a heart rising
To meet the magnitude of its pain.

Give War a Rest
by George Staehle

I have a White House cold.
When I hack,
my cough sounds like,
"Attack Iraq."

Why do I have to be so hoarse?
Why does the U.S. want force?

I don't want this cold anymore.
I don't wanna be cajoled into war.

I don't want this cold
dropping bugs in my lungs.
I don't want a war
dropping bombs on the young.

It's time
my antibiotics prevailed.
It's time
Dubya's histrionics were impaled.

I ask myself,
Is this cold better than flu?
Ask yourself,
Is war the best thing for you?

I want one night's sleep
without coughing.
I want outright peace
in a U.S. offering.

Let's make that sleep cough-free
for a month, at least.
Let's make that offer war-free
forever, in the Middle East.

I Pledge Allegiance to Freedom
by Charan Sue Wollard

We are Americans, free to be who we are,
to say, love, vote and pray who we are,
to shout, march, lie down in the streets who we are,
to wear ribbons of many colors who we are,
to wrap ourselves in flags or chadors who we are,
to cover our heads with mantillas
   or yarmulkes or dastaars who we are,
to write poems, sing songs,
   dance in the streets who we are,
grasp hands from sea to shining sea, light candles,
   hold silent in earnest vigils who we are,
close our eyes in transcendent meditation who we are,
raise our hands to the Great Spirit who we are,
bow our heads to Jesus who we are,
bow low to the ground to Allah, not only in times of need,
   but five times every day of our lives who we are,
to supplicate and merchant and do good deeds who we are,
to promote, provoke, subvert and convert who we are,
to take twelve trembling steps who we are,
to pass by homeless families huddled in abandoned cars
and the illucid street dweller
   whose stench follows him like exhaust who we are,
to drop coins in the basket, adopt an Afghani child,
   endow a university who we are,
to protect our families, protect our forests,
   protect our honor who we are,
to honor or dishonor cops and politicians
   and all other authority who we are,
the ACLU and the NRA who we are,
to commune with saints, ghosts, Tibetan lamas,
to consort with thieves, prostitutes, priests or atheists,
to argue, debate, pontificate the origins of species,
   affirmative action, the efficacy of farm subsidies
   or Batman vs. Superman who we are,
to listen, to hear, to be down with the bros,
   to respectfully disagree who we are.

I salute this flag, which is for all,
I, the unpatriot, the unwashed and the unabashed,
the enemy within, the loyal opposition.
I am Anglo-Saxon, French, German.
I am papist and anti-papist.
I am Arab.
My ancestors fled the potato famine, the kaiser,
    colonialism and fascism,
hunger in the cedar mountains of Lebanon
    and on the blue, icy plains of Norway,
they were farmers and doctors, slavers and enslaved,
immigrants generation to generation who we are.

You may curse me, denounce me,
    revile me for my reckless nonconformity,
imprison me, blacklist me, send your agents
    to investigate my suspicious activities.
I salute this country 'tis of me
                          for me
                                     and by me
of all the people for which it stands,
enemies of intolerance, soldiers of freedom who we are.
Do not call me un-American.
I take my stand for who we are.

Anthology Contributors

J.D. Blair — Since 1957, J.D. Blair has written for radio, television and print. His current projects center on short fiction, poetry and essays. His latest success will appear in "Orchid: A Literary Review" where he won their short, short fiction competition for pieces under a thousand words. Blair lives in Walnut Creek.

Peter Bray — Peter Bray is a member of Benicia's First Tuesday Night Poets, the Ina Coolbrith Poetry Circle, Chaparral Poets, the American Academy of Poets, and the West Coast Songwriters Association. He writes from his home in Benicia, California or while orbiting the planet with his silver *travois*. Samples of his work are at his website, www.peterbray.org

Mark Cabasino — Mark Cabasino earned his BA in English and Communications from St. Mary's College of California. He then returned to St. Mary's to earn an MFA in Poetry in that program's inaugural years. He currently teaches English and Creative Writing at Livermore High School. He would like to thank his family, friends and students for their unending love and support.

Diana Carey — Diana Carey lives in Livermore with her husband and two dogs. She writes for fun and has been writting for about 3 years. Diana also enjoys carving stone pendants which she sells at the LAA Art Gallery on 3rd St.

Pat Coyle — Pat Coyle grew up on ranches along the front range of the Rockies and around his grandparent's plumbing business in Santa Fe. He's worked as a programmer, on a ranch development in Belize, and as an engineer. He and his wife live in Livermore and have two grown children.

Tom Darter — Tom Darter is a musician who has earned most of his living working with words. He was the founding editor of *Keyboard* magazine, and currently works as a technical writer. He recently started to rekindle an old passion, acting, and found himself in two Shakespeare plays in the last six months.

Leslie Flannery — Leslie Flannery is a California native who has been writing full time since she abandoned her big-girl job two years ago. She lives in Livermore California with her husband of nearly 20 years and her two children. She has written several unpublished novels. Life is good published or not.

KE Froeschner — After wasting many years designing nuclear weapons, war games, and other idiocies at LLNL, Ken returned to theatre, writing, directing and producing original adaptations of the operas *Hansel & Gretel*, *The Ring*, *The Impresario* and *Romeo & Juliette*. Current efforts include finishing Tolkein's "Lay of Beren & Luthien."

Harold Gower — In the ten years that Harold was a member, the Alameda Poets published five anthologies. Harold was the chief editor of the fifth anthology, *Landmarks & Landings*. Harold writes strictly for fun not for profit; he hopes to publish his own collection of ramblings in the not too distant future.

Jason Hambrecht — Jason Hambrecht is an exogenous Californian inhabiting Livermore's dust-and-tumble westside. Mister Hambrecht consistently appears on People's Most Eligible Bachelor list. Check near the back of the unabridged edition. Last page. Second from the bottom. Call me!

David Hardiman — David Hardiman was born a small child, but grew quickly and by his mid-fortieshad had achieved full adolescence. As a semi-literate juvenile, he enjoys writing short autobiographical sketches as well as long biographical ones. His probation officer believes he can become a contributing member of society just as soon as his electronic ankle cuff is removed.

Karen Hogan — Karen Hogan, who was nurtured in the 60s by the creative community that centered around May School Theater, has a passion for writing stories, and then sending them out into the air. She returned to Livermore in 2001 after a 34-year absence, and founded People Who Write and Tell Stories in 2004.

Ben Jones — Ben Jones is working his way through MFT night school by working days as a software engineer in a biotechnology firm. He loves biology, gardening, writing and thinking about the mysteries of life.

Bobbie Kinkead — Story is my life. From my education in dramatic Colorado, to school teaching in frontier Alaska, and then nesting with my family in the diversified Bay Area, I have practiced writing and illustrating. As teacher, mother, artist, author, and storyteller I now create stories for others to enjoy.

Annette Langer — Annette Langer received top honors in the 2005 Writer's Digest national writing contest and has recently released her first book, *Healing Through Humor: Change Your Focus, Change Your Life!* Her current offering is excerpted from her upcoming book, *A Funny Thing Happened to Me on the Way to the World*.

Thomas Lofgren — I was born in Eureka, California and raised to young adulthood in Long Beach, California. After graduation from college, I began a career in the retail industry. Married with four grown and disengaged children, I currently work for the Internal Revenue Service and live in Pleasanton.

Ethel Mays — San Francisco resident Ethel Mays grew up in Tulare County where Sierra Nevada foothills protect pockets of unspoiled open range. Her writing is in Canadian and U.S. publications and she reads regularly at the San Francisco Writers Workshop. "Moon Ride" is a chapter from her first novel, *Only the Horses*.

Cara Mecozzi Cara Mecozzi is currently writing this upside-down while watching three friends attempt to juggle four stuffed animals, two bruised Granny Smith apples and an empty water bottle. She is sixteen, easily amused, and currently enrolled in school at Granada High. Wish her luck on her driving test.

Phil Mitchell Phil Mitchell, now retired from the military and industry, enjoys life with his wife in Pleasanton, California. He enjoys writing, mainly short stories. Several stories have won awards and publication locally and in *Readers Break* published by Pine Grove Press, New York and the *Writers' Journal* Horror/Ghost Contest.

Joy Montgomery Joy Montgomery is a process improvement specialist who wants to keep America and Americans working. For fun, Joy is a mom, grandmother, opinionated observer, and short story writer. In October, 2006, Joy presented a seminar on effective communication and team-building at the 2006 APICS International Conference in Orlando, Florida.

Cynthia Patton A Livermore native, Cynthia Patton returned home in 1993 because husband Michael adores rodeos. Cynthia worked as an environmental attorney, technical editor, and habitat restoration manager before adopting Katie, now two. Cynthia's nonfiction has appeared in newspapers, magazines, and two self-published books. She's currently working on a memoir.

Diana Quartermaine Diana Quartermaine's publishing credits include: *East Bay Poets Response to Katrina*; *Voices of East Bay Lesbian Poets*; *Brevities*-mini mag. Recently, she has been writing descriptive memory pieces. She also is known for her lyrical, "jazzy," "Bonsai" style. Raised in San Francisco, she has been, living in Alameda since 1996.

Albert Rothman Since retiring in 1986 as a scientist Albert Rothman has written personal essays, memoir, poetry, and short stories. A book of his Brooklyn childhood is ready for publication. Albert has won numerous awards; his work has appeared in a variety of magazines and anthologies since 1986.

Vanitha Sankaran Vanitha Sankaran is a biomedical scientist and a novelist. Her short stories have been published online and in print. Visit her website at www.vanithasankaran.com!

George Staehle George Staehle has been writing poetry for several years after a career in physics research. He was born in Ohio, lived and went to school in Columbus, and moved to the San Francisco/Oakland Bay area in the mid-sixties. He canoes, hikes, paints watercolors, and invents board games.

Selene Steese Selene Steese is a prolific writer who loves to perform her work. She teaches writing workshops throughout the Bay Area, and immerses herself in words as much as possible. "It sometimes seems," she says, "as though I tumbled out of the womb with a pen in my hand."

Sue Tasker — Sue Tasker is the founding president of California Writers Club, Tri-Valley Branch, and a member of SCBWI. Inspired by her love of travel and history, she writes for various publications in the U.K. and the U.S. Her poem Rhythm of the Rain is precipitated by, and dedicated to, Alice.

Camille Thompson — Camille Thompson grew up in the East Bay, and has been writing most of her life. She won her first writing award at the age of eleven. More recently, her work has appeared in a number of publications and anthologies. Camille lives in San Ramon, California with her husband, Jerry.

Frank Thornburgh — Grew up in rural Indiana, California Police Officer, Physics/Math Degree, OL-5 Greenland Engineer, New Jersey Fireman, Special Forces Reserves + others over 44 years, Parachutist and Marksmanship Instructor U.S. Army, N.B.C. Instructor Army Reserve, Substitute teacher, Purchaser and re-builder of 15 residential homes, Writing short articles for magazines and newspapers

Hector Timourian — Hector Timourian grew up learning and adapting to Mexican and Armenian cultures. After migrating to the U.S., he adapted to the Anglo culture. A biomedical scientist and educator, after his retirement—no longer being restricted by the rigors of technical writing—started writing stories from his life and imagination.

Judy Clement Wall — Most recently, my fiction was published in *Byline* magazine, and I have a story forthcoming in the feminist journal *So to Speak*. I am happy to be included in the *Livermore Wine Country Literary Harvest*! I think all my stories read better with wine. Cheers!

Charan Sue Wollard — Charan Sue Wollard has lived in the beautiful Livermore Valley over 30 years. She is a poet, storyteller, editor, painter and student of metaphysics. In her day job, she helps people she likes buy and sell homes. Her writing has appeared in the *Carquinez Review*, *SV* magazine and other publications.

Steve Workman — Steve Workman has written several short stories that have been published in various anthologies over the past four years. All of the stories are related in some way and will be incorporated into a larger work of fiction once the final story is written.

Proofreaders

Donna Mecozzi — Donna Mecozzi enjoys reading and listening to stories. Being a scientist, she appreciates percision and delights in stories that are well written and technically correct. With four children, now young adults, she has had plenty of proof reading experience. It was her pleasure to contribute her skills to his endeavor.

Delores Peterson — Delores Peterson is a technical writer and editor. A former Air Force brat, Delores lived in cities from Bangor, Maine to Manhattan Beach, California, but considers Salt Lake City her home. Delores moved to Pleasanton in April 2006. In her free time she studies metaphysics and writes creative nonfiction.

Index of Authors

Author	Page	Title
Blair, J.D.	36	Peacocks in Mourning
	48	Damp Eucalyptus
	64	Uncle
	162	Sol
Bray, Peter	46	Life's Just a John Prine Song
	138	On Building a Universal Spam Filter
Cabasino, Mark	8	The Cure
	131	He Lives Alone, Much Like Unloading a Uhaul
	164	The Monologue of Rainsworth, the One-Eared Cat
Carey, Diana	142	The Blue Vase
	170	The Loch
Coyle, Pat	120	Kathy
	125	Bill
Darter, Tom	6	What Am I Saying? What I am Saying
	137	Hollow, Man.
	168	Doctor Visit
	222	The Trilogy of DEATH!*
Druce, Mary	257	Flight Plan
	269	The Ladder
Flannery, Leslie	240	Poor Claude du Bois
Froeschner, KE	69	The Pages
	166	Again
Gower, Harold	70	Death V alley and the "Unknown Prospector"
	119	A Vilanelle
	250	Buckarooing
Hambrecht, Jason	43	The Terrible Haiku
	178	Mono Tome
	206	Nanofiction: One Billionth of an *Oeuvre*
Hardiman, David	110	My Kidney Stones Rock!
Hogan, Karen	10	John and Louise
	140	Amazing Grace Arrives from Cyberspace
	281	America's Rising Heart
Jones, Ben	234	The Island
kay, sandra	44	On a sleepless night in spring
	184	3 of 9: Can't Wait!

Author	Page	Title
Kinkead, Bobbie	101	Tiger and the Fish!
Langer, Annette	152	Eating my Way Through India
Lofgren, Thomas	65	Johanna James
Mays, Ethel	108	touches stone
	132	Coyote Laughing
	221	destiny's token
	270	Moonride
Mecozzi, Cara	116	Death Has Pale Eyes and Greets me With a Knowing Smile
	207	The Sunrise Ritual
Mitchell, Phil	179	Math Attack
Montgomery, Joy	278	Jihad American Style
Patton, Cynthia	75	A Fish in the Desert
Quartermaine, Diana	97	Good Weather Sunday
	98	Effie's Eulogy
	100	Sister's Earthquake Story
Roberts, Calvin	212	Atlas of the World
Rothman, Albert	96	Mirror
Sankaran, Vanitha	217	The Electric Lady
Staehle, George	107	Nearly Bacterial Haikus
	282	Give War a Rest
Steese, Selene	32	Stream of Consciousness
	163	Sometimes I Just
	251	Kiss Dancing
Tasker, Sue	94	Rhythm of the Rain
Thompson, Camille	230	Good Daughter
Thornburgh, Frank	146	A New Thing Called Television
	148	Her Last Smile
	248	My First Enterprise
	252	Hoppe #9
	255	Red Wing Shoes
Timourian, Hector	1	Rubbing Shoulders with an Angel
Wall, Judy Clement	258	Discarded Things
Wollard, Charan Sue	34	Charlene Writes a Poem
	183	Calculus
	192	Shooting Moonrocks
	284	I Pledge Allegiance to Freedom
Workman, Steve	49	The Mailman

People Who Write and Tell Stories

Presents
Saturday Salons
at 4th Street Studio
Livermore's Literary Arts Center
2235 4th Street—Livermore
Third Saturday of every month
7:30 PM

"Livermore clearly has a vital writing community.
I've attended evenings at 4th Street Studio during
People Who Write and Tell Stories readings.
It was invigorating! exciting!
It felt to me as if I were witnessing the
genesis of theater—community members
putting their life experiences into
literary form and then reading aloud.
This is the beginning of theater.
I think Shakespeare would approve."

Lisa Tromovitch, Artistict Director
Livermore Shakespeare Festival

"There is a there, there!" said Gertrude, raising her stein

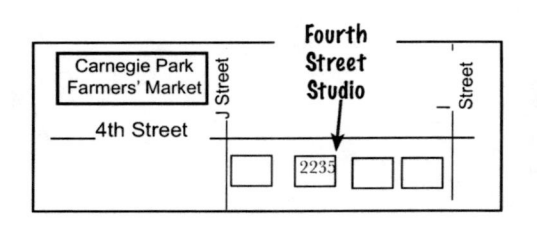

Printed in the United States
62298LVS00003B/1-96